Life Does Go On

Life does go on;
The right and the wrong.
With tears and with song.
A life full of dreams;
Some grown and some died.
We all have our dreams.
Life does go on.

Love does grow on;
The sweet and the sour.
Life travels with it;
Each minute, each hour.
A love full of comfort,
Of laughter and warmth.
We all have our comforts.
Love does grow on.

−Catherine Anderson

Love,
Julie

Jamie Anderson

Love, Julie

To Karen and Krissy
You've got the right stuff

Present Day

From: Julie
Sent: July 3rd 11:59 AM
To: Luke
Subject: Hi

Hi Luke,

I just wanted to check in to see if you were okay. Did you get my texts? I thought maybe I'd give email a try. Maybe email will work.

Love, Julie

Chapter One

One Year Ago

I didn't want to be here.

Slouched in the passenger seat of Kate's oppressively hot car, I tilted my head so the air conditioning blew my long, thick hair off my neck. My stomach flipped as I thought about stepping into the stifling heat and walking through the community centre door. It wasn't just that I was nervous; it was more the lingering stomach ache, the dry mouth, the hint of depression. It was like I was still hungover. But that couldn't be possible, could it? I laid my head back on the seat and softly groaned.

It had been one month since I'd fallen off the wagon. One month since I'd embarrassed myself, and everyone I loved, at my brother Ben and my best friend Kate's engagement party. One month since I'd determined I was "cured" from being an alcoholic and deserved a glass of champagne. After all, I'd been sober for a solid seven months; obviously that was all the time I needed to get my shit together after being a drunk for most of my life. Turned out I wasn't. Cured, that is.

"Julie, you should probably go in." Kate tucked a dark curl behind her ear and gently nudged my elbow with her own. "It's almost noon." She turned the car off and, with it, the comfort of the air conditioning. *Jerk*, I thought, but not without love.

I squirmed in the sticky seat. "You know I don't have to be here, right? I can do it by myself. I was doing fine for the better part of a year. I just slipped a little—it won't happen again." I pulled down the visor and peered above my sunglasses into the tiny mirror, my pleading green eyes touching the deep brown of Ben's. My older brother. My rock. Kindly taking the backseat, knowing my nausea had the tendency to develop into carsickness.

"We're not forcing you to go." He leaned forward and put his hand on my shoulder, squeezing lightly. "This is your choice. If you want to try something else, you have our full support."

Kate turned in the driver's seat to face me and nodded. "Whatever you decide."

I pulled off my sunglasses and then quickly slid them on again, the brightness of the summer sun piercing my eyes and boring a hole into my skull. Mornings like this were the worst, especially when you couldn't temper them with a breakfast screwdriver.

Could I do this myself? I really didn't know. Mostly because I didn't actually do it myself when I tried to get sober the first time. When I first hit rock bottom, when I came close to losing my best friend forever, Kate and Ben were with me every step of the way. And even before that I was always hanging out with one of them; I was never on my own. At night, my multiple online dating conquests kept me occupied, filling the loneliness hole if you will.

Gross. My stomach flipped again.

But since Ben and Kate had gotten together almost a year ago—which, by the way, I fully supported—we'd been hanging out less and less. And since I'd deleted all my online dating accounts, I'd been alone more and more.

So, the question remained: could I do this myself? Maybe. Should I? Probably not.

I sighed dramatically, undid my seatbelt, pushed open the door and rolled out of the car. "See you in two hours," I said, poking my head back in, catching the relief as it pulled the tension from their faces.

"You've got this, Jules!" Ben smiled and pumped his fist awkwardly into the air, the knuckle of his thumb grazing the arm on his glasses. "We'll be here when you're done."

The inside of the community centre was hot and humid, diffused, inexplicably, with the faint aroma of farm animals. I walked down the hallway—the slap of my sandals on the chipped laminate echoing like gun shots—clenching and unclenching my fists, wondering which door I was supposed to open to enter a room I never thought I'd be entering. There was no signage to be found. I guess that's why they called it anonymous.

I was just about to give up and leave—ready to call Kate and Ben, ready to tell them I had failed yet again—when one of the doors swung open from the inside and an older man popped his head out. His lower lip protruded as he blew out a puff of air, stirring the wisps of silver hair that stuck to his brow, and kicked a wooden wedge underneath the door to prop it open.

"Is this…?" I started, eyes darting to the floor.

"It is," he said warmly. "Come on in. Are you a family member or here for yourself?" He guided me into the musty-smelling room, gently touching my shoulder.

I swallowed, for once at a loss for words. "I…myself? I didn't know family members could come to the meetings."

"They don't normally." He started to unfold orange plastic chairs from a stack in the corner. "Today is a celebration day. We have a couple of big milestones to acknowledge. I'm Tim." He held his hand out and I took it firmly in my own.

"Oh. Cool. I'm Julie." This wasn't what I'd had in mind for my first meeting. I already didn't want to be here, and now I was going to have to sit and celebrate some strangers' milestones one month after I'd just tanked my own. Of all the meetings I could have chosen in the entire city of Regina, why did I have to pick this one?

"Isn't the meeting supposed to start at noon?" I asked, one foot out the door, my stomach fluttering with tiny, anxiety-ridden butterflies.

"12:30."

Shit.

"Is there a washroom somewhere?" I asked, wanting to run, wanting to hide from this stifling room, from the part of myself that needed to be here. So much for ripping off the Band-Aid.

I headed in the direction Tim pointed, pushed open the heavy bathroom door and closed it behind me, grateful it was empty, grateful for the quiet. Not super grateful for the overpowering smell of sewage, but beggars couldn't be choosers, I guess.

I took a shallow breath, trying not to gag, and tried to find a spot on the mirror that wasn't stained with water marks. The unflattering fluorescent lights made my eyes appear duller than they actually were, the bags underneath more prominent. My long blonde hair had wilted in the stifling heat and I pulled it back with a pink silk scrunchie I'd been wearing around my wrist.

I looked like I hadn't slept in weeks.

You can do this, Julie, I thought. *You have to do this. If not for you, then do it for Ben and Kate.* The last thing they wanted to deal with was a forty-four-year-old raging drunk while trying to plan a wedding.

I nodded once at my reflection and, no longer able to withstand the stench, forced myself back into the hallway, towards the room. More people had arrived in the short time I'd been gone and I achieved my goal of slipping in unnoticed, surrounded by cheerful chatter.

It seemed that Tim had been busy since I'd left. Two plastic tables had joined the chairs, one holding a silver coffee urn that looked like it had arrived straight from the seventies and one that was slowly being filled with cookies and donuts and all sorts of things I couldn't wait to stuff into my face. This might not be so bad after all.

I made a beeline to the tables and poured some stale-smelling coffee into a Styrofoam cup. "Who even uses Styrofoam anymore?" I muttered.

"They were donated," a deep voice declared, startling

me from my judgmental thoughts. "Ten years ago. They're still not even close to running out."

I turned towards the voice and was almost blinded by his wide smile, brimming with sparkling white teeth and confidence.

"Oh. Sorry." I waited for him to step aside. He was not a small man and he was completely blocking my view of the desserts.

"I'm Luke." He held out his hand, looked at it, wiped it on his shorts, and held it out again.

Do people even shake hands anymore?

"Julie." I tried to conceal my distaste as I lightly gripped his sticky hand. I did not succeed.

"Sorry," he laughed. "It's icing. From the cake I brought." He pointed to a cake on the dessert table: round with white icing and gold piping, the perfect sugary likeness of an AA chip. "You are all my heroes" was written in gold.

Delightful.

I smirked. "Are you the group's cheerleader?" How could someone with a drinking problem be so cheerful?

He laughed. Cheerfully. "No, I'm here for my friend." He pointed at a shaggy-looking man talking to Tim across the room. "I like to include everyone; just in case they don't have anyone to support them."

Of course you do.

"Doesn't it make your heart full to see all of these people achieving their goals?" He tucked a strand of his strikingly auburn hair behind his ear and it seamlessly blended into his similarly hued full beard.

"Sure does." I looked down at the baked goods in front

of me, willing him to leave me alone, pretending I was trying to decide what to choose when I knew full well I was going to choose everything.

He leaned in conspiratorially and stage whispered, "I like to think it's my delicious cakes that keep them coming back."

If he says something about doing God's work, I'm leaving.

"Well," I said, filling a paper plate with a chocolate cupcake, two gingersnaps and a frosted mini-donut and then backing away. "Enjoy the celebration."

"You too!" he said with a jaunty wave.

I sat and watched him cut the cake as I shoved pastry into my face. His solid thighs pressed against a pair of worn cargo shorts; a short-sleeved green-and-grey plaid shirt stretched over his stocky frame. I stared until he caught me and then quickly looked away, flipping my ponytail over my shoulder. *Sorry, buddy. I'm not really into hipster lumberjacks.*

I confidently crossed my legs and then lowered my eyes, lids hooded over a flash of guilt. Why was I being such a bitch? Just because he was annoying didn't mean I had to be a jerk.

I sighed. This meeting had better start soon or I was going to start voicing my crabby opinions out loud instead of safely in my head. I glanced back towards the door, trying to calculate the time it would take to flee through the crowd, trying to ignore the uncomfortable pressure in my chest. *Would it be too much to ask for someone to crack a window?*

And, just like that, the meeting started. Tim walked to

the front of the room and cleared his throat and everyone rushed to their seats. After a short speech about how lucky he was to be among so many courageous people, followed by about five minutes of enthusiastic clapping—Luke leading the charge—the meeting officially began.

One of my pre-set conditions for attending this meeting was that I would just sit and watch for my first time. I wanted to see how things were done before I made any rash decisions.

So, I sat. And I watched. For two hours. Two hours of shifting my hips in an unyielding plastic chair while members went up, one at a time, and basked in the glory of their lengthy sobriety, proudly pocketing various colours of round plastic chips.

Two hours of twelve steps and greater powers and making amends and whispering prayers while I sat in silence, tired and ashamed, the sting of self-hatred forming a lump in my stomach.

My tongue was like paste as I sipped on terrible coffee, desperately wishing it were water, breathing deeply as tiny prickles of sweat buzzed on the surface of my skin whenever someone rose to celebrate their success. That had been me once. It wasn't that long ago that I had been on my way to being a better person. Positive and motivated. Ready to face whatever challenges lay in front of me.

I ached to share their joy, but instead I gritted my teeth, stewing in my own self-pity, gripping the edges of my summer skirt as I tried to hold my horrible, unfair feelings inside.

Until I couldn't.

Until I completely lost my shit.

"I am so proud of all of you who are celebrating your milestones today," Tim said as the meeting started winding down. I could tell I wasn't the only one who was tired—hands raw from clapping, bellies full of sugar—but, by the end, I had firmly convinced myself that I was the only one who was also carrying the additional draining effects of withdrawal. I slowly blinked as the combination of nausea, dehydration and mental defeat swallowed me whole.

"Those who are celebrating have worked so hard to get here." Tim beamed. "They made, and continue to make, a decision to turn their will and their life over to a higher power—over to the care of God." He smiled, his eyes sweeping the room, slowing down and then stopping when they touched on mine. "All we need to do is ask for His help and He will take care of the rest."

I could have stopped my eyebrows from furrowing. I could have stopped the scowl from tugging at my lips. But as my stomach roiled with each new, shallow breath, dense with the exhales of a room full of converts, all I could think about was the immensity of shit that I had slogged through in the four decades I had been alive. And how there hadn't been even a whiff of a higher power helping me out then.

Who had taken care of Ben when he'd had panic attacks at school and all the other kids had made fun of him?

Me.

Who had watched as our parents pretended everything was fine and that Ben was just "quiet for his age" because they didn't understand social anxiety?

Also me.

Who had made Ben come home from university, the only place where he had friends, the only place he could be his real self, merely because I had let some man get the better of me?

I closed my eyes, dizzy from exhaustion and irrational rage.

And then.

"You know what? No." A brash voice burst from the silence.

My voice.

I jumped up, ready for a fight. Ready to unleash my frustration onto a room full of innocent people. "I may be powerless over alcohol, but there's not a chance in hell that I'll be turning my will or life or anything over to the care of Him or anyone else. Men are what got me here in the first place."

I looked around, my tired eyes meeting those wide with shock. I knew I should stop; I knew it wasn't their fault I was such a mess. I knew I was ruining what, for most, was a very special day. But I couldn't.

"I may be a drunk, and I may be a fuck-up," I raged, "but this is my life, I'm responsible for it, and the only one I can depend on is myself. Not you, not a higher power, certainly not 'God.'" I air-quoted. "If *she* even exists."

A collective gasp rose from my rightly offended audience and I turned to leave, thankful I had chosen a chair at the end of a row.

My vision blurred and my ears buzzed as I moved towards the door, feeling like I was walking in slow motion; like my feet were trudging through sand. My breath caught at the sensation of a hand on my arm and I turned towards what was sure to be a well-deserved biting remark.

But when I blinked, I could only see kindness. Luke, the cheerful lumberjack, was looking up at me like he understood. Like he could see past my hateful words to something I didn't even have access to.

I didn't like it.

"I don't need your pity," I hissed and tore my arm away.

"And I'm taking these brownies!" I yelled to the rest of the room as my clever parting shot, grabbing the paper plate upon which they were sitting. "They're fucking delicious!"

"So, how was it?" Kate's wide smile faded as I slid into the front seat. "Uh oh, what happened?"

"Can we go get something to eat?" I pulled on my seatbelt. "I'm at the bottom of a serious sugar crash right now and I could go for some real food." I held up the paper plate. "Brownie?"

I glanced over at Kate as her eyes flickered to the rear-view mirror, knowing they were meeting an equally concerned set on Ben.

"I'm fine," I said. "I'll tell you more when we get to Vic's. This is more of a sit-down conversation." I pulled down the visor and poked the dark circles under my dull eyes with the tip of my finger. "Yuck. I look like death."

"Don't say that." Kate gently slapped my thigh with the back of her hand. "You are the most gorgeous woman I know. I know you feel bad, but don't be mean to yourself. Many women, myself included, would be quite pleased to look like you on your very worst day." She smiled encouragingly.

"Well, I'm glad you look like you," Ben said to Kate from the backseat, squeezing her shoulder.

"Ugh, get a room," I muttered, a smile tugging at the sides of my lips.

We drove in silence to Victoria's Tavern, what used to be our weekly lunch spot, but considering Ben and Kate had cancelled twice last month, I wasn't sure we could call it that anymore.

Kate parked on one of the side streets in the deserted wilderness of what was once a bustling downtown.

I looked around, eyes blurred with nostalgia. "Remember how busy it used to be down here when we were kids? Remember the Christmas displays at The Bay? I feel like the whole city would be downtown on the weekends. Am I misremembering?" I shook my head and kicked an empty soda can down the sidewalk.

"No, I remember that too," Kate said. "I remember going to the Cornwall Centre with my dad before he left and it was always really busy. Now the mall is empty when I come here on Saturdays. If I come down here at all."

"Sad," I said and looked up to find them standing in front of me, both trying not to look concerned, both failing miserably.

"Please don't look at me like that," I said as we walked towards the pub. "I'm not dying, I'm just a drunk."

Kate grabbed my hand. "Don't say that. You're not a drunk. Before the engagement party you'd been sober for, what...how long?"

14

"Seven months," I said, swallowing my regret.

"Exactly!" She lifted her hands in an awkward little cheer before pulling open the heavy door of the pub and letting me and Ben through. "And that's great. You just had a bit of slip-up, like you said." She nudged Ben in the stomach.

Ben jumped and a "hell yeah!" burst awkwardly from his mouth.

"Hell yeah?" I raised my eyebrow. "Since when is that something you say?" We slid into our usual booth in the corner.

Ben looked at me and then at Kate, who shrugged as if to say, *Don't ask me why that came out of your mouth.*

We took out our phones, scanned the QR code on the table and scrolled through the online menu.

"We're just worried about you," Kate said. She put her hand on Ben's and he visibly relaxed. "Are you going to tell us what happened?"

Even though Kate and Ben had been dating for almost a year, it was still hard to think of them as a single unit. Now it was always "we" think this and "we're" doing that. At some point they had ceased being distinct people and had morphed into a solid entity.

I closed my eyes and put my head in my hands. "It was a milestone celebration meeting," I said, "which, in normal circumstances, would have been great. But as someone who recently ruined seven months of sobriety, I wasn't feeling all that celebratory."

"Shit, I'm sorry, Julie." Ben looked at me, knowing me better than anyone. "So…what did you do?"

I took a deep breath, not sure where to start, and was (thankfully) interrupted by the server who set down three waters on the table, condensation sweating from the glasses. I picked one up and held it in my hands, wishing I could dive into its icy coolness and escape this wicked heat wave.

"Anything else to drink?" She pointed her pencil at me. "I've noticed you haven't had your usual Shiraz for a while. We have half-price bottles on until six."

Kate's head shot up and Ben cleared his throat.

"No thanks," I said, meeting her eyes, trying to pretend my mouth hadn't just gone dry. "I'm an alcoholic now." I shifted in my seat, peeling my bare legs off the vinyl-covered booth, instantly regretting that I had worn a skirt.

"Cool." She put her pencil in her pocket and walked back towards the bar.

"Why do you need to do that?" Ben asked after she was gone, his face flushed.

I shrugged. "I like making people feel uncomfortable?"

"Well, you nailed it." His hand automatically went to the back of his neck, the place it disappeared to when he was nervous.

"You always feel uncomfortable, so that doesn't count." I grinned.

He rolled his eyes. "So, are you going to tell us what happened or what?"

"Wow," Kate breathed after I'd finished.

Ben didn't say anything. He just kept opening his mouth and closing it again, like a stunned goldfish.

"It's fine," I said, swirling the ice cubes around in my

glass with my cardboard straw, pretending it was true. Pretending I wasn't so ashamed that I wanted to cry. "I'm just not going to go back."

They were both silent, trying to look at each other without me noticing.

"Oh my God, you guys, what?" I said in a burst of exasperation. "Stop looking at each other like you're my disappointed parents. I get that enough with my actual disappointed parents."

"Sorry," Ben said. "We're just worried."

"I know," I said, my voice softening. "You don't need to worry though, I'll find something else."

"What was actually wrong with this one?" Kate fanned herself with a cardboard beer coaster. "I mean, why did you get so angry?"

"I don't know." I rested my chin on my steepled hands. "I know it works and has saved people's lives and is great in so many ways. But, honestly, besides the celebrations pouring salt into my gaping wounds of failure, I just didn't feel connected to the program itself; the rigid structure and rules. I don't think I could consistently deal with the twelve steps and the depressing introductions and everyone chanting the alcoholic's name like we were all in a monastery."

They both nodded, wanting to understand.

"They just weren't my type of people, you know? They were all really nice. Too nice, maybe. Especially this one guy, he was like Barney the dinosaur. If Barney wore plaid. He kept looking at me with, I don't know…."

"Sympathy?" Ben offered.

"No…more like…."

"Pity?" Kate jumped in.

"No. But thanks," I said dryly. "More like empathy. Like he really cared."

"Yeah, that *would* suck," Ben said. "I hate when people care." He smiled.

"I don't know," I said, ignoring his sarcasm. "It was just… too much, I guess." I sat back, wanting the conversation to end. Not wanting to dig any deeper. Unable to put into words the fact that somehow, in a room full of people who had struggled just as I was struggling, I had never felt more alone.

Ben leaned in and grabbed my hand. "Listen, Julie, I know you're strong and I know you're dedicated, and for a solid seven months of sobriety you did it without any formal help."

"Well, I couldn't have done it without you guys," I said. It was true. Without Ben and Kate's love and support— their endless patience with my shitty moods when I was going through withdrawal, their willingness to come over at the drop of a hat when I wanted to drink—I very likely would still have been barrelling down my own unique road of self-destruction.

"And we'll always be here for you," Ben continued. "But I know what it's like contending with the battle of unreliable mental health. And maybe"—he looked at me, trying to gauge my reaction—"maybe this time you need a bit more help than just us. I know you don't think we've noticed, but we can tell you haven't been doing well this past month."

I opened my mouth to argue and then closed it as my mind went back to a month ago. Ruining the special night of my brother and my best friend, the two people I loved the most. Disappointing my family and friends. Disappointing myself.

And Ben was right. Having dealt with anxiety his whole life, he did know a thing or two about surviving mental health challenges.

And honestly? More than anything, I owed this to them. They had stuck with me through everything. Through a life of fuck-ups; through endless mistakes. At what point did I stop being a burden? I had to do this. I had to truly get my shit together before they gave up and left like everyone else. I had to turn my life around; for real this time.

"All right," I relented and then laughed at the barely contained shock on both of their faces. "I know you're right. One of the things I've learned is that, sometimes, you need to trust the people who love you more than you trust yourself. And I trust you both. I'll get the support. I'll start looking for another group. But," I added, "it's going to be my type of group. Something with people I can relate to. No steps. And no religion."

"Good," Kate said. "And, like we've said several times before, we'll support you in whatever you do." She raised her eyebrows. "As long as it doesn't involve having a glass of champagne."

Ben put his head in his hands, tufts of dark hair poking through his fingers.

Kate looked back and forth between us both. "Too soon?"

And then I laughed. Like a real, cleansing laugh, releasing the knot of stress that had taken root in the centre of my shoulder blades.

"This is why I love you, Kate," I said wiping tears from my eyes. "You always know the wrong thing to say."

Chapter Two

That evening, after Ben and I had spent an hour in our childhood home—perched on the worn leather sofa, awkwardly engaging in stilted conversation with our parents, pretending that everything in our lives was grand—I stared out of his passenger-side window and pondered whether or not to ask the question that had been hovering in my mind since I'd gotten in the car. The question I knew Ben didn't want me to ask. Ben was terrible at keeping secrets and I had a feeling he was holding on to a pretty significant one.

"So…is tonight the night Kate is finally going to ask me to be her maid of honour?" Ben had dropped Kate off at home after lunch, ostensibly to prepare for the long-overdue dinner they had invited me to a month ago.

"I'm not sure what you're talking about." Ben cleared his throat.

"Why are you holding the steering wheel so tightly?"

"I'm not," he said as he flexed his fingers. "I'm just being a safe driver."

"Of course," I said. "I mean, studies have shown that strength of steering wheel grip is directly correlated to the frequency of car accidents."

Ben's eyes narrowed.

"I mean, obviously I'm going to be her maid of honour. We've been best friends for over thirty years."

"Just let her do her thing," Ben said with relief, dropping the façade. "She has a whole presentation planned. She's very excited about it. It's actually pretty adorable."

"Of course I will," I said, an unexpected lump in my throat. I loved them both so much.

We drove the rest of the way in silence, giving me time to prepare for whatever Kate had in store. As much as she loved weddings, I despised them. I used to be a big fan of cheap drinks and a good excuse to party, but now I would prefer to pretend they didn't exist.

"I refuse to spend my hard-earned money on funding a misogynistic social construct," I'd say when nosy friends and relatives would ask why I hadn't yet walked down the aisle. Or, if I was feeling more generous: "I haven't met the right person yet." But deep down, I knew why I would never get married. Even if I did find the right person, which seemed less and less plausible every day, they wouldn't be the right person forever. They would learn what I was really like. And they would eventually leave.

We pulled up to the front of their apartment, which had once only been Kate's, and I looked at it with new eyes. It wouldn't be long until I would be parking in their guest parking stall for the last time. Another thing Ben and Kate had recently announced was that they had started looking for a house. Now that they had a double income, and Kate had a full freelance roster of PR clients, they both felt comfortable taking on a mortgage payment.

"It's actually cheaper than both of us paying rent," Kate had said the night they told me. "We'll be saving money."

Of course I was excited for them, but I couldn't help but feel a bit sad. Kate had lived in this apartment since we were in our early thirties. Since way before Ben had finally worked up the nerve to tell her he'd always been in love with her. Since she'd realized she felt the same. I had spent many a night sleeping on her comfy couch after we'd had one too many bottles. I was going to miss this place.

"Remember," Ben whispered as we walked up the stairs, "pretend to be surprised."

It turned out, I didn't have to pretend. There was nothing that could have prepared me for the sensory explosion that Kate had so lovingly—and aggressively—created.

As I walked into the kitchen, precisely timed to my entrance, the melodious rhythms of New Kids on the Block's "The Right Stuff" burst out of her unexpectedly powerful iPhone speaker. She was dressed to look like Donnie—my favourite "kid" in our favourite boy band—navy bandanna wrapped around her head, sleeveless jean jacket over a white T-shirt, ripped jeans tucked into chunky white running shoes, and lip-syncing the lyrics with such passion that I had to put my hand over my mouth to force the laughter back in.

As the chorus got closer, I knew what was coming. And she didn't disappoint. Hand on her pretend belt buckle, feet kicking out to the side, arms crossed at her chest, face bobbing up and down. Just like we'd done hundreds of times as we watched the video in high school. Laughing each time twelve-year-old Joey McIntyre drove away in the stolen car.

So, I did what was only natural. I enthusiastically joined

her. And we danced and laughed and played the song over and over, just like when we were young. Before any of the bad stuff happened. Before we had to grow up.

After we were done, I sat on the kitchen chair, exhausted.

"I probably should have stretched before I started." Kate wiped her face with her sleeve. "I'm going to feel this tomorrow."

"I can't believe I remembered it all," I said, trying to catch my breath. I looked around the room, which was decorated in posters from our old teen magazines, cassette tapes set up in a row on the counter. "I can't believe you did all this."

"Julie." Kate knelt in front of me, taking my hand. "Girl, you've always had the right stuff. And while you don't turn me on, you've been my closest friend for decades. I would be so happy if you would be my maid of honour."

I laughed and was startled when it turned into a sob.

"Oh, shit, are you okay?" Kate jumped up and grabbed a Kleenex from the box on the counter.

"I'm more than okay." I sniffed and looked at Ben, whose eyes had widened to an equally concerned expression. "I'm just so happy for you both. Of course I will. I would be honoured to be your maid of…wait, is that why they call it that?"

My final words were muffled as Kate jumped into my arms and squeezed. Ben, not knowing what to do, put his hand on my head and patted it a couple of times.

"I'm so happy you're going to be a part of our wedding!" Kate pulled away. "And, no rush, but do you have anyone you think you might bring?"

Ben stifled a cough and I saw him subtly shake his head out of the corner of my eye.

Kate sighed. "I know we weren't going to ask yet, but it's coming up in less than a year and I know that seems like a long time, but it really isn't when you think about it. And we'll need, among many other things we don't have, an accurate idea of numbers." Her voice started to both rise and speed up and Ben looked at me and shrugged like this was basically his life now.

"Easy there, Bridezilla." I put my hands on her shoulders, gently pushing them down. "Deep breaths. I don't have anyone in mind now, but I promise I'll let you know before June, okay?"

"Okay," she said, her breath slowing. "But I'd really be more comfortable if you could let me know by the end of November."

"If I fall madly in love with someone by the end of November, I'll let you know," I said. "I promise."

She visibly relaxed, my sarcasm not registering. "Sorry," she said, not sounding sorry. "We just have so much to do and neither of us has time to do it. It's causing me a lot of stress, which, in turn, is causing Ben a lot of stress."

"No, it isn't, it's totally fine." Ben pulled her into a hug while mouthing to me, "It's not fine," as his eyes bugged out of his head.

"Why don't I help?" I said before I could stop myself.

"What?" Kate looked at Ben both of their expressions skeptical.

"You're both really busy, right?" *What am I doing?*

"Right," they said in unison.

"So busy," Kate added. "I'm barely home. Mittens hates me right now."

"Hey, I'm here." Ben tried to look offended, but he knew Kate's cat would always be just that. Kate's.

Actually, I thought, whatever irrational brain break that had caused me to suggest helping plan an event I dreaded in the first place could be just what I needed. Planning an amazing wedding for Ben and Kate would be the perfect way to show them that I had my life together; that I was not going to be a mess forever. Not only would this challenge keep me occupied, but if I succeeded at this, I could succeed at anything. I could finally prove to them that I could be more than a burden.

"Well, guess who's not busy?" I said. "And guess who needs something to keep her mind off drinking?"

Their faces were blank.

"Really?" I held my hands up in defeat. "Me! Who else do you know who's trying not to drink?"

"Lots of people, actually," Ben said.

Kate nodded. "The sober-curious movement has really taken off."

"I hate you both." My eyes narrowed then softened. "Seriously though. I could do it. I would have something to do and the two of you wouldn't have to add anything else to your already full plates. It's win/win."

"But, and how do I say this gently?" Ben started. "You are, without hyperbole, the most unorganized person I've ever met."

"Not that we don't appreciate your generous offer." Kate shot him a warning look.

"Of course, yes, very generous," Ben said, backtracking. "And we do appreciate it."

"I can handle it," I protested. "I can. Really. Just give me a chance. Please." My eyes lowered. "I already ruined your engagement party by getting embarrassingly drunk; the least I can do is plan you an amazing wedding."

I could feel them looking at each other over my head, silently communicating in the irritatingly adorable way they always did.

"Okay," Kate said.

"Okay?" Ben's eyes widened. "That's not what I was—"

"We trust you and we know you'll do a great job." Kate took my hand, ignoring Ben, who seemed to be having a mini-stroke.

"What about Hudson?" he yelled like a man gasping out his final breath before drowning.

"Hudson?" Kate looked confused. "What about him?"

"That guy you used to hang out with at university?" I was also confused. I knew of Hudson but had never actually met him, despite the fact that he'd moved to Regina from Toronto the previous year. I knew he had helped Ben with his anxiety a lot in university, but I guess I hadn't realized they were still close. Time flies when you're trying to stay sober.

"Yeah," Ben said. "I asked him to be my best man. It was either that or Dad. And, you know—" he shrugged "—Dad would probably just be uncomfortable."

"Why is this the first time I've heard you mention Hudson in relation to your wedding?" I looked at him skeptically. "And, yes, good call about Dad." He and Mom, while supportive, would definitely be more relaxed on the sidelines.

"You've had a lot going on."

Fair.

"Anyways." He took a deep breath. "What if Hudson helps? He still doesn't know many people here and he offered to lend a hand. And, best of all, he's a project manager. I mean, this is a no-brainer, right? Right?" He looked back and forth between me and Kate frantically.

"I hate that phrase. 'No-brainer'," was all Kate said. But then she shrugged. "Makes sense though."

"Sure," I said. I knew this was the only way I was going to be able to plan the wedding without causing my brother to have a nervous breakdown. "Hudson can help. But I get to make the decisions. Remember that wedding we went to when we were kids and everyone had to get their picture taken in KITT, the car from *Knight Rider*, before going into the church? I guarantee you a man planned that."

"I thought it was pretty cool, actually," Ben said quietly.

"Exactly."

Chapter Three

It was a rare occasion when Old Julie woke up on a Saturday without a hangover. My weekends used to start around noon with me rolling over to reach for a bottle of water from the case I kept under my bed. Breakfast was a handful of Advil and a glass of orange juice, often containing a couple shots of vodka. It was only then that I could face the day.

I wished I could say my Saturdays were now filled with waking with the sunrise and healthy breakfasts and restorative yoga. That I didn't still lie in bed until 10:00 a.m. waiting for the rolls of nausea to pass. Waiting for the cravings to subside. That I didn't spend most of the morning in bed watching re-runs of *Friends* on my iPad.

Now, though: now I had a wedding to plan. Now I had a goal to achieve. Almost a month after I had volunteered, the day had finally arrived. Today was the beginning of something important. Today I would start the process of proving to myself, and everyone around me, that I was no longer a hot mess in heels. And today was also the day I would get to meet the famous Hudson. I honestly didn't know what to expect. What kind of dude wanted to help plan a friend's wedding anyways? Men don't even like planning their own weddings.

I forced myself out of my warm cocoon of blankets and trudged into the bathroom, hoping a shower would provide the energy of the healthy breakfast I now didn't have time to eat.

I chose one of my more flattering outfits—a burgundy halter dress that hugged my slim frame and hung just below my knees and a pair of chunky black sandals. I wanted to look like I was put together. Like I could handle things by myself. Like I wasn't a recovering alcoholic that needed something to do to keep her mind off drinking.

We were meeting at Kate and Ben's apartment at 1:00 p.m. so I stopped at Tim Hortons for a tray of coffees and a box of Timbits. I hoped Hudson enjoyed coffee. Actually, I didn't really care; if he didn't want it, I'd drink it.

I arrived just before 1:00 p.m., early for once, and took a sharp right into the parking lot, ready to slide into the guest spot.

"Shit!" I yelled as I slammed on the brakes, almost smashing into the car that was already parked there, coffee splashing all over the passenger seat. "What the fuck?" I said, looking around for the jerk who had parked in their guest spot. Each apartment was allowed one guest spot and this one was basically mine.

Someone is in the guest spot. I texted Kate, refusing to back out and park farther away.

It's Hudson. Sorry! She texted back immediately.

Tell him to move.

LOL

I wasn't joking.

I sighed, deep and dramatic, reversed my car and continued through the parking lot to (the very far away) group of extra guest parking spots, instantly regretting my chunky heel footwear selection.

Well, I didn't know I would be HIKING.

I wiped the coffee off the seat the best I could with a dirty napkin I found on the floor and blew off the Timbits that had escaped from the box. *These can be Hudson's.*

Ten minutes later, I yanked open the lobby door, set the coffee and treats on the ground and groaned as I peeled the strap of my right sandal away from a newly formed blister. Beads of sweat had darkened the back of my dress and I uselessly fanned my glistening face with my hands, trying to will away the scowl. I couldn't.

By the time I made it up the stairs to the apartment, I'd had about enough. For the first time in a long time, the only drink I wanted was a tall glass of ice water. I lifted my hand to knock on the door and took a deep breath. *It's all right,* I told myself. *This is the worst of it. The day can only get better from here.*

It's funny how life can kick you when you're down. Because when the door opened and a familiar, wide-grinning, red-bearded, irritatingly cheerful face greeted me, I knew my day was about to get much worse.

"Oh!" I blinked, astonished. "What are you doing here?" I couldn't move. The fact that the overly chatty lumberjack from the infamous AA meeting was standing in front of me had stunned me into stillness.

"Oh good, you're here." Ben pulled the door open

wider and grabbed the cardboard tray of coffee from my hands, scrunching his nose at the mess.

"This is my sister, Julie," he said, gesturing that I should come inside. "And, Julie, this is my good friend and best man, Hudson. Luke Hudson."

Fuck. Me.

"I'm not working with that guy," I said to Kate, who was staring at me with equal parts confusion and wariness.

Right after Ben had announced who Hudson was and confirmed the role he was going to play in the tragic comedy that was my life, I had grabbed Kate and pulled her into their bedroom, shutting the door behind us.

"Why?" she asked. "Hudson's great! He was a rock for Ben when they were in university and, since he moved here, they've started hanging out again. If it wasn't for Hudson, Ben would likely never leave the house." She smiled and her face softened in the way it always did when she talked about my brother. It now shocked me that it had taken them decades to get together. If Kate hadn't abruptly decided in her forties that she wanted to try online dating, giving Ben the kick in the pants he needed to tell her how he felt about her, who knew what would have happened?

"Stop calling him Hudson," I hissed. "His name is Luke. And if you had called him Luke from the beginning, I would have asked more questions."

Kate looked taken aback, her face contorted into her own unique expression of bewilderment, head tilted, brows furrowed. Which was fair; she had no idea how I knew him. How embarrassed I actually was about the whole "I will not give my life to God" breakdown.

I sat on the cracked leather recliner that was tucked into the corner of their bedroom, one of the few pieces of furniture that had migrated from Ben's apartment when he'd moved in. I closed my eyes, breathed slowly, and counted in my head, just like Ben had taught me.

"He was at the meeting," I finally said.

"What meeting?"

"*The* meeting, Kate. The meeting where I irrationally screamed at a bunch of innocent people trying to get their lives together. If I ever mention a meeting again, that will forever be the meeting I'm referring to."

"Okay, sorry." Kate held up her hands. "*That* meeting, I get it."

"You know that super cheerful guy I told you about? The one who kept looking at me with concern?" I rolled my eyes to emphasize that I thought showing genuine concern for a stranger was ridiculous.

"Yeah, that sounds like Hud…Luke. He's a really nice guy."

"Well, I don't care if he's Keanu Reeves," I said. "He's not only annoying, but he saw me at my absolute worst. The last thing I want to do is plan a wedding with him, especially one that is this important." I did not want some outsider ruining my chance of proving to Ben and Kate that I had my shit together. Despite the fact that, at this moment, I clearly didn't.

Kate opened her mouth to speak when the door opened and Ben slid into the room, closing it behind him.

"What are you both doing in here?" he whispered. "You're being rude." His eyes darted in my direction.

I scowled, ready to protest, but grabbed the glass of water Ben had been drinking and drained it instead.

"Someone please catch me up on whatever is happening." Ben looked at Kate.

"Julie hates Luke because he was at the AA meeting, and he's super cheerful, and he cares about strangers and now she doesn't want to plan the wedding with him," Kate said all in one breath, glancing at me to see if she had gotten it right.

Ben nodded as he took it all in, his hand sliding to the back of his neck.

It was at that moment that Luke chose to burst through the door like the Kool-Aid man.

"What's going on?" He looked around the room with concern. "Is everyone okay?"

"We're fine, *Luke*," I said as I got up to close the door, trying to nudge him backwards with my look of disdain. "We're having a private conversation."

He didn't move.

"With family," I added and moved my hands in a sweeping motion towards the door.

"Well, technically Kate isn't family yet," Luke said with a grin, unfazed.

"Listen, buddy," I started but was interrupted by a hand placed firmly on my shoulder.

"Please stop." Kate sighed, brushing away a tired curl that had fallen from her scrunchie. "You both offered to help with the wedding and I am incredibly grateful for that.

But I am also very stressed right now and, honestly, I don't care who hates who and who finds who irritating."

Luke opened his mouth to speak, but after a look from me promptly shut it.

"If this is truly a deal breaker, you need to tell me now," she continued. "I took on an extra client to help pay for this wedding because, thanks to your generous offers, I had room in my schedule, which means, if I don't actually have your assistance, I'll need to find someone else. And that person will cost a lot of money. And we don't have a lot of money. And all I want to do is marry Ben in June and, if we don't get married, I may very well never be happy again," she concluded, matter-of-factly.

By this point Ben had scooped their cat Mittens into his arms and slowly backed into their walk-in closet, always one to disappear at any sign of confrontation.

"So?" She looked at me and I nodded.

"Of course I'll still help," I said.

"And you?" She looked at Luke and he nodded and shrugged, not really having any idea what was going on.

"Good." She gently pulled Ben out of his hiding place and walked him over to the door. "Thank you both for your help. I appreciate it," she said as they left.

"For the record though—" Luke stepped through the doorway and yelled down the hall "—I never said I hated anyone."

"Ugh," I groaned quietly from the chair, head back, eyes toward the ceiling.

This was going to be a long ten months.

Present Day

From: Julie
Sent: July 8th 9:05 PM
To: Luke
Subject: Hi again

Hi Luke,

I know you're mad. And I get it. I'm sorry that you're mad. But maybe we can get past this? Maybe we can just try again?

Love, Julie

Chapter Four

Eleven Months Ago

If you had asked me twenty years ago what my professional life would look like in my mid-forties, I would have probably envisioned something corporate. Likely a senior management role at a downtown office where I would confidently stride into work every day in expensive blazers and Louis Vuitton heels. I'd be one of those women who got their hair coloured every month and enjoyed a mani-pedi every second Friday. I'd work somewhere important where people did what I said and got me fancy coffees without me asking. People would admire my exceptional performance and hard-core dedication. I would be both respected and feared.

What I would not have envisioned was making a career out of temping in a variety of shitty administration positions because my life had fallen apart due to trauma and booze. I would not have predicted quitting or getting fired from so many jobs in the past twenty years that I hadn't developed any valuable skills. Not that administrative positions were somehow beneath me—they were great for someone who did them well—but my limited computer abilities and extremely poor organizational skills ensured that I was not one of those people. And yet, those were the only positions in which I got placed.

I looked at the address on Google Maps, smack dab in the centre of downtown Regina, and then up at the crumbling, red brick building looming in front of me. No name plate, no number on the door. Based on the numbers on the two identical brick buildings flanking it, though, this had to be it. *This had better be it*, I thought. If I had to walk any further in this heat, I would be a mess for my first day. And even though I didn't want this job, I did need it. This was going to be my next step in turning my life around.

I opened the door and stepped into a dim lobby, chin tipped as my eyes followed a long, carpeted staircase leading up to another blank door. For an advertising agency, they sure didn't advertise themselves very well.

There didn't seem to be an elevator anywhere, so I trudged up the stairs, pulled open the second door and poked a cautious foot into what I assumed was the agency. A brightly coloured mural competed for my attention with pastel posters hanging in frames. Gold and silver awards were showcased in glass cabinets, gleaming in the warm light. A wooden swing was inexplicably hanging from the ceiling.

This had to be it. If any company was going to have a swing hanging in their lobby, it would be an advertising agency.

The sound of my heels echoed across the cement floor as

I made my way up to the reception desk that was currently missing a receptionist.

I looked around. Was this the job I was temping for? Was I supposed to start right now?

I checked my phone to see if I had missed an instruction in the email. Nope. I was just supposed to meet "Quinn" at the front desk. "Quinn?" I peeked around the corner. "Hello?"

Quinn, or who I assumed was Quinn, burst through a side doorway, arms full of files.

"Ah!" She screamed when she saw me, dropping the files on the floor. "Crap."

"Shit, sorry," I said as I bent down to help. I was instantly mortified as she started to cry. Good Lord, what kind of hot mess had I gotten myself into?

"Sorry." She sniffed and dabbed her eyes with the flared sleeve of her billowy cotton blouse. "My emotions are a bit all over the place. I've been working late and haven't been sleeping and, you know?" She swept her hand around the room, blouse sleeves trailing like streamers.

I didn't know. But I nodded anyway. "Sure."

As I picked up the files and stacked them in a pile on top of the raised desk, I watched Quinn do the same, sizing her up, wondering what kind of a person cried after dropping pieces of paper. And who had paper files anymore?

With every few files she added to the pile, she ran her hand across her glistening forehead, tucking wayward strands of dark hair streaked with purple back into her messy top-knot. She was sweating a lot for someone who was wearing nothing but a light blouse and a flowing floral skirt. I considered asking if she was pregnant (maybe I was covering for her maternity leave?) but then remembered that one should never ask that question unless one sees a baby actually coming out of a vagina.

"Thank God you're here," she said as she finished stacking, hands on her hips, breathing deeply. "You *are* Julie, right?"

"I am. Julie."

"Oh good." She relaxed, relief softening her already kind face. "The last temp was met at the door by one of our staff dogs and freaked out. And the temp before that didn't show up. Do dogs freak you out?"

"No, I love dogs." I didn't love dogs.

"Okay, good." She blew her bangs out of her eyes, seamlessly reached into a pocket in her skirt, pulled out a bobby pin and used it to secure the offending hair behind her left ear.

"Sometimes people bring their dogs here. Which is great, but sometimes they poop on the floor. And guess who has to clean it up?"

"The dog owners?"

She laughed an empty, humourless laugh. "You'd think, right?" She slid to the floor and rested her head against the wall.

"So," I thought I'd try, "am I taking over for you when you go on…holidays or…leave or something?"

She sighed and pushed herself up to a standing position with the help of the tall reception desk. "I'm actually not the receptionist," she said, a flash of resentment in her eyes. "I'm an account manager."

"Oh." I glanced around. "Why are you—"

"Because I'm the only woman on the accounts team." She rolled her eyes.

"Ah ha." I nodded. Now everything made sense. "How did you manage to carve enough time away from planning birthdays and stocking the supply cabinet?"

A burst of uninhibited laughter escaped from her mouth. "I like you," she said after she'd recovered. "Here, take these." She handed me a stack of files and motioned for me to follow her into a back room. "Our old receptionist got fired after sleeping with one of our clients. One of our married clients. So, the first thing I'm going to teach you is don't do that. Or"—she reconsidered—"if you *are* going to sleep with one of our married clients, don't get caught."

"Got it." I laughed. "Should I be writing this down?"

"I like you," she said again as she piled more files into my arms.

"How long have you been here?" I asked as she opened a large metal filing cabinet and indicated that I should drop the stack into the drawer.

"About ten years. I got my first job here as an account coordinator after I moved from Vancouver." She shut the drawer. "We'll deal with these later."

"Cool." I leaned back and perched on a large table holding, of all things, a giant paper cutter and laminator. "But, also, why?" I love Saskatchewan, and I love Regina, but I was born and raised here. I still don't fully understand why people come here and stay by choice. Especially when they're from somewhere cool like Vancouver.

"Don't judge me, but I followed a man here." She

fiddled with the sleeves on her blouse. "It's a long story, but in the end, even though we broke up, Regina felt like home. It rains too much in Vancouver. It's way sunnier here, which I love. Even when it's bitterly cold for half the year, which I also love. Give me a cozy sweater and a fireplace over a bikini and a pool anytime."

I nodded.

"Don't look so horrified." She laughed and swept her hands over her large frame. "Obviously I don't wear bikinis very often."

"I wasn't—"

"Anyways," she said, wiping her hands on her skirt, "let's return to the front and I'll start giving you the lay of the land, maybe even introduce you to some people. Have I told you I'm glad you're here? Please never leave."

We'll see, I thought. Lord knows I certainly was not one for longevity.

By early afternoon, I'd met most of the staff and learned so much about how an advertising agency functioned that my head felt full.

"Well." Quinn checked the time on her phone. "I guess I better get back to my actual job. Those client briefs aren't going to write themselves. Are you okay here for a while?" She turned to leave and then glanced back. "Oh, I almost forgot, we're having kitchen drinks after work. Did you want to join us?"

I swallowed, my mouth suddenly devoid of all moisture. "Kitchen drinks?"

"Yeah, it's our art director's thirty-fourth birthday. He's

been at an off-site meeting all day or I would have taken you over to meet him—he's a bit of a bro-dude, but he's actually pretty decent to work with. We're going to do a special Monday bar cart in the kitchen."

One thing I'd learned about agency life, through the many sordid stories Quinn had told while she was training me, was that the drinking culture was on par with a university frat house. Every Friday one of the interns pushed a cart filled with booze around the office and everyone, and I mean everyone, started the end of the work week having a drink at their desks. Apparently, this was on par with most Canadian advertising agencies.

"I don't think so," I said, desperately trying to produce some saliva. "I mean, I have plans." I'd thought I'd have at least a week to come up with a good story to explain why I didn't drink. I didn't want to start a new job by instantly not fitting in.

"We're starting early though. Your plans aren't until after work, right? You can at least have one drink before you go." Her blue eyes sparkled, urging mine to join in their excitement.

I looked at my lap. I wasn't sure what to say. Until eight months ago, I was one of the first people to look down on those who didn't drink. Those who were more responsible than I was. The boring people. But I guess I would have to own my new reality one of these days. Maybe not to everyone here, but I wanted to be honest with Quinn. Despite the fact that I'd just met her, I had really started to like her. And I didn't make friends that easily.

I took a deep breath. "I don't drink. Alcohol. I don't

drink alcohol." I looked up and held her eyes, searching for the derision, waiting for them to roll, waiting for the inevitable "Why?"

"Cool, okay." She shrugged. "We can get some pop or fun soda water or something. You should still come though, it'll be fun."

Well, that was easier than I thought. "Sure, I'll think about it," I said as she walked away, grateful for her understanding. Honestly, the hardest part about being sober wasn't the not drinking part (although that part was very challenging), it was the not drinking around other people. The socializing part. I had no idea how much alcohol was tied to social conventions until I stopped drinking it. I mean, I knew I drank a lot, I would have a drink any chance I got; the old Julie would have already been in the kitchen pouring a glass of red. But I hadn't realized how much a part of the social fabric drinking was, how people didn't just use it to forget—to get through their lives like I did—they also used it to connect. It was a way to form and strengthen relationships. An excuse to go out; a way to bond.

Co-workers formed friendships, and, as friends, they were more likely to open up. I hadn't realized how hard it would be not to participate in that anymore. How out of place I would feel at my other jobs. When you were the only one not drinking in a room full of uninhibited, after-work drinkers, you really noticed it. And, in my mind, so did everyone else.

Around 3:30 p.m., I heard the first rustlings in the kitchen. Bottles clinking, glasses being taken out of the cupboard, the fridge door opening and closing, the crisp pop of a can being opened. My mouth actually started watering.

A few subdued voices turned into more as people decided they were done for the day, shedding their work armours as they took their first sips. Carbonated bubbles loosened tongues and lifted laughter. Louder voices rode on the giddy relief that work was finally over. Someone turned on some music.

I locked my computer and took a deep breath. There was only so long I could sit here before someone asked if I was going to come and join the fun. Or no one would, which would be worse. I guess I would have to do this eventually. If I stuck to my contract, I was going to work here for at least six months. I doubted I was going to be able to skirt on the surface of the social scene here like I did at my other, month-long terms. I might as well get it over with.

I walked into the kitchen and was met with a slightly tipsy yell; the kind of yell that I had once been so familiar with. "What are you drinking, new girl?"

I stopped in my tracks, my eyes glued to an alarmingly attractive man wearing a cardboard hat announcing that he was, indeed, the birthday boy. He looked like he'd just stepped out of a *Men's Health* magazine. How had he slipped by my desk unnoticed? His cheek bones alone would have piqued my interest. And the rest of him? My goodness.

"You were away from your desk when I came in." He stuck out his hand and winked like he knew me. "I'm Ethan. What are you drinking?"

Wine, please! I wanted to shout as I ignored the wink

and shook his hand, his palm twice the size of mine. I wanted a drink so badly I was having a physical reaction. I discreetly wiped my palms on my pants and breathed deeply, trying to slow my pounding heart. I could smell the sweet heaviness wafting out of an opened bottle of Cab Sav and the pleasure centres of my brain started firing. I could almost feel the buzz. The comfort. The safety of cloudy thoughts.

With the greatest amount of effort I had ever put forth, I opened my mouth to politely decline when suddenly Quinn was shoving an icy can of sparkling water into my hands. "Have some of this," she said. "I'm not drinking tonight."

"Because she sucks!" someone yelled in the background.

"And," she continued, rolling her eyes, "I hate not drinking alone. Would you be my not-drinking buddy?" She grinned.

I met her eyes, stunned into silence, my mouth open; then it softened into a grateful smile when I realized what she was doing.

"Sure," I said, opening the can. "I don't need to drink to have fun," I said a bit louder, my voice met with a few cheers mingled with some low boos.

"Thank you," I whispered, watching Ethan out of the corner of my eye as he rejoined his buddies.

Quinn just smiled and turned back to the group. "Now, which one of you jerks said I sucked?"

"Does everyone else always leave before cleaning up?" I asked as Quinn stacked glasses on the counter and I put them in the dishwasher.

"Yup," she said. "Often our fearless leaders will sit at the table drinking wine and chatting while the women clean up the mess, so everyone else thinks it's fine."

"Amazing." I picked up a piece of crumpled paper someone had thrown on the floor and tossed it in the garbage. "And thanks again, by the way. For, you know." I held up my empty can of sparkling water and gave it a shake.

She smiled. "Speaking of...that." Her bright eyes dropped to her hands. "Please tell me if I'm out of line, the last thing I want to do is offend you."

"I'm not easily offended." I returned her smile. "Try your best."

"I don't know why you don't drink, and you don't have to tell me." She pulled on her sleeve. "But one of my friends runs a support group and it's really great. She's really great. And I'm always looking for ways to help her out. And maybe you already have a group or maybe you don't need a group, but if you do, I could give you the information."

She was looking everywhere but at me and my heart went out to her, knowing she was trying to help in what, for many, could be a very delicate situation.

"I am actually looking for something new," I said and she relaxed.

"It's not super formal," she continued, now meeting my eyes. "Just a bunch of people dealing with the same issues, getting together and talking." She shrugged and her words disappeared into her shoulder.

"It sounds interesting," I said, not knowing how much I wanted to reveal but at the same time somehow knowing that Quinn wouldn't judge me. "I tried a different kind of group a month ago and it didn't go very well." I hesitated. Should I tell her why? Did I really want to introduce someone I'd just met, and more importantly liked, to the barely functional train wreck that was my life?

I decided I did. I might as well be totally honest with at least one person I worked with.

I watched her closely as I told her the story of my meltdown, and subsequent realization that I needed to get my shit together, searching her sunny face for signs of disapproval.

"You know," she said after I was done, "I admire you for standing up for what you believe in. Most women wouldn't do that in front of a group of people."

"Well, most women aren't dangerously close to falling into the abyss of insanity."

She tipped her head to the side, clearly questioning my logic. "Most women I know are."

Fair point.

"You know what?" she said as she closed the dishwasher door and draped the cloth over the side of the sink. "I think we're going to be great friends."

I smiled, secretly pleased that she thought so. With the exception of Kate, I hadn't had many real friends who were women. Or who were men, for that matter. When I was younger, I was too busy looking after Ben; his anxiety had often displayed as silence, making him a prime target for bullies. My parents did their best—I knew they loved us—but when presented with something they didn't fully understand, something that no one talked about when they were our age, they preferred to pretend everything was fine, never really evolving into the kind of Boomers who felt comfortable talking about emotions. If it hadn't been for Kate sticking by my side, I likely would have started drinking much earlier than I did.

I wondered if Quinn would feel the same once she found out about everything else.

Chapter Five

This place is a dump.

I hung back outside the door of yet another dingy room, in yet another stifling community centre, and watched as people of all shapes and sizes walked past me, some with a flicker of interest, most with friendly smiles.

I watched as they cheerfully greeted one another, feet scuffing on worn Berber carpet, claiming seats on chairs the colour of safety pylons. Did all of these groups have orange plastic chairs? Was it in a handbook or something?

I watched as the last couple of people walked into the room: both women in their twenties, both blonde and perky. Both with the wherewithal to start conquering their demons before completely wasting their youth.

I took a deep breath and walked into the room, grabbing a stale muffin off the grey plastic table on my way to one of the folding chairs. As much as I wanted to spin around on my strappy sandal heel and never come back, I made myself sit, tore off a piece of the muffin and popped it into my mouth.

Gross, raisins.

Off to a great start, I thought, forcing myself to swallow the mouthful and then setting the muffin down on the floor.

As much as I knew I needed to be here, as much as I'd promised Kate and Ben, I would have much preferred to be lying on my couch right now, pretending my brain wasn't heavy with depression, that my hands weren't shaking so much I had to tuck them under my thighs, that I really, *really* wanted a drink.

"Thanks for joining us, everyone." A friendly looking woman who looked to be in her late fifties stood at the front of the room, and everyone quieted down. "We have some new people here today." She looked in my direction and gave me a warm smile. "Welcome, I'm Corie."

I nodded in acknowledgment and tried to smile back at the woman I assumed was Quinn's friend. She had none of the flamboyant brightness of my new favourite colleague—comfortably neutral in her beige yoga pants and light brown T-shirt—but her kind eyes gave her away as someone who could be worthy of Quinn's recommendation.

"Did you want to introduce yourself?" Corie adjusted her wire-framed glasses and tucked a piece of silver hair behind her ear. "No pressure."

I leaned back and crossed my legs, flattening my sleeveless silk tunic top over my robin's egg blue capris. "I'm Julie," I finally said, biting the bullet. I waited for the inevitable, "Hiiii Julie," but it didn't happen. Did I keep going? Did I have to say I was an alcoholic? I chose to pass. "I had a bit of a breakdown at the last meeting I attended," I said, keeping my tone light.

"Is that why you're here?" Corie tilted her head like

she was looking at a bird who'd just flown into a plate glass window.

"No, I'm here because I'm a drunk," I said and then lowered my eyes. I hadn't meant for it to come out sounding so harsh.

The room was silent, but I held my ground, refusing to be vulnerable. *I am not here to make friends,* I thought, like I was on a reality TV show.

"Thanks, Julie," Corie said, her kind smile never faltering. "Welcome to the group. If you have any questions or need anything, don't hesitate to ask." She looked away. "Does anyone have anything they want to share today?"

I sat silently for the rest of the meeting, listening as people shared their stories. I felt nothing when a lady broke down because she'd shattered two years of sobriety by getting drunk at a party and sleeping with her best friend's husband. I felt numb as people held her hand and hugged her and told her they were there for her no matter what. I refused to feel compassion. I couldn't allow myself to take that risk again. I had let everyone in my life down. I had let myself down. The emptiness I felt inside was all I truly deserved.

At the end of the meeting, all I wanted to do was escape. I grabbed my purse off the floor, threw my muffin in the garbage and strode purposely towards the door. *I have somewhere important to be,* my face screamed. *Don't even attempt to talk to me.*

"Julie, wait a moment." I looked at my watch and frowned. I was going to be late for the pretend thing that I was rushing out for.

Corie quickly caught up with me, accurately interpreting my impatience. "I just wanted to make sure you were okay," she said softly. "Obviously, I don't know what your story is, but I know it's hard to be new. If you don't want to talk, that's absolutely fine. You can just come here and listen every week. Whatever you're comfortable with." Her face was warm and open, in direct contrast to mine.

I smiled, finally, and allowed my shoulders to lower from their protective stance. Despite my unrestrained hostility, she was being very kind and seemed genuinely interested in my well-being. And, if she was going to let me show up every week and listen to everyone else's problems without participating, who was I to argue? That was basically my dream.

"I'm fine," I said. "Thank you for asking. I'm just a bit...." I struggled to find the words. What was I, really?

"Tired? Going through withdrawal? Feeling hopeless? All of that is perfectly normal." She put her hand on my shoulder and I softened even more, feeling the warmth pull the depression from my bones.

"Can I ask how long you've been sober?" she asked.

"Almost two months," I said. "Before that, though, I'd made it seven months."

"That's great!" she said without mockery. "And you're still going through withdrawal?"

"A bit," I lied. It was definitely more than a bit. "But not as bad as the first time I quit," I lied again. "I'm just always kind of a jerk." I grinned and she laughed.

"You know, we get all types. The fact that you're here is important. You don't have to be all glitter and rainbows.

All we ask is that you treat everyone here with respect, and you did do that. Maybe one day you'll be able to extend that kindness to yourself."

I opened my mouth to speak and she stopped me by holding up her hand. "It's okay," she said. "You don't have to say anything. It was your first day; of course it was going to be hard. It might never be easy, but it will get easier."

I nodded and moved away, not wanting her to see my eyes fill with tears. I wanted to tell her how awful I felt. How disappointed I was in myself. How I wanted to stop being scared. But instead, I said, "See you next week?"

"You bet," she said. "Take care, Julie."

Chapter Six

I was in my late teens when Gwyneth Paltrow and Brad Pitt dated. Along with many people, I barely remember this happening, but I have a surprisingly accurate recollection of one thing: what she was wearing when they attended the Oscars in 1996. A gorgeous white slip dress that hung on her perfectly; at once both sexy and glamorous. While Kate cut out pictures of puffy princess gowns with capped sleeves and winding trains to slip into her wedding binder, I coveted the simplicity of the slip dress. Kate envisioned herself getting married as Cinderella, but when I thought of my wedding, I wanted to be Gwyneth Paltrow.

Now on the rare occasions when I thought of weddings, they did not feature me in a slip dress, or any dress for that matter. Now weddings were just events that needed to be attended. Parties where I tried to determine how long a couple would stay together based on the length of their tedious speeches.

Which is why no one was more shocked than I was when I volunteered to help plan one. I knew in my heart that Ben and Kate would defy the odds, that their love would last forever, but I was probably the last person who should have been planning the event that would send them on their journey. And knowing that I was planning it with Mr. Cheerful Pants didn't make getting out of bed on Sunday morning to go meet him any easier.

But I wasn't doing this for fun. I was doing it for Ben and Kate. And I was doing it to prove that I could. So, after a solid ten-minute pep talk, I forced myself out of bed and got ready to go meet Luke.

Kate had organized the first wedding planning meeting and I was grateful she'd picked a Starbucks; at least I would be drinking good coffee while I hated my life. Pumpkin Spiced Latte season had started early this year and, while out loud I scorned the pumpkin spice lovers of the world, inside my soul I secretly was one.

I stood at the glass door, peering in, trying to see if Luke had arrived. The trademark Starbucks smell made my mouth water, but I was still not super eager to go inside.

"Hey there!"

I jumped and spun around to face Luke's giant grin.

I put my hand on my heart. "Jesus, you scared the crap out of me."

He laughed. "Sorry. I may be big, but I'm also super stealthy. Like a ninja." His hands karate-chopped the air between us. "Are you going to go in or just stand outside?"

I opened the door with a sweeping gesture. "After you."

He walked in with a spring in his step. "Nice! I didn't know Pumpkin Spice season started in August!" He beamed. "I'll have a grande pumpkin spice latte, extra whip," he said to the barista and then turned back to me. "Can I get you one?"

"Sure," I said, secretly pleased I didn't have to pay for my expensive treat. "No whip on mine though." He held his hand up when I did the obligatory reach into my purse for my wallet.

I nodded a "thank you" and sat down at a nearby table.

He walked over to wait for the coffees, his navy soccer shorts cheerfully swishing. I peered at him through my eyelashes as he shoved his hands into his pockets. I mean, I wasn't dressed up by any means, but at least I'd made a bit of an effort with my teal polka dot dress. It wasn't like he'd just come from the gym. He certainly didn't look like an athlete.

He sure was friendly though. He spent another five minutes chatting with the barista after our coffees were ready. Were we going to be here all day?

"Sorry about that." He sat down and took a sip of his coffee. "It turns out I went to high school with her sister in Toronto. Small world, eh?"

"Saskatchewan is relatively small," I grumped as I sipped my coffee. "Everyone is connected somehow." I refused to buy in to his cheerful attitude.

"Right you are!" And he clearly refused to be taken down by my shitty one.

"So." He leaned in, narrowly missing a sticky glob of something in the centre of the table. "Aside from planning weddings, what do you like to do for fun?"

And there it was. I had been wondering when he was going to ask me out. I'd been doing my best to make it clear that I was only here to get a job done, but I guess Luke was just like any other man.

"First of all, planning weddings isn't really my idea of

fun, and secondly, sorry, but I'm not interested." I sipped my coffee and forced a smile.

He tilted his head in confusion. "Interested in what? Doing things for fun?"

"Listen." I jumped right in with my standard spiel. "I'm sure you're great and everything, you seem very…unique… but I'm not interested in dating at the moment."

He looked absolutely clueless for half a second and then burst out laughing.

"Oh, you thought I was asking you out?" he said after he calmed down. "No, sorry, you misunderstood; I was just trying to get to know you better because we'll be working so closely together."

Oh.

"Oh," I said, flipping my hair back. "Well, good."

"Good!" He grinned like I didn't just embarrass myself. "I'm glad we got that cleared up. Now, let's talk wedding. Question though, if you don't like planning weddings, then why are you helping to plan this one?"

I sighed, not wanting to reveal that planning this wedding was basically my lifeline. "I'm doing it for Ben and Kate," I said. "So they won't be stressed out."

"Makes sense. That's very kind of you." He pulled out his laptop and flipped up the lid to reveal a sticker that said *Good Vibes Only.*

"Good Lord," I said softly.

"Cool hey?" He turned it around so he could admire it. "My friend gave it to me, the one I was with when we first met at the AA meeting. He makes them, you know, to keep his mind off things."

"Is that why you were at that meeting?" I asked. "To help your friend?"

He nodded. "I find it rewarding to help those who are close to me."

I nodded in return, unsure of what to say. Luke appeared to be very good at expressing his feelings, something I was not able to do as easily.

By the time we finished our coffees, we'd gone over a list of potential venues—prioritized by need and then price—and had made a good start on a guest list to send to Ben and Kate for review. Both of them had been sporadically texting me names throughout the week, and, while Luke was giving me his thoughts on gift registries, I compiled them all in a Word document. I was pretty proud of myself.

Luke knew a graphic designer who worked at a print shop, so we chose some sample invitation designs for Ben and Kate to look at as well.

Before I knew it, two hours had gone by and we'd accomplished quite a bit. I didn't want to admit it, but I wouldn't have done that much on my own in two hours. I probably wouldn't have done that much in two weeks. I guess having Luke help hadn't been such a bad idea after all.

"That was a great planning session," he said when we were finished, closing his laptop with a satisfied grin. "This wedding is going to be epic."

Epic? Who still said epic?

I stood up and grabbed my purse as he slid his laptop into a puffy red case.

"Thanks for coming, Julie." He reached out his hand

like we'd just settled an important business transaction and I shook it half-heartedly. "I know I wasn't your first choice for co-planner."

"It wasn't that it was you," I lied. "I had just thought I was going to be planning it by myself."

He nodded as if he completely understood. "I hear ya," he said. "But I appreciate you letting me help. I love stuff like this. I'm used to planning construction projects. It's nice to be able to do something fun."

"Well, if this is your idea of fun, you're welcome to it." I pushed my chair in. "It seems like you're good at it," I added.

Luke gasped and I jumped.

"What?" I said, looking around anxiously. Did a bird fly into the window? Did Starbucks run out of oat milk?

He put his hand on his chest in mock astonishment. "Did you just compliment me?" he asked with a twinkle in his eye.

"Don't get used to it." I tried to hide the smile that was tugging at the corners of my lips.

We said our goodbyes in the parking lot and made plans to meet back at the same Starbucks in a week—"our office," he called it. And, of course, we both had homework. We each had to contact five venues on the list and inquire about availability and cost, something I had already started to feel anxious about. I needed this wedding to be a complete success, which meant starting with a perfect location. It was already less than a year until the wedding; I really hoped we hadn't left it too late.

After I left Starbucks, all I wanted was a drink. I longed for the buzzy comfort, thoughts hiding in the cloudy residue, tension draining from my body with every sip. In the past I would have easily given in to the temptation, but now, whenever I felt that way, I knew I needed to stop those thoughts in their tracks. So, Sunday night, I went back to Group.

I quietly slipped in after everyone had sat down. The plastic folding chairs were arranged into a not-quite circle and Corie was getting ready to start. She smiled and winked as I joined, her hands stuffed casually in the back pockets of her loose-fitting sweatpants.

Someone had propped open a couple of windows and the room, while usually hot and stuffy, was actually a comfortable temperature. The sweetness of the end-of-summer evening wafted in, masking the stale, old-building smell. My shoulders relaxed and the tension started to dissipate.

"Okay, everyone." Corie clapped her hands together. "Tonight, I'd like you to think about who you're here for and, if you're comfortable, share that with the group. I hope, above all, you're here for yourself, but there is no wrong answer. As long as you're here, that's all that matters."

The room went silent. Everyone looked at the floor, at the walls, anywhere but at Corie or at one another. She smiled and looked around the room. "Anyone?"

I shifted in my chair.

"Julie, great!" she said.

"Um, no...I was just...."

"Go ahead," she said gently. "This is a safe space."

"Well," I started. I wasn't used to this, being uncomfortable in front of other people. I was always the extrovert, the centre of attention, the life of the party. Opening up was harder than I thought without the comfort of a medium booze buzz.

"I'm here because I fell off the wagon almost two months ago." I glanced around, still somehow expecting judgment, despite the genuine friendly smiles and faces alert with encouragement. "Before that, I was sober for seven months." I paused among the murmurs of support. "Until I mistakenly thought I could have a drink at my brother and best friend's engagement party."

When Ben and Kate had announced their engagement, I'd been as thrilled as anyone. I'd known it was coming; they were perfect for each other. So, who could blame me when I'd wanted to have a glass of champagne to celebrate? I'd been sober for seven months. I knew what I was getting into.

"I thought I could handle it," I said, remembering saying the same thing to Ben and Kate as they'd both looked anywhere but at my face, Ben's hand on his neck, Kate's expression somber.

"I thought I'd conquered my demons. I knew my limits. I could totally drink casually now, you know?" I said to the room. They knew.

Turned out I couldn't.

That first sip was pure bliss. The tang of alcohol on my tongue, the fuzzy warmth in my stomach. My whole body relaxed. I was finally able to breathe again.

I tried to only have one. But that glorious feeling, the

heightened joy, the crystal clarity, the comforting glow. If I felt this way after one, I would surely feel even better after two. And then I'd stop. Once I'd hit the peak of boozy nirvana, I'd allow myself to gently float back down.

Two glasses of champagne had turned into three, which had then turned into who knows how many as I'd continued my one-person party by sneaking sips or finishing off bottles when people weren't looking. Or, at least, when I thought they weren't looking.

"And, as anyone who has ever had a drinking problem knows," I continued to explain to a room full of people who surely did, "once you hit that peak, you've already passed the point of no return. The more you chase the joy the more elusive it becomes. And then, before you know it, it's gone. And you're alone. And miserable. And all you want to do is lie down and close your eyes and sleep for days. Until the nausea stops. Until the spinning subsides. Until everyone stops looking at you like they've just eaten a bad piece of shrimp."

After being sober for seven months, I couldn't hold my alcohol. And I couldn't hide it like I used to. But, more importantly, I didn't want to hide it. When Kate found me in the bathroom at the engagement party, splashing my face with water, wiping the mascara off with a paper towel, I didn't lie. I didn't say I'd eaten something bad. I didn't suggest that maybe I had the flu.

All I said was sorry. And I let Ben carry me to the car. And I let them take me home.

"I guess I won't ever be able to drink like a normal person." My face flushed with shame as I recounted the end of the night, Kate holding back my hair, watching me puke the hardest and well-earned seven months of my life into a bucket by the side of my bed.

"So, of course, I got back on the wagon," I finished, looking around, meeting eyes filled with kindness, feeling the power of everyone's trust. Everyone nodded, a couple of people even clapped.

But I wasn't finished.

I cleared my throat and wiped my palms on my dress, knowing my body was trying to tell me something that my brain refused to align to.

Stop lying, it was saying.

And so I finally did.

"Except," I said, my eyes lowered, "I actually fell off the wagon two more times after the engagement party. I guess I really wasn't on the wagon to begin with." I looked up, surprised I'd said anything, surprised I'd revealed a secret that I hadn't even told Kate.

Kate had been so busy with Ben and her freelancing work, and I had been so sure I could do it myself, that I'd fallen back off the wagon not once but twice. And I'd fallen hard. Back to drinking a bottle of wine by myself before 6:00 p.m. Back to trolling online dating sites and inviting randoms over to play. Back to trying to hide from my life, the life I'd been trying to hide from since my early twenties.

The second time I'd fallen, I'd almost gotten caught. Ben had stopped by to check in and I was still sleeping at noon. Luckily, I'd had the good sense to hide the wine bottle outside in the trash the night before. He didn't say anything, but I'm pretty sure he knew. I'd seen that look in his eyes before. Disappointment. Worry. Fear.

"That's when I decided to try AA," I said. "It had worked for so many people. All I had to do was pretend I was super motivated to hop back on that wagon and be a better me; pretend that I wasn't full of shame and remorse for wasting almost a year of my life; that all I needed was twelve steps and a higher power."

The truth was I wasn't motivated to hop back on the wagon. I wasn't doing it for me at all. I was doing it because, once again, I'd let down the only people I loved. The truth was that taste of champagne at the party, that taste of being able to relax and feel good about myself and say what I wanted, and do what I wanted, and not have to try so hard to be perfect—that was something I had missed desperately. I'd missed the taste of being able to forget.

The room was silent as I finished, the heads that had been nodding knowingly throughout had stilled. "So, that's why I'm here. I'm here because I messed up. I'm here for Ben and Kate. I'm here so they don't have to carry me for the rest of their lives."

"And what about yourself?" Corie asked.

"What do you mean?"

"Aren't you here for yourself as well?"

"Sure, I guess." I shrugged. "I mean, I mostly just want to prove to them that a Julie can exist in their lives who isn't a fuck-up. I've even volunteered to help plan their wedding and I hate weddings. Maybe you guys could give me some wedding ideas?" I joked, my go-to strategy for digging myself out of something uncomfortable.

Corie nodded and laughed along with the rest of the group. "Thanks so much, Julie," she said. "We appreciate your honesty." She looked around the room. "All right, who's next?"

I sat back in my uncomfortable chair and breathed out slowly. I hadn't realized my shoulders were raised until they'd lowered back into place. Telling the truth had been easier than I thought. Maybe this group would really help. Maybe I wouldn't have to do this alone.

Present Day

From: Julie
Sent: July 12th 11:16 PM
To: Luke
Subject: Are you okay?

Hi Luke,

I know you probably hate me right now, but I just need to know you're all right. Are you? All right? Please let me know.

Love, Julie

Chapter Seven

Ten Months Ago

It had been one month since I'd started temping at the agency and, against my better judgment, I was actually enjoying it. I mean, the work was mindless and leadership was a bit lacking, but working with someone like Quinn made up for the fact that the place was run purely on the fumes of burnout. In any case, it didn't really affect me. No one cared about administrators.

Today, however, Quinn looked extra haggard. The circles under her eyes were a bit darker, the blue a little less sparkly.

"Are you okay?" I asked as she placed three more files on my desk. She was wearing a flower-printed purple dress with pink leggings and a green silk scarf draped around her neck. Her dark hair was pulled back into two teased pigtail buns. Despite the fact that her outfit didn't quite suit her mood, she was totally pulling it off. I loved it.

"Is it the weekend yet?" Her crossed arms rested on my high desk and her head fell to meet them.

"Are you going out for drinks after work?" I asked,

hoping that would put a smile on her face. Her head rose and I was rewarded with a weak one.

"I'll go if you go."

"Done."

"I'm going to drink this time though. Probably a lot." She stood up straight and pulled her shoulders back in a stretch. "It's been a week."

"As you should." I pulled the files off the top of my desk and placed them beside me. "I'm a big girl. I can take care of myself."

Quinn smiled as she rubbed the back of her neck.

"Looks like someone needs a massage." Marc, the head of Creative, walked into the lobby, hands outstretched, fingers wiggling.

"No thanks." Quinn's expression darkened and she turned her back towards the wall.

"But you love my massages!" Marc hung his head, pretending to be hurt. "You've never said no before." He smoothed his hand over his greying hair, which was currently slicked back into a man bun.

"Mostly because you always start before I have a chance to say anything." She crossed her arms.

"Ha!" Marc barked and leaned on the desk towards me. "Don't listen to her. I give great massages."

"Good to know," I said as I rolled my chair a few inches back. He was so close I could smell the stale coffee on his breath.

"Your loss," he said, brushing off the rejection like a piece of fuzz from his bespoke suit jacket. "See you ladies at Pile O'Bones for drinks?"

We both nodded.

"What a creep," Quinn said after he'd left. "I've got a bit more to do; then do you want to walk over to the brewery together?"

I nodded. "You bet."

"Marty!" she squealed, her eyes brightening then disappearing along with the rest of her.

I peeked over the top of my desk to find Quinn kneeling on the ground, skirt splayed, Marty's furry rear end wagging back and forth frantically underneath it.

She giggled as I sighed and sat back down. Marty was one of our office dogs, Marc's dog to be exact. A loveable, scrappy Boston terrier. If you liked that sort of thing. Apparently, Marc didn't even like dogs but had fought for him in his divorce proceedings just to piss his wife off. Marc was a real gem.

"Who's a good boy? Who's a goodsie woodsie boysie woysie?" Quinn's voice had suddenly taken on the quality of someone several IQ scores lower than possibly even the dog.

"Julie, come pet Marty," she said, her voice shifting back to human form. "He looks so cute today! I think he got a new collar."

"I'm good." I clicked on my keyboard to show I was, indeed, too busy to go pet a dog.

"But he's so cute!"

"Yes, I believe I heard that somewhere."

"Don't tell me you hate dogs." She pushed herself up to standing and brushed off her skirt, narrowing an eye in my direction.

"I don't hate dogs," I said, arms crossed. "I just don't love them like everyone else on the planet seems to. I leave them alone; they leave me alone. It's a mutually acceptable agreement." I peeked over the desk again. "I don't hate you, Marty," I said in a normal voice. "I'm sure you're delightful. But I also don't think we need to be friends, OK?"

Marty looked up at me, sneezed, and then trotted off in the direction of the kitchen.

"Is it bad to say I like you a little bit less than I did this morning?" Quinn smiled in a half-joking, half-serious kind of way.

"I would believe you if I wasn't so likeable." I smirked. "Now go finish that work or I'll tell Marc you changed your mind about the massage."

"Are you going to get a beer?" Ethan slid onto the distressed wooden bench beside me and ordered a pint of Nokomis Brown Ale from the server as she walked by. "We could share a flight." I looked around, wondering why Ethan had chosen our table to sit at when he usually sat with the Creative department. Our office was very cliquey that way.

"No, thanks." I moved over to give him room as Brian, an account executive, slid in and Ethan's thigh pressed against mine. Old Julie wouldn't have moved her legs, she would have kept them pressed up against his, office inappropriateness be damned. New Julie, however, slid over a bit more in the opposite direction.

He was incredibly attractive though. And just my type. Dark blond hair hung below his chin like a curtain. My fingers twitched as I thought about reaching up and tucking a strand behind his ears. As if reading my mind, he ran his hand through the silky strands, pushing them back from his broad face. My thighs buzzed as his biceps flexed under his tight blue dress shirt, buttons straining over his broad shoulders and wide chest.

He works out, I thought automatically and found myself wanting a drink now more than ever. Alcohol was always my excuse for doing things I would never do when I was sober. It loosened my moral resolve. And I used to use it for just that purpose.

I slowly inhaled a deep, shaky breath and swallowed the lump of panic that had started forming in my throat. *I can do this,* I told myself. *I've come this far.*

Despite it being challenging, after-work drinks had become really fun. I hadn't realized that the more other people drank the more comfortable I would feel. At the beginning, when everyone was just starting—feeling things out, letting go of inhibitions—it was more obvious that I was the only one without something boozy in my hands. But after an hour or so, when people started to relax, when I started to relax, it was easier to be sober. People stopped asking if I wanted a drink. Everyone was more involved with their own. No one really cared. So, I stopped caring too.

"I'm glad you came out." Ethan leaned in so I could hear him over the din. The trendy brewery wasn't just a popular place for my co-workers; it was packed. Corporate folks seamlessly blended with trendy hipsters, sitting around polished wooden tables, playing pinball, draining glasses of one of the many craft beers on tap.

"Can I tell you a secret?" Ethan whispered in my ear and I involuntarily shivered.

"Sure," I said, immediately wary.

He leaned closer. "When we first met, I thought you were going to be 'too cool to hang'." He air-quoted, incorrectly.

"What does 'too cool to hang' mean?" I air-quoted right back at him.

"You know, like you thought you were better than everyone or something," he said, his sexy grin softening the bluntness of his statement.

All of sudden it became really important that he knew I used to be fun. That I used to party. That I was never too cool to hang. *That's totally not me!* I wanted to scream. *I'm always the life of the party!*

But instead, I said, "I was just a bit shy," and then laughed. Even I didn't believe that. The server came back and placed Ethan's beer on a cardboard coaster and then nodded at me.

"I'll just have a soda water and cranberry, please." I smiled, face flushing, pretending it was what I really wanted, ignoring the speed of my craving-fueled heartbeat.

"Oh, come on," Ethan teased, nudging me with his elbow. "It's Friday. Live a little."

A flash of irritation dimmed my forced smile, igniting an uncomfortable revelation: *This used to be me.* I used to be the asshole pressuring people to drink when they didn't want to. Why didn't anyone tell me to fuck right off because it was none of my business what they drank or didn't drink?

And then, just like that, I wasn't embarrassed. I was angry. It truly was no one's business but my own what I decided to do and what I chose to put into my body. Ethan had no idea what my story was. Just like I'd had no idea what everyone else's story was when I'd looked down on them for not being as cool as I thought they should be.

"I don't drink," I said finally, holding his gaze. "And I'd appreciate it if you respected that."

His eyes widened and he briefly looked like he'd been slapped. Clearly no one had ever told him what he couldn't do before and he wasn't quite sure how to handle it.

The table went silent and my face turned an even brighter shade of red, but I held my resolve. I didn't apologize for "being a bitch," I stuck by my words. This was me now, and if he didn't like it, that was his problem. I didn't have to be friends with everyone I worked with.

His face softened. "Hey, you do you, bro. I was just having some fun. Good for you for taking care of yourself. That's totally dope." He grinned. People started talking again. I looked over at Quinn and she smiled and gave me a thumbs up. I had done it. I had told my truth. And I had survived.

Later, when everyone was leaving, Quinn leaned over from across the table and touched my arm. "You know," she said, "if you ever want a non-drinking buddy, I'm always up for it. I mean, I often drink, but I don't have to. Like I said before, you don't have to tell me anything, but for whatever reason you're choosing not to drink, I respect that, especially when our culture—both in agency and in general—doesn't always welcome non-drinkers with open arms."

I smiled gratefully. She was right. Non-drinkers had a tough time in our "it's five o'clock somewhere" poppin' bottles zeitgeist. I didn't realize how much I had needed an ally. And now I had one. And a pretty cool one at that.

"Thanks," I said, not quite ready to reveal more. "I really appreciate it."

Chapter Eight

I woke up on Saturday morning to no fewer than fifteen texts from Luke.

How's the venue list going? Haven't started.

What about the museum? Hard pass.

Do you think they'd want to get pictures done at Mosaic Stadium? Doubtful.

Here's the link to the updated spreadsheet! Don't you have a job?

"I feel like we won't have anything to talk about considering you've been texting me all week," I said when I arrived at "our office" and sat down at the six-person table he had set up as what looked to be mission control. He had the sleeves rolled up on his shirt, plaid of course, like he was ready to get down to business.

"Oh, we have plenty to talk about," he said, ignoring my tone. "Let's see your venue list."

"Hold on there, quick start." I held up my hand. "I need to get a coffee first."

"Here." He pushed one towards me. "Pumpkin Spice latte, no whip, right?"

I stood there, stunned. He was right. How did he know what I liked after only having one coffee together?

"I pay attention," he said, reading my mind.

I sat and pulled the coffee towards me, nodded a quick "thank you," and took a sip. Heaven.

"You're welcome. List, please."

Surprising both of us, I had made a list. And I'd talked to Kate to get her thoughts. I figured he probably thought I wouldn't do it so I was pretty proud of myself when I handed it over.

"Looks good." He nodded. "Almost exactly the same as mine. So, we agree that the Hotel Saskatchewan is our first choice?"

I nodded. "It's expensive, but it's basically Kate's dream wedding venue. The perfect combination of history and class. She actually had pictures of the Regency Ballroom hanging up on her wall beside her New Kids on the Block posters when we were in high school." I smiled, remembering a simpler time. "I'm not sure if she would ever be completely happy without getting married beneath a ceiling dripping with extravagant chandeliers. And the best part is, if people don't want to stay there overnight, there are a lot of other options close by. That's the beauty of being downtown."

"Great!" He clicked a few buttons on his laptop. "Location, done!"

"Sorry to burst your achievement bubble, but don't we actually have to book it before we're done?"

"I did already."

What?

"What?"

"When I was phoning around to see if the venues were available, I booked this one, just in case. I knew it was one of their top choices, but I wanted to see what you thought before I confirmed."

"What if I hadn't agreed?" I asked, moderately impressed by his sneaky initiative.

"The deposit is refundable if I cancel within ten days."

"Oh. Well, okay." I sipped my coffee, attempting to hide the fact that I couldn't think of anything else to say. Part of me wanted to be angry because he'd booked the venue without involving me, but another, larger, part of me was relieved because booking a venue was a huge thing off our plates.

"Sorry," he said, a concerned expression on his face. "I didn't mean to exclude you. I just thought that venues were hard to book so we might as well get a jump on it. I promise, for everything else, we'll move forward together."

"No, it's fine." I smiled. "It was smart. You're right. Venues are hard to book."

He stared out into space, a wistful gleam in his eyes, his mouth softening into a goofy grin. "It's going to be so romantic. Don't you love weddings?"

"Not really."

"Why not?"

I opened my mouth to give my standard answer about extravagant social constructs but instead said, "I don't know, they just make me sad." *Where did that come from?*

"How so?" he said, giving me his full attention.

For a brief second, I considered telling him the truth.

That the idea of taking part in an event requiring a healthy relationship and long-term commitment was something I'd considered myself so far removed from for so long that the only thing I could feel now was grief.

But the moment passed and I came to my senses. The last thing I wanted to do was to be vulnerable in front of someone I'd only met a couple of months ago. After this wedding was over, I would never see him again.

"You know, the money," I said, snapping back to reality. "Weddings cost a fortune; it's depressing. Okay, what's next?"

"The Stag and Doe," he said after a pause, his voice wavering between questioning and accepting what I'd just said.

Being from Saskatchewan, I had never heard of a Stag and Doe before, but, in Toronto, Luke had assured me, combining the bachelor and bachelorette parties was all kinds of fun.

"Ah, yes," I said, pushing my phone towards him with my list of ideas. This was one thing I could take control of. If anyone knew how to party, it was me.

Luke scrolled through my list. "Gabos? Really? I mean, no offence, but isn't that club full of twenty-year-olds?"

I shrugged, blew on my coffee, and took a sip.

"Well," he said, "I know I don't know Kate as well as you do, but do you think she really wants to attend a party where she has to wear a T-shirt that says, 'My last night of freedom,' with balloon penises taped all over it?"

And that's when I spat out my coffee.

"Oh, shit," I said, jumping to grab some napkins from

the nearby counter. "I'm so sorry." I wiped the coffee drops off his laptop and handed him the rest of the napkins.

He didn't take them. He just sat there with a stunned expression, lips tight, not saying anything.

Well, I guess I'd done it. I'd finally overstayed my welcome in his space of cheerful grace.

I continued to hold out the napkins like a tragic statue, waiting for him to crack, to move, to do anything.

But then his right eye twinkled, and the corner of his mouth twitched, and like the burst of a geyser, a guffaw escaped his pressed-together lips.

"Oh, man, you should see your face," he said, slapping his thigh. "You look like you're about to cry."

"I do not." I twisted my face into a neutral expression.

"You did." He chuckled. "And really? If you wanted to go to Gabos so badly, you just had to say so. You didn't have to spit coffee all over me."

"To be fair," I said, my lips twitching, "I wasn't expecting the words 'balloon penises' to come out of your mouth at our meeting today, so I was a bit taken off guard."

"Totally fine." He dabbed at his keyboard with a napkin. "To be honest, I wasn't either." He smiled and tapped a couple of keys. "It's fine, you didn't wreck it. I can wash it off when I get home."

"I don't get you." I shook my head. "Why are you so smiley all the time? I mean, I just spat coffee all over you and you barely even flinched. You're not mad. You're not irritated. You're just so…happy."

"It bothers you, doesn't it?" He smiled even wider.

"Yes!"

He laughed. "Well, not to get into any great detail, but one day I decided my life was better when I smiled. When I didn't sweat the small stuff. Because the small stuff is easy. If I could smile through the small stuff—like someone spitting coffee all over my laptop—I shouldn't have much to complain about. If I can bring cheer to the table rather than sorrow, I can deal with the bigger stuff much more easily. And hopefully help others do so as well."

"You know, some studies show that positivity psychology is more harmful than saying what you truly feel," I said, not wanting to buy in to his healthy attitude.

"But that's the thing." He leaned in close. "The more I focus on what makes me happy, and the less I care about what other people think"—he looked at me knowingly—"the more cheerful and positive I truly feel." He shrugged as if to say I could take it or leave it. "You only get one shot at life. You better never let it go." He smiled.

"Did you just quote Eminem?"

"Sorry," he said. "I'm just caught up between being a father and a prima donna."

He looked up, face straight, completely serious. I shook my head and looked down, trying desperately not to smile. Trying not to laugh. Trying to keep my face an impenetrable wall of stone.

But no matter how hard I tried, I couldn't stop the giggle from bubbling up from my chest and coming out as a snort.

I looked up and his shoulders were shaking, his hand over his face as he tried not to burst. But it didn't matter. Because I had already fractured. And people had started to look.

"Human emotion looks good on you," Luke teased,

passing me a napkin as I continued to giggle. "Here, this one already has your spat-out coffee on it."

I took the napkin and dabbed at my eyes. "Man," I said. "I haven't laughed like that in a while."

"Feels good, doesn't it?" He wiped his eyes with the back of his hand. "Laughter is such a great stress release."

"Are you actually a father?" I crumpled up my napkin and put it in my empty cup. "Or was that just part of your rap performance?" I lowered my eyes to my hands. Whether or not Luke had a kid was something I should have known; he was my brother's close friend after all. Had I been so preoccupied with staying sober that I had withdrawn from those around me? Maybe it wasn't just Ben and Kate cancelling dinners that was the problem.

"No, I am actually a father." He picked up his phone and swiped so I could see the lock screen unencumbered. An adorable little girl with wild curly red hair and Luke's sparkling green eyes stared back at me. She was hamming it up for the camera, all smiles and teeth. Definitely Luke's child.

"She seems very sweet," I said. I never knew what to say about kids. I wasn't around them very much.

"She is," he said, his eyes full of pride. "Her name is Hannah. She's seven. She's my whole world. You don't have kids?" he said in a way that told me he took the time to learn about his friend's family.

"I don't," I answered. "By choice," I added. "Not that I don't like kids; I've just never really thought about being a mom."

That wasn't entirely true. I definitely didn't want kids

now, but I had thought about it when I was younger. I had thought I'd settle down. I thought I'd quit partying. I just never did. And now, in my mid-forties, I was well past my parenting prime. I probably couldn't have kids even if I wanted to.

He put his phone back down on the table and I waited for him to say something about Hannah's mom. Was she still in the picture?

"Hannah's mom passed away right after she was born," Luke said softly, as if reading my mind. "She was in a car accident."

"I'm so sorry," I breathed. "I didn't know."

"Theresa was the kindest, most generous person I had ever met. Never judgmental, always there to lend a hand. She was truly beautiful, both inside and out." A warm smile brightened his face. "I miss her every day, but I still consider myself very lucky. Do you know why?"

I shook my head, trying to swallow the lump that had formed in my throat.

"Because every day Hannah looks more and more like her. And every day I get to enjoy the wonderful little person she's becoming. She has so much good in her. Just like her mom." He looked at his watch. "Speaking of which, I have to go pick her up from Theresa's mom's. The time's gone by quicker than I thought; we didn't even get to the guest list. I don't suppose you can meet before our normal time next week? We really should have a gift registry link to send out with the save the dates."

"Sure," I said, shaking myself off, trying to recover from the emotional shrapnel.

"What about Wednesday after work?" he asked as I scrolled through the calendar on my phone, knowing that I had literally no plans. "I can drop Hannah off at her grandma's again after school and meet you somewhere."

"That works." I shoved my phone in my purse and walked towards the door. "In the meantime, why don't you send me your edited guest list and I'll send it to Ben and Kate for approval. That way we can focus on the save the date design and get that moving forward."

"Great!" He beamed as he held the door open for me and we stepped outside. "Does Excel work for you?"

I nodded, praying Quinn could show me how to use a spreadsheet. "Perfect."

I got in my car and watched him pull out of his spot and drive by, his waving hand as wide as his toothy grin. I chuckled softly, guessing that his over-the-top joviality was now purely for my benefit. "Well played, Luke Hudson," I murmured.

As I put my car into reverse and slowly backed out of the lot, it suddenly occurred to me why I found these meetings so uncomfortable. Why I found it so difficult to be nice. I'd never had a real friendship with a man before. With the exception of Ben, most of my interactions with men consisted of either one-night stands or brief chats in the halls at work. I'd learned long ago that putting any more effort in was not worth my time. It was best to get what I needed and go, before I was left behind.

With Luke it was different. I was going to be stuck with him for the good part of a year whether I liked it or not. I needed him to help plan a successful wedding and I wouldn't be able to just up and leave before I reached my goal.

I was just going to have to get used to this new dynamic and figure it out as I went along. And more importantly, I was going to have to do it sober.

This was going to be a challenging ten months.

Was it weird that I was kind of looking forward to it?

Chapter Nine

The end of September brought with it the beginning of a season in which our wedding plans were truly going to be carried out in earnest. After hearing what Luke and I had accomplished so far, Kate, who had once been the kind of person with a binder full of bridal preferences, appeared to be embracing the stress-free bliss of having people she trusted take on most of the tough wedding-related tasks.

The four of us celebrated our progress at Ben and Kate's apartment by eating a meal of pasta and garlic toast, Ben's specialty, while Kate entertained Luke with all of her terrible pre-Ben online dating experiences.

"That dinner was amazing." I patted my very full tummy when we had finished. "I'm going to feel this tomorrow." One thing I especially loved about being in my forties was that I had started getting hungover after eating too much. It was fun.

"Here." Ben handed me a couple of fruit-flavored antacids. "Consider this dessert."

Luke smiled. "If I recall, you were always very well stocked in the antacids department when we were in university. That was actually my first clue that you might be struggling with anxiety."

"Really?" Ben's eyebrows rose. "I thought it might have been the panic attack I had in our first chem lab." He grinned, now able to joke about something he had once found so difficult to talk about.

"How were antacids a clue?" I peeled one from the package and popped it into my mouth.

"My sister suffers from anxiety," Luke said, resting his forearms on the table. "And, as a result, has wicked heartburn. She pops those things like candy."

"It really meant a lot that you encouraged me to talk to you about it," Ben said softly. "Until I met you, Julie was the only one who knew."

Luke's chair creaked as he sat back. "I'm happy to have been there for you. Although, I will say, I'm still surprised your parents weren't more involved."

"They mean well," Ben said as we shared a glance. "They just don't know how to deal with things they can't comprehend."

"And they prefer not to," I added.

Luke looked at me. "So, they don't know about your...." He trailed off.

"No," I said. "They don't know about my drinking problem."

"That's kind of sad," Luke said. "I can't imagine not being close to my mom. I tell her everything."

"Well, I guess we're not all that lucky." I shrugged away his concern. I was used to my parents being emotionally absent and I no longer had the energy to feel bad about it.

There were a lot of things they didn't know about my past. Me being an alcoholic was just the tip of the iceberg.

I glanced at Kate, who was swirling the remnants of her soda water in the bottom of her glass. Our mom might have been distant, but at least we knew she loved us. After Kate's dad left, her mom basically quit trying. We never did determine if it was because she knew her incessant bullying had driven him away or if she was just incredibly self-involved. Either way, Kate spent a lot of time at our house when we were kids.

"Are you going to have any other groomsmen?" I asked Ben, knowing that if he wasn't going to ask our dad, that didn't leave many other options.

"I'm actually going to have a groomswoman." He beamed at Luke, who returned the grin. "My friend Sherri, also from university," Ben said. "Luke introduced me to her actually. The three of us were pretty inseparable once upon a time."

"Isn't she also your ex-girlfriend?" I looked at Kate, eyebrow raised.

"It's fine." Kate smiled. "I would actually love to meet her. She helped Ben so much and, for that, I love her already."

"You're a bigger person than I am," I said and gave Ben a look that said he was a very lucky man.

He nodded. He knew.

"How's the new job?" Kate handed Ben her plate as he and Luke cleaned up.

"Good actually," I said. "The work isn't super challenging, but I don't mind it. The people are really nice."

"Any great men at your new place of work?" Her expression was hopeful in a "maybe Julie will find a boyfriend so we can double date" kind of way.

"Not really," I said. "There's one guy named Ethan who's fun. And super cute. But no one boyfriend-worthy."

"Why don't you invite him to the wedding?" Kate said like she'd just discovered the idea and hadn't been thinking it as soon as I'd said "there's one guy."

"I'm pretty sure he has a girlfriend." I shrugged. Quinn had given me the unsolicited intel that Ethan's supposed relationship had been a hot office gossip topic for years. No one had ever seen his girlfriend, and he rarely mentioned her, so everyone was always trying to determine whether or not he actually had one.

Disappointment flickered across Kate's features. "I just want you to be happy," she said.

"I am happy. Well, as happy as I can be. And, believe me, dating someone right now would not increase my level of happiness. Besides, the one thing I did take away from your engagement party is that staying sober is my priority. And while my primary goal is to make it day to day, my main goal is to make it to a year. And beyond, obviously.

"One of the things everyone says—the books and programs and such—is that you shouldn't date anyone during your first year of sobriety. And I'd like to stick to that. I think focusing on myself will really help."

"When you say 'dating,' do you mean...?" Kate's eyebrow rose comically.

"No sex either."

"Hmm," she said. "Interesting."

"You don't think I can do it."

"Well, considering…you know."

I did know. I had slept with a lot of guys over the past couple of decades. A lot. And, I'll admit, a large part of that had to do with the amount of booze I'd consumed in an effort to feel something other than sadness about my shitty past. But staying away from sex for a year was going to be a lot harder than not dating someone for a year, especially considering I hadn't actually dated anyone since I was in my twenties.

"I can do it," I said. "I have to do it. And thanks to your newfound willingness to hand over the reins of your wedding, I'm going to be too busy to even think about it."

Chapter Ten

"You're doing what?" Quinn's fork, stabbed through a tater tot, was suspended halfway between her plate and mouth.

"Planning Kate and Ben's wedding. I thought I told you that already." I looked up and frowned. I hadn't expected her response to be one of overwhelming disbelief.

"I'm pretty sure I would have remembered if you'd told me. Mostly because I thought you didn't like weddings."

I shrugged. It might have been on purpose that I hadn't told her.

"So, not only are you planning one, but you're planning one with a guy you don't like?" Her skepticism was a bit disconcerting.

"I like him," I corrected. "He's just annoying sometimes. We have very different personalities."

"Do you think that's good for your mental health right now?" She raised an eyebrow and pointed her fork at me.

I had recently confided in Quinn about why I didn't drink. How I'd hit rock bottom and almost slept with someone Kate had had a crush on before she and Ben had gotten together. If I hadn't stopped myself, my best and longest-lasting friendship would have been ruined. I still wonder what my life would be like now if I hadn't finally admitted I had a drinking problem. My chest tightened as I remembered the other secret I had revealed to Kate that night. But, as I was wont to do, I swallowed all of my terrible feelings and soldiered on.

"My mental health is fine." I peeled the plastic lid off my take-out Cobb salad. "I'm sure I'll be able to handle a hearty dose of positivity a couple times a week. Besides, he's very organized; something that I am not."

"I've noticed," she said, not unkindly.

I glowered.

"Is he cute at least?" She popped another tater tot into her mouth.

I shrugged. "I don't know. If you like bigger men, I guess."

"Bigger how?"

"I don't know. He's very tall. I wouldn't say he was slim by any means." I thought about it for a minute. "He's stocky. Like, not super muscular, but, you know, sturdy."

"Fat," she said bluntly.

"It doesn't matter to me how much he weighs," I protested. "He's just not the kind of guy I usually go for. It has more to do with his personality than anything. I prefer men to be more…."

"Like assholes?" Quinn smiled.

"Basically."

Quinn laughed in response as Ethan walked in, Marty the office dog trotting along behind him. From his bag, Ethan pulled a giant Tupperware container of what appeared to be spiral pasta and plopped it on the table.

"Carb loading," he said when he saw my eyes widen. "I'm training for a winter half-marathon." He looked at Quinn and then back at me and then back at Quinn. "What's going on? Did I miss something?"

"Nothing," Quinn said. "We were just talking about how what someone looks like isn't always the best measure of what kind of a person they are."

I raised my arms in protest. "That's not what I was say—"

"Totally," Ethan said as he sat down, seemingly oblivious to the fact that I was speaking. "I mean, I work hard to look like I do. I take care of myself." He beamed. "But if that's not your jam, whatever." He shoved a forkful of pasta into his mouth.

"So, if people don't look like you, that means they don't take care of themselves?" Quinn tipped her head in mock confusion.

Ethan's smile started to fade and he looked at me, eyes widening, begging me to help. I smiled as if to say, "Sorry, buddy, you're on your own."

"No. I mean, um…." He swallowed his pasta. "I just said that I do. Other people can do whatever they want. I don't care if people are thin or…whatever."

"You can say fat," Quinn said.

"Fine, fat." Ethan cleared his throat. "I've dated people who weren't super skinny and I still thought they were hot."

"How very big of you." Quinn rolled her eyes again.

Ethan glanced at me and I shook my head. I did not want to be a part of this conversation.

"Well," he said, putting the lid back on his pail of carbs, "I should probably get back to work. Award-winning artwork doesn't create itself." He got up from the table and basically jogged out of the kitchen.

"People like him are the reason body image issues exist." Quinn popped her last tater tot in her mouth and pushed the container away.

"Ethan? I don't think he meant any harm. He's just not very smart," I said, registering a flicker of motion to my left and noting Marty staring up at me, eyes wide, head tilted. "I don't have anything for you," I whispered. "Go find Marc."

Quinn shook her head. "I don't mean what Ethan just said; I meant how he acts in general. Have you seen his Instagram?"

I shook my head. I'd deleted all my social media accounts when I stopped hooking up with randoms. I didn't need the temptation.

Quinn grabbed her phone, clicked on the app and started scrolling.

"Look at these," she said, holding her phone up to my face. "All pictures of him in the most flattering positions possible, all filtered almost beyond recognition. I bet he takes ten pictures before he posts the best looking one."

I shrugged. I honestly didn't see the issue. I used to do the same thing. Why would I post unflattering pictures of myself? And if filters helped smooth out my face or make my eyes look brighter, what was the harm?

"Do you know how many kids—and also adults, by the way—look at manufactured pictures like these and think that it's normal? That this is what beauty looks like? That this is who they should strive to be?"

I shook my head. I guess I had never thought about it that way.

"Look at how many followers he has. I wonder how many of them think that if they just worked hard enough, they could look like him one day." She sighed. "And the sad thing is they will all be disappointed because no one can look like someone who has been digitally manipulated to this extent. If you hadn't noticed, he doesn't look this good in real life."

She flipped her phone over. "Whatever. I'm just glad there wasn't social media when I was younger. I had enough problems feeling like an outsider in high school because I didn't look like the popular girls. But I just had TV and magazines to show me that I didn't belong. I can't imagine what it's like to be a kid these days." She rubbed the furrowed space between her brows with her thumb. "Sorry, this kind of stuff just gets to me."

I nodded like I understood.

"Anyways," she said, her anger dissipating on a long-exhaled breath, "have you noticed that Ethan has been coming in here at lunch more and more lately?" She grinned.

"Hard pass," I said and she laughed. "And even if I was interested, which I'm not, past events have taught me that hooking up with colleagues isn't the best idea." I looked down, suddenly uncomfortable.

Quinn nodded slowly, giving me an opening to tell her more. "Okay," she said, after it was clear I wasn't going to. "You don't have to tell me anything you don't want to, obviously, but, at the risk of overstepping, I will leave you with this: a lot of people, women especially, who have had something bad happen to them in their past have the tendency to self-sabotage. Have you considered that perhaps that might be the reason you tend to go after assholes?"

I truly hadn't.

"Something to think about," she said as she got up and stretched. She walked out of the kitchen with a tired wave, leaving me to digest that nugget with my new best friend Marty, who was currently staring at me like I had a treat hiding in my pocket.

"I don't have anything for you," I said, looking at him pointedly. "Why are you always hanging around me? Go find your owner." I stood up and returned his steady gaze. "Stay," I said, holding out my hand and stepping back, ready to return to my desk alone.

Marty sank to the ground with a sigh, head resting on his legs, sad eyes lifting to meet mine. *Dammit,* I thought as my heart broke. I hated when my emotions got the better of me.

I sighed. "Fine. I would prefer not to be alone with my thoughts right now anyways." His head lifted and his ears perked up, likely knowing he had found his mark. "Come on then," I said and he jumped up, tail wagging furiously.

Poor lonely Marty, I thought, looking around. Confident that there was no one else within hearing distance, I squatted down, cupped his tiny face in my hands and whispered, "I know how you feel, buddy. I know how you feel."

Present Day

From: Julie
Sent: July 15th 1:05 PM
To: Luke
Subject: Me again

Hi Luke,

I went to 13th Avenue Coffee House today. I ordered a white chocolate brownie and thought of you. I miss you. Please email me back.

Love, Julie

Chapter Eleven

Nine Months Ago

On the second weekend of October, Luke and I started having our meetings at 13th Avenue Coffee House. Now that we had become friendlier, I thought we could move somewhere that was less business and cozier.

The coffee shop was full, so we took our coffees to the patio outside to enjoy the unseasonably warm afternoon. We had to keep our jackets on, but the sun was glorious. We sat at the wooden tables, nodding to the few other folks who were taking advantage of the weather, knowing that soon it would be so cold our faces would hurt.

"I've never been here." Luke sipped his coffee from the cardboard take-away cup. "It's really nice. I love that it's an old house."

"This is where Kate and I always go, or used to go anyways. It's the best," I said as I dug into my white-chocolate brownie with a disposable bamboo fork.

One thing a lot of people don't know about recovering alcoholics is that many of them not only crave the booze they are no longer consuming, but they also crave the sugar. Alcohol, especially wine, contains a lot of sugar. And wine was almost always my drink of choice.

I craved the sugar so hard that there were still some days when I would get the shakes. The difference between constantly craving booze and constantly craving sugar, though, was that I was allowed to have sugar. So, I could justify stuffing my face with it. It was my reward for staying away from what I wanted the most.

Luke sat back and sighed contentedly. "I love the Cathedral area, it's so artsy. I was admiring the murals painted on the sides of some of the shops while I was walking here. The benches even look like art! I would love to buy one of the old character houses and fix it up."

"That's ambitious of you." I smiled. "Some of them are in pretty rough shape."

"All the better to put my own mark on one." He sipped his latte with enthusiasm. "Yum! This is delicious."

"Are you always this excited about everything you do?"

"Mostly, yeah." He nodded. "Like I said before, why not try to make the most of everything?"

I shrugged in response.

"You seem to be the exact opposite," he said.

I shrugged again and he laughed.

"What *do* you like to do for fun? You never answered me before; you seemed more interested in ensuring I knew you didn't want to date me." He winked and reached forward, stealing a chunk of my brownie.

I gasped in mock anger. "No. My brownie. I asked you if you wanted one."

"I didn't, but yours looks really good."

"It is good. And it's mine." I put the brownie on a napkin on my lap.

"Fine." He sat back in good-willed defeat. "So?"

"Well…." I thought about it. "I used to drink for fun. Now I don't know what I do. Watch TV, I guess."

"TV doesn't count," he said.

"Buy things online?"

"Nope."

"Nothing then. I mean, I guess I used to date. Sort of."

"What do you mean sort of?" he asked, eyebrow raised.

"I didn't actually go on dates; I just had a lot of… sleepovers."

"Oh."

"You don't have a perky retort for that?" I raised my own eyebrow in response, wondering if I had found the limit of Luke's seemingly endless amount of non-judgmental composure.

I hadn't.

"I don't," he said. "There's a huge double standard for men and women. It sucks that women are looked at differently when they behave the same way that men are lauded for."

"I've never met someone as genuinely open-minded as you." I sat back and brushed the brownie crumbs off my lap. "Are you a real person, Luke Hudson?" I teased.

"I am happy to inform you that everything in this larger-than-life package," he said as he opened his arms wide, narrowly missing his coffee cup, "is fully and completely the real deal."

I laughed, moving his coffee cup closer to the centre of the table. "Good to know."

"Why did you stop? Dating, I mean," he asked, his expression genuinely curious.

I slipped a strand of hair behind my ear and laughed again, this time with less humour. "It got a bit out of control."

"How so?"

I sighed. "It just got to be too much." I sipped my coffee. Normally, this would be where I ended the conversation, but with Luke, I inexplicably couldn't make myself shut up. He was just so easy to talk to.

"I stopped because it wasn't healthy," I said, eyes on my lap. "It was part of the addiction. And it had gotten to the point where I wasn't enjoying it anymore. I was just going through the motions. Poking at a bruise to see if it still hurt."

He nodded, his eyes soft. "Do you think you'll try again now that you're back on track?"

I shook my head. "Not right now. The one thing I took away from AA is the idea that you shouldn't date anyone until you're a year sober. I need to work on me for a while without having anyone else in the picture. I still have a lot of work to do."

He closed his mouth, seemingly satisfied. "Hey, I have an idea."

"Oh God. What? I'm not starting a gratitude journal with you."

He leaned forward, eyes sparkling. "Let's do something fun next weekend."

"And what would that look like?"

"Instead of meeting here to talk about wedding plans, let's do some kind of activity; shake it up a bit. Maybe try out one of Ben and Kate's Stag and Doe ideas. It could be fun. At the very least, it could take your mind off wanting a drink."

"How is doing an activity conducive to wedding planning?" I was not sold on this idea. Planning this wedding was important to me. I didn't want to get sidetracked by "fun." "Where would you put all of your spreadsheets?" I asked.

"My spreadsheets are all up here." He tapped his head. "And, besides," he spoke slowly as if speaking to a child, "there's this really cool invention, it's amazing. You can download something called an 'app' and see everything on your phone."

"Are you making fun of me?" I tried hard to scowl but failed miserably.

He put his fists to the sides of his head and opened them, driving home the point by demonstrating that his mind was blown.

"Hmm," I mused. It wasn't like I had anything better to do. If we had to hang out together, we might as well try to do something fun. Plus, if it was even half as fun as Luke clearly thought it was going to be, it would at least be better than sitting on my couch feeling sorry for myself.

"Sure," I said. "Let's do it. As long as we still do wedding stuff," I added.

"Yes!" He raised his hand for a high five.

"No."

"Fine then." His bottom lip poked out in a fake pout. "I got some sweet invite design options from my friend yesterday; did you want to see?"

I was amazed to realize that I really did.

One of the things I learned after I first stopped drinking was that alcohol affects women differently than it does men because it takes us longer to metabolize it. Which is why, I learned after the engagement party, women should really pay attention to what their bodies are saying to them when they drink. I was thinking about this one night after Group as I helped Corie fold up the plastic chairs and put them away.

"That was a good session," I said.

"Thanks." She grabbed a chair from me and added it to the stack. "I often don't know if anyone gets anything out of them, so it's nice to hear when one goes well."

"How long have you been a therapist?"

"I'm not a therapist." She smiled. "This group is self-sustaining. It's mostly just a place to talk. My job is to mediate; to encourage conversation and to get the conversation back on track if it gets out of hand. Is it okay that I'm not a therapist?"

"Fine by me," I said as I passed her another chair. "I tried therapy and didn't love it. This group is helping more than anything I've tried in the past."

She smiled. "Good. I'm glad you keep coming back."

"It's honestly pretty surprising," I said.

"Why surprising?"

I shrugged. "I don't know. I guess I just thought…." I trailed off.

"You thought what?" She unfolded the chair she was holding and sat down, gesturing for me to do the same. "You can be honest with me; I won't judge."

"I guess I just thought it wasn't for me. The idea of a group. I mean, I did it without a group the first time. Why couldn't I do it this time?" I sat heavily on the unfolded chair beside her. "Seriously, why couldn't I?" My eyes unexpectedly welled up with tears and I swiped at them impatiently.

"I'm curious to know how you managed to do it by yourself the first time," she said. "That's an amazing accomplishment."

I paused, trying to get my emotions in check. "Well, I wasn't by myself." I ran my hands through my hair and twisted it around so it fell over my right shoulder. "I had a lot of support. My best friend Kate and brother Ben were there for me every step of the way."

"The ones who are getting married?" she asked.

I nodded.

"So, what do you think happened? What's different now?" she asked.

Good question. "I don't know. I guess Ben and Kate are more involved with their own stuff. They don't have as much time for me. I guess I didn't know how much I depended on them for support." I swallowed the lump in my throat.

It's amazing how sometimes you don't know what you're feeling or why you're feeling it until you say it out loud. How you can still surprise yourself. I really hadn't realized how much I had depended on Ben and Kate after I quit drinking the first time. I hadn't realized how much they had always been there, ready to hold me upright when I couldn't do it for myself. Ready to pick me up off the floor on my bad days and help me celebrate my good ones. I hadn't known how much I needed someone else to help me shoulder the burden.

"Everyone needs support," she said, "especially during challenging times."

I nodded, not trusting myself to open my mouth. Not wanting more tears to fall.

"Can I ask you something?" Her voice was hesitant.

I nodded again.

"Do you think maybe—and don't get upset—but do you think you might have, subconsciously, decided to have the glass of champagne at their engagement party because you knew you *couldn't* handle it?"

I shook my head. "I don't understand."

She continued, "Maybe, because you were feeling left out, because you were missing the support, maybe you subconsciously decided that the only way to get that support back was to show them how much you needed it."

The shock of what she was saying, and the anger the shock turned into, hit me like a punch to the stomach. I cleared my throat, trying not to choke on the fire rising in my chest. "So," I began as I struggled to control my breathing, "what you're suggesting is that I deliberately got super shit-faced at my brother and best friend's engagement party, completely embarrassing myself and deeply disappointing all my friends and family, erasing an incredibly hard-earned seven months of sobriety, just so I could get more attention?"

As I was speaking, her face blanched. "I'm sorry I offended you," she almost whispered. "That wasn't my intent."

"I'm sorry too." I stood up and yanked my coat off the coat rack, causing the wire hanger to fly across the room. "I'm sorry because this group was helping me. I was actually starting to get my life together. And now I'm going to have to find another one."

"You don't have to find another one." She stood up and followed as I stomped towards the door. "You can still come back. You should still come back."

I ignored her and opened the door, closing it behind me. There was no way I was coming back to this place. After what she'd accused me of? The idea that I would deliberately sabotage such an important event for the two people I loved most in the entire world just so I could get more attention. Just because I'd been feeling lonely.

I jammed my key in the lock and pulled the car door open so forcefully I almost dislocated my shoulder. Rubbing my arm, I slid into the driver's seat and threw my purse on the floor.

How dare she? I thought. And then, *What if she was right?*

Chapter Twelve

My favourite part about Monday mornings was meeting Quinn in the lunchroom for an early coffee while she told me about her weekend. Quinn was like I used to be, in a sense. She dated a lot; she was on every online dating app. But whereas I had only been on the apps for hook-ups, she truly wanted to find a partner. And, no matter what happened, she never gave up on her dream of becoming a character in one of the romances she was always reading.

"Ladies." Ethan walked in just as Quinn finished telling me she'd deleted her Tinder account. Again. "How were your weekends?"

Quinn sipped her coffee and gave him the thumbs up.

"Mine was good," I said, lifting Marty up and placing him on my lap. "How about you?"

"Good." Ethan sat down beside me. "Hit the gym, crushed a run; you know, the usual." He looked at me and grinned, his blue eyes flashing. A faint flutter in my stomach surprised me. Man, he was attractive; in another time, in another world, I would have definitely swiped right. I looked down at my mug as I tried to force away my impure thoughts. I was taking care of myself right now. And besides, he had a girlfriend.

"How's the artwork for the new digital ad campaign looking?" Quinn asked.

"Oh, man, super sexy," he said, sitting back and linking his hands behind his head, his pecs straining against the thin material of his cotton golf shirt.

Stop looking at his chest. Stop looking at his chest.

"Sexy?" I said, trying to be flippant, hoping I didn't sound like a breathless teenager.

"You know," Ethan said. "Cool, trending, interesting. That's what sexy means in the advertising world."

"Oh, I know what it means," I said, my eyes twinkling, back in control. "I just haven't heard someone use that phrase since the early 2000s."

"Burn!" Quinn squealed, her finger in Ethan's face.

"No one says 'burn' anymore, Grandma." Ethan brushed her finger away and laughed.

"I say it." Quinn stood from her chair and mimed a mic drop. She looked at me and rolled her eyes. "Kids these days," she scoffed.

"I'm only, like, a year younger than you!" Ethan called as Quinn walked out the door. He sighed. "Look what you did," he said to me.

I laughed and gently placed Marty on the floor before getting up to put my mug in the dishwasher. "That's what you get for using the word 'sexy' in a sentence where it doesn't belong."

"And where does it belong?" He walked over to the sink and stood in front of me, eyes flickering to my lips.

"Nowhere." I forced myself to hold his gaze. "It's a degrading description." I refused to show any signs of being flustered.

"So, what if I thought a person was sexy?" His eyebrow rose and the side of his mouth followed in a sly half grin.

"You would keep it to yourself." I closed the dishwasher and spun on my heel, ready to leave the conversation.

Didn't he have a girlfriend? He hadn't mentioned her lately, but that didn't mean anything. Was this just harmless flirting or did it mean something? If he did still have a girlfriend, flirting with another woman was not cool. If he didn't, I guess I would find out soon enough. Gossip had a way of moving around this place at the speed of light. Either way, I had a promise to myself to keep. And getting involved with someone, especially someone I worked with, would only lead to trouble.

Hanging out with Luke was, unexpectedly, turning out to be something I started to look forward to every week.

After almost three months of wedding planning, Luke and I had become—dare I say it—friends. I'd had my doubts; his cheery personality was in direct contrast to my "everything exists to make me miserable" attitude, but his idea to shake things up by doing activities was a good one. I'd actually started to have fun. And I hadn't had fun in a long time.

"So, how did you get into project management?" I asked one Wednesday after a lengthy evening searching for the perfect wedding guest book.

"Why can't we just use a regular notebook?" I'd asked,

turning over yet another white, satin-covered, encyclopedia-sized, overly priced, bound bundle of perfectly normal notebook paper.

Luke had gasped, half serious. "Don't even joke about that." He snatched the book from my hands and held it in front of me. "Do you know how many times Ben and Kate are going to read this?"

"Once?" I guessed.

He scoffed. "Many more times than once. It will hold all the words and memories of their family and dearest friends. We need it to be beautiful."

Now, leaving the final store with a fifty-dollar guest book in hand, I couldn't help but smile thinking of how seriously he was taking this and, because of how much I needed a win with this wedding, how much I appreciated it.

"I started building houses with my dad when I was eighteen, so, I guess, twenty-four years ago," Luke said as he held the door open for me and we walked out into the cool evening. "I worked for a bunch of companies and then realized I liked the coordinating part better than the building part, so I went back to school in the evenings to get my project management certification and started managing the projects instead. I still like the construction side, but I've been able to satisfy that part of me by doing projects around the house. You know, building planters and a deck and stuff," he said as we got into his truck.

"No wonder you want to fix up a house in Cathedral," I said. "You could actually do it." I closed the door to his truck and shivered. We were back to the normal, freezing cold, end of October weather, and the vinyl seat was like ice underneath my jeans. "I'm surprised you don't have a career that has something to do with helping people. Like training therapy dogs or bringing elderly people food in a van."

Luke smiled. "Are you cold?" he asked as I blew into my un-mittened hands. "Dumb question, of course you are. As soon as the car warms up, I'll crank up the heat. There's a blanket in the back if you need it."

I reached behind me and my hand landed on a colourful fleece blanket, which I pulled onto my lap. "Disney princesses, hey? This suits you."

"Ha ha," he said dryly. "Obviously it's Hannah's."

"Obviously."

He was looking behind him to check before he pulled out of the parking spot when his phone buzzed in the coffee cup holder.

"Speaking of which," he said as he read the message. "Hannah's grandma has to go help out a friend and needs me to pick up Hannah early. Would you mind if we did the wedding planning part of the evening at my place instead of a coffee shop?"

"Sure, no problem." I shrugged. It was no problem, right? Going to his home, meeting his daughter? Nothing weird. Nothing to feel nervous about.

"Aren't you going to ask how I got into admin work?" I asked as I gazed out the window, saddened by how many shops and restaurants now stood empty since the pandemic. "I actually used to be in HR," I said. "Before the booze got the better of me."

"I kind of knew that already," he said with a sly grin.

"Really? How?" I turned in my seat to face him. "I'm not on social media anymore. Kate or Ben must have told you."

He looked down, uncharacteristically shy. "We've actually met before."

"What? When? I can't believe I don't remember!" But I could believe it. Old Julie always went for pecs and abs over substance. I looked down at my hands as my face flushed. "Was I mean to you?" I asked quietly.

"Meaner to me than you usually are?" He smiled, glancing at me sideways.

"Seriously, was I?"

"Nah." He shook his head, brushing it off. "It was, like, three or four years ago. We met at a party at your boss's. I was there with a friend. You didn't talk to me much."

A sharp inhale stuck in my throat as I remembered that boss. His breath on my neck as he stepped behind me to help with something on my computer. His hand brushing my thigh under the boardroom table. My inability to make sound decisions after drinking a bottle of wine.

I rubbed my hands on my legs. "I'm sorry I don't remember you. I wasn't in the best place back then. And I wasn't always that nice. I'm still not that nice. You might have noticed."

"Totally fine," he said as we pulled into the driveway of a cute little bungalow. Halloween decorations covered every inch of every window, orange-and-black streamers hung from the trees and a big inflatable pumpkin towered over neatly trimmed shrubs. "And, for what it's worth, I think you're nice."

"Wow," I said as I exited the car, ignoring his compliment. "Someone sure likes Halloween."

"Daddy!" A tiny voice squealed through the darkness, followed by boots on pavement. Luke strode across the street and a blur of pink clothes and red hair jumped into his arms.

"Hi sweetheart." He buried his face in her curly mop and kissed her forehead. "Where's Grandma?"

"She's watching from the window." Hannah pointed across the street to where an older lady was smiling and waving, likely much cozier and warmer than I was.

"You live across the street from your...from Hannah's grandma?" was the only thing I could think of saying.

Luke crossed back over the street holding Hannah's hand and the three of us walked towards the house. "It was kind of a lucky coincidence." He pulled out his keys and unlocked the front door, warm air wafting out as he pushed it open. "I had been applying for jobs in a variety of cities, and when I got an offer here in Regina, I decided to take it. Theresa's mom—her name is Janet, by the way—moved here a few years ago and I already knew Ben, so I figured I'd give it a shot. When the house across the street from Janet went up for sale, I had to grab it. It was kismet."

"You're pretty." I looked down to see Hannah gazing up at me with Luke's green eyes. "I like your hair."

"Thank you." I smiled and reached down to, I don't know, pat her head? I didn't really know what to do with kids.

"She's not a dog, she's a little girl," Luke whispered loudly as we walked into the house and Hannah giggled.

"Hannah, this is my friend, Julie. She and I are going to do some work, okay? Can you go and brush your teeth?"

"Hi, Julie," Hannah said, poking her head out from behind the security of her dad.

"Hi, Hannah." I grinned. She really was adorable. I couldn't tell from the picture Luke had showed me, but she had the most delicate sprinkle of freckles across her nose.

She threw me a shy smile and then turned around and sprinted down the hall.

"She's a sweetie," I said.

Luke smiled a smile that said it all. She was indeed his whole world.

He took my coat and cleared some newspapers and a couple of cereal boxes off the kitchen table so we could sit down. With the exception of the table, the kitchen was very neat and tidy. The house wasn't lavishly furnished by any means, but it was definitely cozy. You could tell Hannah had helped with the decor.

My quick glance around the living room revealed a big, overstuffed beige couch with what looked to be another Disney princess blanket neatly draped over the back. An older-looking bookshelf was wedged between the couch and the wall, stuffed with both adult books and colourful books that could only be Hannah's.

I sat at one of the wooden chairs in the kitchen and set my purse beside me, pulling out my phone. "I got one of those newfangled spreadsheet apps you told me about." I smirked. "How on earth did we survive before digital technology?"

"I know, right?" He pulled his laptop out of his bag and

flipped up the top. "I noticed you added some 'dones' to the task list; the save the date e-cards all went out okay?"

I nodded. "I even got some positive responses." Luke was not on board with digital invites, but he had agreed to send the save the dates via email. Apparently, as long as we weren't digitally inviting people to the actual wedding, we were fine. And, more importantly, Kate and Ben thought they were great. As Kate had repeated several times to me over the past few weeks, the less they had to do the better. "I'm in my forties," she'd said over a recent group Zoom call. "I've realized that marrying the man I love is more important than any wedding binder used to be."

"I really like the design work you chose," Luke said as he brought the invite up on the screen. "For someone who doesn't like planning or weddings, you've come up with some banging ideas."

I smiled to myself, secretly touched by his compliment. I should have said "thank you" but instead I said, "I quit that job. Also, please never use the word 'banging' in that context again."

He looked up from his laptop, confused. "I think I missed something. Quit what job? And I reserve the right to use 'banging' as an adjective whenever I please."

I rolled my eyes. "The place where I don't remember meeting you. I quit after the first time I stopped drinking. It was pretty toxic."

"Oh, good for you then. Trying to get sober around anything toxic is a losing battle." He'd stopped clicking around on his laptop and was giving me his full attention. "Do you like working at the agency?"

"For now," I said. "I don't really have any other skills at the moment. I honestly haven't thought about what I want to do long term. Right now, I just want to plan the crap out of this wedding and then hit my year of sobriety. After those milestones I'll start thinking about something else. Until then, being sober and less of a hot mess is where all my effort is going."

"You'll do it," he said, his eyes warm and sincere. "I'm getting the feeling you're a very strong person."

For someone who'd only known me for a few months, he sure had a lot of faith in me achieving my goals. Faith I wasn't always sure I had.

His eyes left mine and I turned to see Hannah slowly sliding into the kitchen on pink fuzzy socks, hesitant to interrupt.

"Ready for Charlie?" Luke asked.

She beamed and nodded enthusiastically.

Luke slid off the bench and turned to me. "I'm reading her *Charlie and the Chocolate Factory.* Sorry, I won't be long."

"Take your time." I smiled, remembering when Ben had read it to me when we were kids, sitting in my childhood bed under mounds of comforters, snug and safe. It would always be my favourite book.

"It was my favourite book when I was a kid," Luke said at the same time I thought it, taking me by surprise. He took Hannah's hand and I watched them walk down the hall to her bedroom.

Maybe we had more in common than I thought.

Present Day

From: Julie
Sent: July 19th 10:52 PM
To: Luke
Subject: Guess who?

Hi Luke,

Okay, I get it, I messed up. Again. And I'm sorry. Again. Ben told me you aren't dead so that's a relief. But he won't tell me anything else other than you took Hannah on a summer vacation.

I kind of want to drive by your house to see if I can find any clues as to your whereabouts, but I feel like that might tip me dangerously close into stalker territory. I wish I could see you again though. I wish I could say I was sorry. I am truly sorry, Luke.

Please come home.

Love, Julie

Chapter Thirteen

Eight Months Ago

Now that I had someone to do things with, my weekends didn't seem quite so bleak. After months of planning with Luke, we had settled into a comfortable routine. So much so that it felt like we had known each other for much longer than we had. That said, there was still a lot he didn't know about me. And, if I was being honest, I preferred that it stayed that way.

"I don't like the outdoors," I said on a Sunday afternoon while we were sitting in the tented patio of Bar Willow looking out over the glittery, snow-covered landscape of Wascana Park. I had just gotten design approval from Kate, and Luke was in the process of sending the final invitation proofs to the printer while I composed an email requesting a block of hotel rooms at the Hotel Saskatchewan. An accomplished multi-tasker, he was also trying to convince me to go hiking.

"We're basically outdoors now." He gestured towards the gorgeous winter wonderland outside the tent's plastic windows. "And look how beautiful it is." He was right.

From where I was sitting, I had a clear view of the hundred-year-old Saskatchewan Legislative Building, its stately dome poking through soft, fluffy clouds.

"I like this kind of outdoors." I pulled my winter jacket tighter around my shoulders. "The kind where there are heaters so you can enjoy the beauty, be cozy and exert as little effort as possible. This I can do."

"What about walking?"

"If it's not freezing, I could give you a slow stroll."

"Possibly a meander?"

"Anything over and above a saunter and I'm out."

He laughed. "You sound like Hannah. Despite begging me to take her camping this summer, her love for outdoor activity is marginal at best."

"Sounds like a smart girl," I said as he passed me his iced virgin margarita so I could have a sip. "I don't know how you can drink something like this in the winter. I know we're basically inside, but it's still cold."

"I've always run hot," he said, unzipping his jacket to reveal a pale blue T-shirt underneath. He patted his stomach and grinned. "I've got a lot of insulation. I'm basically like a bear."

"Like Winnie the Pooh?" I picked up the drink he had set down in front of me and smelled it.

"I was thinking something more manly like Baloo, but sure, I'll take Pooh." He raised his eyebrow. "Are you going to drink that or just smell it?"

"You know this is pure sugar, don't you?" I stirred it with his straw.

"Yes, I do, that's why I offered you some."

I looked at him with suspicion. "I don't know if I should pretend to be offended or legit be scared because you already know my greatest weakness." I finally gave in and took a long sip from his straw. "Mmmm…pure sugar…." I slid the drink back with a contented smile on my face, sugar craving satiated.

Luke laughed. "You look like you're high."

I answered in the form of a delicate burp and then giggled. "I feel pretty good actually. This is the first time I've been here when I didn't look at the wine list. When I didn't imagine what I'd get if I were drinking. This is the first time I didn't need to do that."

"I'm glad," he said and drained the rest of the margarita. "It must be hard to be around temptation all the time. Sticking to your resolve takes a lot of courage. I admire that."

"I'd hold my applause until after I've made it more than four months," I said, brushing off his compliment but touched that he'd said it.

One of the things I liked about Luke was that I could be myself around him. I didn't have to pretend to be put together and in control of my life. I loved Kate and Ben, but sometimes, because I knew they worried about me, I had to hold things back. With Luke, I could let everything hang out. There was no one to impress. Nothing to lose. I didn't have to be perfect, put-together Julie. I could just be Julie, swears, scars and all.

"Okay." I flipped a page in my notebook. "Let's talk cake tasting."

He sat up, ready to get back to business. "All right. So,

the last time we talked"—he searched through his notes—
"was right after you ate all the cake at the first tasting,
angering both Ben and Kate."

"They weren't *angry*," I clarified. "They were more…."

"Disgusted?"

"Definitely more accurate."

He laughed. "Did you want me to go to the next one?"

"That's probably for the best." I stretched and groaned.
"So, do you want to do this stupid walk around the lake in
the snow or what?"

His eyes lit up, clearly surprised at my willingness.
"Sure!"

"I should probably start fitting some exercise into my
schedule." I wrapped my cream-coloured scarf around my
neck and hiked up my jeans. "The older I get the harder it
is to walk up the steps in my apartment."

"I could always introduce you to snow shoeing." He
pulled a green woollen hat out of his pocket and pulled it
down over his ears.

"Nope, I'd rather be wheezy." I zipped up my puffy
blue coat.

He laughed. "I do have a question before we leave
though," he said.

"Go for it."

"Will we need to budget for a security guard for the
wedding to make sure you don't eat the cake before the
couple has a chance to cut it?"

"Hilarious," I deadpanned as I laid a twenty on the
table. "Next time, drinks are on you."

I was up early on Sunday morning, ready to power through my to-do list. Thanks to planning this wedding, I could use my newly non-hungover self to do something productive. Now I was surprisingly eager to get out of bed on the weekends, knowing there was something to do; knowing I had a purpose. I was so eager, in fact, that I barely acknowledged that the nausea I usually felt when I woke up had subsided; the craving to have a drink barely there. I was finally turning a corner again. I had almost made it through the remnants of withdrawal.

I would keep my mini-celebration to myself though—today was an even bigger day than most. Kate had texted to say the alterations to the bridesmaids' dresses were complete and we—me and her twenty-five-year-old cousin Marnie—were going to meet at her place to try them on at noon. I had just enough time to put in a few solid hours researching party favors for the wedding guests before I left.

I arrived at Kate's apartment at 11:45 a.m., Tim Hortons coffee and muffins in hand, to a wide-open door and an alarming high-pitched squeal coming from inside. Kate's cat, Mittens, was sitting in the hall, clearly not impressed with the noise level.

"Hey buddy," I said as I scooped him up under my arm and closed the door behind me. "I'm here!" I yelled. "I found your cat outside."

"Oh shit." Kate ran up to the door to greet me, her dark curls bouncing. "We must not have closed the door properly when we brought in the dresses." She grabbed Mittens out of my arms and murmured sweetness into his furry neck. "Come see your dress!" She grabbed my arm. "It's gorgeous."

I put my purse on the kitchen table and followed her down the hall. I was looking forward to trying it on again.

"You both look stunning," Kate had said when Marnie and I had tried the dresses on two months ago. I hadn't argued; some dresses fit me better than others and this one actually fit pretty good. I'd turned around in front of the three-way mirror, admiring how the clingy fabric hugged my curves in all the right places. Kate's colours were going to be rose and gold and the smoky rose colour of my dress went perfectly with my blonde hair and green eyes. If I couldn't drink at the wedding, at least I could look good.

"I might even wear this again after the wedding," I'd said and turned to Kate. "Thanks for letting us pick dresses that are functional."

"I look so hot," Marnie had said as she'd piled her caramel-coloured waves on top of her head, puckered her lips and snapped about twenty-five selfies. Despite how much she got on my nerves, I had begrudgingly smiled in agreement.

Marnie personified everything I disliked about women her age. She was young and perky, entitled and opinionated and, above all else, incessantly online. Every time I saw her she was either scrolling through her phone or taking a selfie. She was never present. She never paid attention. And the only thing she talked about was herself. I knew deep inside that I probably disliked her because she embodied everything I'd taken for granted when I was in my twenties—minus the online part—but more often than not, I pushed that logic away and continued to treat her with disdain, like the sullen, cynical Gen-Xer that I was.

I was greeted by her giggles as I walked into the bedroom. She was sitting on Kate and Ben's bed, legs crossed, scrolling through her phone, sipping on a mimosa.

"Julie!" she shrieked and jumped up, sloshing the drink so it came perilously close to escaping the glass. The sharp tang of champagne and orange juice tickled my nostrils and my brain buzzed with the anticipation of dopamine.

Excellent. The cravings are back.

"Hi Marnie," I said through gritted teeth as she gave me a tight, boozy hug. I shot Kate a "Please get your cousin off of me" look but she just smiled and shrugged, taking the champagne flute out of Marnie's hand so she wouldn't slop the rest down my back.

"I'm so glad you're here," Marnie said, blue eyes dancing, plucking the glass out of Kate's hands and taking a slug. "I can't wait to try our dresses on." She thrust a half-empty champagne bottle in my direction. "Want some?"

I was about to politely decline when she interrupted me with an aggressive "Shit!" causing Mittens to jump off the bed and sprint out of the room. "Shit, sorry," she said again. "Oh my God, I totally forgot you don't drink anymore. Unless…." She raised her eyebrows.

"Still no." I wrestled one of the coffees out of the cardboard take-out container and held it up. "I'm good though. I've got coffee."

"Do you mind if I still—" she started.

"Of course not," I said, used to people asking, knowing

they were rarely sincere. "Just because I don't drink doesn't mean you can't."

She breathed a noticeable sigh of relief and took another sip. "Phew! I don't think something as momentous as this could be celebrated with just coffee." She turned to me. "No offence. I'm going to go get more juice. Want a refill, Kate?"

"No thanks," Kate said. "Sorry," she whispered after Marnie had flounced out of the room. "I told her you were getting coffee and she brought champagne anyways. I'm glad I had orange juice to mix with it or she probably would have finished it off by now."

"Out of all the people on the planet you could have chosen to be your bridesmaid, why did you have to pick someone I don't like?" I sat on the edge of the bed.

"To be fair," she said, "you don't like a lot of people."

"True." I opened the plastic lid on the coffee and took a sip. "But I dislike her the most."

"I know," she said. "Sorry. I thought if I asked Marnie, her mom would do my flowers for free. And she is. So it's kind of worth it." She sat down beside me and put her head on my shoulder.

"I guess." I sighed. "I'm going to have to keep my distance at the Stag and Doe. Since I've stopped drinking, I have a very low tolerance for the innocence of youth."

Kate laughed as Marnie came back into the room. "What's so funny, chickees?"

"Nothing." I got up, put my coffee on the dresser and, for my best friend Kate, plastered the biggest, most excited smile I could muster on my face. "Let's try on the dresses!"

When would I learn not to get my hopes up?

It turned out my bridesmaid's dress didn't fit. I guess eating what amounted to handfuls of sugar to try to temper the effects of alcohol withdrawal hadn't been the best plan after all.

"Suck in just a bit more," Marnie grunted as she tried to force the zipper over my newly acquired additional curves, my breasts pushing up against the not-as-generous-as-I-thought V-neck. "I almost have it."

"You don't almost have it," I snapped, swatting her hand away, irritation camouflaging embarrassment. "It's no use; we're fighting a losing battle. If you pull any harder, you're going to wreck the dress."

"Do you have your period today?" Marnie asked, hands on her hips, looking slim and stunning in her dress, all of her parts inside of it. "Maybe you're, like, retaining water."

Shut up, Marnie, I wanted to say, but instead I said, "No, I don't have my period. I must have gained some weight." I peeled off the dress and covered it back up with the garment bag, pressing my lips together, trying not to cry.

"It's okay!" Kate said brightly. "We can get it taken out. I'm sure the seamstress will be able to make it work." She smiled.

"Let me take care of it," I said and grabbed the dress. "Or maybe I just won't eat for seven months," I joked.

"Ha!" Marnie scoffed. "It takes longer than seven months to lose weight when you're in your thirties."

"I'm in my forties." I glared at her.

"Yeah." She took another sip of mimosa, peering at me over the glass.

I opened my mouth, ready to tell Marnie where she could shove the champagne glass, when Kate wisely steered her out of the room, asking her to go check on Mittens.

"It's okay," Kate said again, her eyes full of sympathy. "It will all work out."

I sat on the bed in my slip and sighed. "I know. I'm sorry for losing it on Marnie. This should be an exciting day for you and I've, once again, made it all about me. I'm really sorry, Kate." My eyes filled with tears, but this time not because of the dress. This had been my first big test to show that I was getting better. That I could be unfazed and completely in control. My first chance to show Kate that she didn't have to worry about me anymore, and I had failed.

"It's a good thing all the champagne is gone," Kate joked, shaking the empty bottle, trying to make me laugh.

She had no idea how right she was.

Chapter Fourteen

Quinn and I were living the dream, working late into Monday evening, mindlessly going through print material, photocopying competitor advertisements and converting them into PDFs to send to one of our clients.

"So, you can't get the dress fixed?" Quinn gently lowered the printer lid over a splayed magazine.

I sighed dramatically. "I can get it fixed, yes, but it's way harder to let a dress out after you've taken it in. The seamstress said she'd try, but she couldn't promise anything."

"So, what are you going to do?"

"Get it let out again, I guess. If I can't have booze, I most certainly can't take away food. What would I have left?"

"Me?" She looked at me and batted her eyelashes.

"No, I mean things I *like*," I teased.

"Marty?" She smiled, knowing how much I had started to love the little guy.

"I wish Marc had stayed at work a little longer," I sulked. "I miss him. Marty, I mean, not Marc."

"Thanks for clarifying." She laughed. "Speaking of

things people like, I think Ethan has a thing for you," she said as she flipped through a newspaper.

"Really?" I pretended I was surprised, but I'd had my suspicions. Ethan wasn't exactly the subtlest person in the world. He was always hanging around my desk, usually for some dumb, made-up reason. The other day, he'd come over to ask me what time it was. He was eating with us at lunch more and more. He always seemed to find a way to sit near me when we went out for drinks. It was honestly pretty flattering to have someone so attractive (and young) pay attention to me, especially now that I was sober.

It's funny how a drunk woman will attract the attention of way more guys—certain types of guys—than a sober one. Funny in a "not funny at all" kind of way. Ethan seemed to still like me even though I no longer presented as someone who would be easy to sleep with because the part of her brain that made good decisions was drowning in booze. I did wonder something though.

"Doesn't he have a serious girlfriend?" I asked.

Quinn shrugged. "I'm not sure anymore. He hasn't brought her up in a while. Not that he ever really talked about her that much. I'd been working here for two years before I knew her name."

An unanticipated single butterfly fluttered in my stomach. I mean, hooking up with Ethan probably wouldn't be the best idea, but if the rest of his body looked like his biceps, it might be worth the risk. A small shiver of excitement buzzed through me. I hadn't run my hands over a good set of abs in so long I'd almost forgotten what it felt like.

"Well," I said, "I'm not looking for a relationship right now."

"Who said anything about a relationship?" An adorably sly grin played upon her lips.

I laughed. "I still have seven months left until I've been sober for a year, which means no sex for seven months. Ugh, that sounds terrifying when I say it out loud."

"You can still have fun without sex." She wiggled her eyebrows.

"I can't." I laughed. "I mean, I can, but I like the actual sex part. I'm not really a fan of the foreplay prelude and the cuddling interlude. I like to get right down to business and then go to sleep." I lowered my eyes to the magazine I was holding. "I know that's not a popular stance for a woman to take." I looked up and put my shoulders back, newfound sober courage coursing through my veins. "But that's how I am, and if people don't like it, that's their problem."

"Heck, yes!" Quinn yelled, pumping her fist in the air. "I wish more women said that out loud or, more realistically, I wish more women *could* say that out loud without being labelled as heartless or cold or slutty. Men can have that attitude all over the place and it's totally fine. The second a woman says she just wants sex and not a relationship, it's like everyone's minds go back to the 1950s. Like, how dare they get to make that decision?"

"I'll admit," I said, "I haven't said it out loud to that many people."

"Girl, you have to say it. And when people react negatively, and you know they will, turn around and walk away with your head held high, knowing that you've made a tiny hole in the reigning patriarchy!" she cheered, her face flushed. "Women just wanting to have sex." She shook her head. "What will they think of next?"

Now that Ben and Kate were so busy, I could pretty much bank on one or both of them cancelling plans. I couldn't get too angry about it though; I knew they didn't mean it personally, but I did still like to throw myself a little pity party every once in a while. Another thing a lot of people don't know about recovering alcoholics is that, for many of us, there is the additional bonus of dealing with surprise bouts of depression.

So, when Kate cancelled Friday night movies at my place because one of the clients she did PR for posted something "slightly misogynistic" on social media and she had to "clean up his fucking mess," I decided to go all in and eat an entire pint of ice cream by myself.

Thank goodness Luke texted after I was about a quarter of the way through.

Hannah's sleeping over at Grandma's and I'm bored. What're you up to?

Right now, I'm pretty busy eating my feelings.

Cool, do you want some company?

Do you like *Bridesmaids*?

The movie or the concept?

Both.

Yes?

Bring popcorn.

Luke arrived with both popcorn *and* chips, which made me like him even more, and we settled onto my well-worn couch to watch one of my favourite movies of all time: *Bridesmaids*.

"It's basically like we're working on the wedding," I said. "We're just in the research phase. Do you want a blanket?" I jumped up and grabbed a couple out of the hall closet. We'd had another good snow the night before and the temperature had dipped pretty significantly over the course of the day. And, seeing as I was just working a temp job, I couldn't really afford to keep my thermostat very high.

"I'm not sure," he said. "Should I have ice crystals in my nose or no?"

I threw a blanket at him, narrowly missing his face. "It's not that cold. Don't be such a baby. Anyways, I thought you ran hot, Baloo."

He laughed and wrapped himself in the blanket. "I'm pretty sure it's warmer outside."

"We'll just have to sit close," I said. "Body warmth. Just like the cavemen did." I sat down and scooted closer, throwing my blanket on top of our laps. As our thighs touched, I felt his twitch.

"Are you okay?" I asked. "You twitched."

"Really?" He looked under the blanket. "Muscle cramp maybe."

"A painless muscle cramp?"

"Or maybe my leg was reacting to the frozen block of ice that just touched it," he said, purposefully shivering. "Were you rolling around in the snow before I got here?"

I nudged his calf with my toe. "I only feel cold because you're so warm. You're basically a furnace."

He swallowed and laughed. "What every man dreams of hearing."

"Okay, no more talking." I held up the remote like a torch and then brought it slowly down towards the TV. "This is where the magic happens."

"Can I ask you something?" Luke turned to me as the movie credits started rolling and set his bowl of popcorn down on the table.

"Wow, this must be serious," I said. "Should I put my chips down too?"

He smiled. "No, feel free to keep eating your chips."

"I was planning on it," I said, my mouth half full of chips.

"Classy." He brushed chip crumbs off the blanket.

"Why do you like this movie?" he asked.

"How can you not like this movie?" I gasped, prepared to fight to the death. "It's so good! I mean, Wilson Phillips is in it!"

"Calm down." He put his hand on my shoulder. "I'm not saying I don't like the movie—I do like it—I'm just wondering why you do."

I sighed. "I don't know. It's funny. It's about strong women. It's romantic. I like that she gets the guy at the end."

He smiled and nodded like he'd just won Final Jeopardy. "I knew it."

"You knew what?"

"I knew you were a romantic. You try hard to hide it, but I could tell. No matter what happened to you in the past, you still believe in happy endings."

I crossed my arms and puffed out a small grunt of disgust. A romantic was not a noun I would ever use to describe myself. If anything, I was an anti-romantic. Romance was stupid. I knew more than anyone that happy endings didn't exist, especially for people like me.

Except.

Except, I also knew that wasn't entirely true. Despite all the crap I'd been through, and despite all the walls I'd put up because of it, there had always been a tiny, almost insignificant, part of me that had hoped my ending would eventually be happy. That one day I would meet someone who didn't just want to sleep with me because I was drunk. One day I would find someone who I felt more than apathy towards. Someone who made me want more than sex. Someone who made me feel safe.

I had never admitted that to anyone though. Maybe it was time that I did. Luke was so easy to talk to. He didn't judge. He just listened. I guess if we were going to hang out more often, I might as well get all of my baggage out of the way.

"I don't deserve a happy ending," I said as I set the chips aside.

"What?" The shocked look was back. "How can you say that? Everyone deserves a happy ending. How can you say that?" he said again.

"You don't know the kinds of things I've done," I said quietly.

"Tell me."

I wanted to tell him. I wanted to tell him about how much I used to drink. About the poor choices I'd made.

About the one night I would never forget. But I couldn't. Not yet.

So instead I said, "You know, the drinking and stuff. I used to drink a lot. And I made some bad decisions." I shrugged. "I've learned that men don't stick around to deal with the hangovers and regret. It's just easier this way. If I don't get my hopes up, I'm never disappointed."

He nodded, his eyes locked on mine, laser focused but also searching.

"So, that's me," I said, throwing my arms up, trying to circumvent an uncomfortable silence.

"I feel like there's more," he said as he stroked his beard. "But that's okay. I won't force you to talk about something if you're not ready. When you are, though, I'm a good listener." He put his hand on the part of the blanket that was covering my knee.

"Thanks," I said and meant it. "I feel like you would be a good listener. But I also feel like you won't want to spend any more time with me if I reveal all of my past indiscretions." I smiled like I was joking, but part of me was scared it would be true.

And then he surprised me. He looked at me with his kind green eyes, opened his arms, and gave me a hug. And, even more surprising, I let him. I let him hold me. This guy who I'd only known for a handful of months but, against all odds, was fast becoming a good friend. I breathed in the comforting smell of fabric softener from his hoodie, allowing myself to relax into his warmth. What would happen if I told him everything and he no longer wanted to be friends?

It was at that point that I felt it. A small shift inside me. Like a tiny fracture where a sliver of light shone through. Something that wasn't anger or self-loathing or sadness or dread. Something real. Something good. Something bright.

Something vulnerable.

I pulled away. I couldn't do it.

And everything closed back up.

"Thanks," I said, smoothing the blanket over my lap and averting my gaze. "I appreciate the support."

He tipped his head, confused.

"You know you have to forgive yourself eventually, right? You may have done some things in the past you're not proud of, but the important thing is you acknowledged them, you stopped the pattern and you're trying to get better. You're trying to *be* better. Just because you've done some shitty things doesn't mean you're a shitty person. You're a good person, Julie. If these last few months of getting to know you have taught me anything, they've taught me that."

I smiled a smile that didn't quite reach my eyes.

"You're doing your best," he said. "You're doing great."

"I'm doing my best," I repeated.

"I stand by my statement though." He grinned. "I still think you're a romantic. I think you believe in happy endings. I just think that belief is buried underneath your past. I have full confidence that one day it will push its way to the top. One day, the brightness will poke through."

"Well, as I've said before, I'm not having sex until I've been sober for a year. So there won't be any brightness poking through anything until June."

He snorted. "I'll make note of that in my calendar." He paused thoughtfully. "Is that the only reason you're not dating? Because of your sobriety commitment? Or is dating not really your thing?"

My stomach sank. I brushed my hair back over my shoulder as I thought of what to say. "These are the kinds of conversations I find easier to have after a couple of drinks." I looked at him slyly.

Not even a tiny spark of humour flashed across his face.

I sighed. "Fine. I have dated, I used to date; I just don't date anymore."

"Why not?"

"I don't know." I did know. "It's just not worth it."

"What do you mean?"

"You know how people say that you need to take risks because even if you have to go through pain, it's totally worth it once you fall in love? And even if that love falls apart, it was still worth it just to have had that feeling? That one great love is worth all the heartache?"

"I have heard that, yes."

"I don't subscribe to that way of thinking."

He leaned in, the groove just above his nose furrowed. "I'm not following."

I squeezed my eyes shut, trying to push away the image of the man I always thought of in relation to the notion of love.

"His name was Todd," I said, all emotion draining from my face. "We met when I was in my late twenties."

I had been working as an HR assistant at a shipping company, back when I'd thought I would actually have a career. I'd been young and eager, ready to explode into my thirties with purpose. I had already started drinking a lot by then, but it had not yet overtaken my life.

"He was a contractor at a company I worked at and we started hanging out on Fridays when everyone went out for drinks," I said, eyes down, feeling Luke's steady gaze as he gave me his full attention. I wondered if he could tell that what I'd just told him was only half true.

The true part was that we did eventually start hanging out on Fridays, but I left out the part where Todd had figured out what was, back then, my greatest weakness. When someone was accustomed to being pursued, the best way to get their attention? Ignore them. Todd understood that about me pretty fast. He could almost sense my need to be wanted. And he used that knowledge to always have the upper hand. Even at the beginning.

Every Friday was the same. Todd would be there and I would try to pretend I didn't care. But I would try even harder to entice him to initiate a conversation: laughing at everyone's jokes, wearing my shortest, yet still work-appropriate skirts, flirting with anyone who would look my way, getting progressively more frustrated.

After two more weeks of pub performances, I exhaustedly admitted defeat. He was hot and I was determined. I finally went over to officially introduce myself and he grinned like a Cheshire cat as he offered me one of his newly purchased beers. Despite the fact that I hated beer, I accepted. And when I did, I noticed a twinkle in his eyes. He'd won and he knew it. But I didn't care. I had already fallen. Hard. And back then, I didn't know how to stop it.

"Once we started hanging out, we moved pretty fast," I said to Luke. "I'd gone through some stuff in my early twenties and, honestly, I was pretty desperate to find someone I could trust. Someone who would take care of me."

"That doesn't sound like you," he said. "You seem very much able to take care of yourself."

I smiled. "Well, I was much younger then." He was right though. It wasn't like me. I just hadn't known how much I'd wanted the safety until it had become a possibility.

"We always had so much fun when we went out," I continued. "He was hilarious and charming. Even Ben liked him. Ben, who, as you know, had a hard time talking to anyone back then, was grateful that one of the guys I was dating took the time to find out about his interests. Most of the men before Todd had just wanted to get into my pants."

Luke shook his head as if apologizing for all of mankind.

"We were a couple before I even registered it was happening," I said. "He'd moved his stuff into my apartment bit by bit and suddenly we were living together. Living the dream. Living for love." I clasped my hands together and held them at my heart, mocking the very idea.

"We fought, of course. Like all couples. But our fights seemed different, often intense. And sometimes they came out of nowhere. One minute Todd was laughing at a funny story I was telling and the next he was screaming at me, calling me stupid and selfish, throwing a can of green beans at the cupboard door."

"Jesus," Luke breathed. "Did he hurt you? Please tell me you left him after that."

"No, he didn't hurt me," I said, my face expressionless, my voice flat. "And no, I didn't leave him after that. The first time I thought about leaving him was after he punched a hole in the wall. I wish I could say it was the *first* time he'd punched a hole in the wall, but it wasn't. It was just the first time it had happened inches from my head."

Luke leaned forward reflexively as if in retroactive protection. His hand rose in the direction of my face but then slowly lowered back to his lap.

"After that, every time he had one of his 'fits,' as I began to call them, I'd think, *This is it. This is the last time. I'm leaving.*" I lightly punched my fist into my thigh for emphasis. "But every time he would just as quickly turn back into normal Todd. Normal, fun-loving, charming Todd. He would apologize and beg me to forgive him. And I did. He loved me after all." I shrugged as if to explain away my own naivety.

"So I stayed. And I convinced myself his behaviour was acceptable. And, most importantly, I didn't tell anyone. It wasn't like he hit me or anything; he never laid a hand on me. I'd just thought I had to work harder at not making him angry."

Luke tipped his head and I nodded. I knew now how foolish I sounded.

"It got to the point where I was always walking on eggshells, trying to be quiet, agreeing to whatever he said, never wanting to set him off. His good moods became few and far between. His anger would often settle into the deepest of depressions.

"Then, one day, I woke up to find him in our sparsely

decorated living room with his bags packed. He was leaving. It wasn't me; it was him. He'd met someone else. Someone younger."

"He said that?" Luke's face was a contorted mixture of protective anger and disbelief.

"No." I shook my head. "But I knew. I'd seen pictures of them on Facebook. When I'd asked about her, he'd snapped and said they were just friends so I'd left it alone. And yet, somehow, I was still surprised to find out they really weren't. I was devastated after he left. I felt like such a failure."

"You were not a failure," Luke said, the anger in his expression triumphing, his fists clenched at his sides. "He sounds like a terrible human and you were lucky to get out of that relationship before you got hurt. Physically, I mean. I imagine he did quite the number on you emotionally."

He was right. No matter how long ago it had happened, when I thought of love, Todd would always be in the way.

"So that's why I don't believe love conquers all," I said. "Because I have felt love and I have felt pain. And the love was not worth it. I would rather not take a risk and feel nothing than feel shitty like that again."

Luke's face softened, the anger drained from his features. "Maybe you just—"

"I swear to God if you finish that sentence with 'need to meet the right person,' I will cut you." I held up a jagged potato chip.

He clamped his mouth shut.

"What about you?" I asked, ready to change the subject. "Why aren't you dating anyone?"

"I just need to meet the right person?" He grinned tentatively, relaxing when I returned it.

"Seriously though." He sat back. "I have to be careful. It's not just me who would be dating this fictional woman; I also have to think about Hannah. Because of her, I can't go around poking just anyone with my brightness." He burst out laughing. "Oh, man I'm funny."

"Hilarious," I deadpanned. "But good point. You're a good dad."

"Thanks," he said. "I try my best. Speaking of which"—he looked at his watch—"I should probably go. Like I said, Hannah's at a sleepover tonight and I want to be there in case she wants to come home. She sometimes gets homesick."

I don't blame her, I thought. If I had a cozy place like that to come home to, I'd never leave.

Luke slipped on his boots and I watched as he walked down the hall, waving goodbye when he turned around. I closed my apartment door and surveyed the empty space, sparingly furnished with crappy odds and ends I had purchased for the sole reason that they were on sale.

I pulled my cardigan tighter around my shoulders and breathed in the stale, old apartment smell that had suddenly become more noticeable. How was it possible that I now felt lonelier than I had before he came over? And why did my apartment suddenly feel so empty?

Present Day

Hi Luke,

Remember when you asked me what I liked to do for fun
and I didn't know? I never told you this, but I figured it out
a few months after we met. Everything we did together was
fun. Even walking around the lake in the winter. But it wasn't
because I really liked walking around the lake in the winter
(I didn't), it was because I was doing it with you. So, what I
like doing for fun is: anything with you.

Don't you think that means something?

Love, Julie

Chapter Fifteen

Seven Months Ago

Monday morning, the phone at reception rang, startling me from my desk nap. "Quinn, the client isn't here yet," I said into the receiver. "I told you I'd let you know."

Quinn sighed on the other end. "I know. I'm just so nervous. Ethan and I worked really hard on this presentation and I want it to go well." She sighed again. "But mostly I want it to be over."

"First of all," I said, "if you keep sighing like that, you're going to hyperventilate, and secondly, you've been practising all week. You nailed it last time you presented it to me. You're going to do amazing."

I waited for her to respond, but all I heard was dead air. "Quinn?"

She walked around the corner, professionally dressed in navy, wide-legged tailored pants, a crisp white blouse and a navy blazer. Her hair was slicked back into a no-nonsense bun. I missed her purple leggings and billowy blouses. I missed her unruly tri-coloured hair.

"Sorry," she said. "I just thought I'd come out and talk, I can't sit down anymore."

"You look great." I reached behind her collar and pulled.

"Ouch, what?" She jerked back.

I handed her the tag I'd ripped off her top.

"Oh. Thanks," she said, leaning on my desk. "So, I lied. I really came out here to ask how the wedding planning was going. Tell me about it to distract me."

"It's going well," I said. "It's actually going much better than I thought it would. Luke is pretty fun to hang out with."

"By fun, do you mean sexy?" She leaned in like she was hoping to get some dirt.

"I wouldn't say 'sexy'," I air-quoted. "Not in the stereotypical sense anyways." I trailed off. Now that I thought about it, he was good looking. Not the kind of guy I was normally attracted to, but there was something about him. His humour maybe? Definitely his personality. And his eyes turned a special kind of sparkly green when he smiled, which was basically always.

"Babe," Quinn said, waving her hand in front of my face. "I think we lost you there for a minute. Where did you go?"

I shook my head to clear it. "Sorry. Nowhere."

She looked at me like she didn't believe a word.

"How did your date go last night?" I asked, trying to divert her train of thought.

"Ugh." She laid her head on her hands. "Turned out he had a surprise wife."

"Oh no, really? What an asshole."

"Yeah." She flopped onto the comfy lounger by my desk. "I told him I wasn't going to be his mid-life crisis, grabbed my purse and left."

"Hey!" I stood up. "I have an idea."

"I'm not dating Luke," she said, laying her head back against the chair.

"Fine." I sat back down. "You're missing out though. He's really nice and smart and fun. He's funny and kind. He's a great listener. I always feel better after hanging out with him."

"Sounds like you should set him up with yourself." Her head popped up and she cocked an eyebrow.

"Nah, he's not really my type." I shuffled some papers.

"Why not? He sounds great."

"He is great. He's just...I don't know. He's just not the kind of guy I usually go for."

"Because he doesn't look like he spends three hours at the gym every day?" She rolled her eyes.

I didn't know what to say. Was she right? Was I discriminating against Luke because he didn't look like the men I'd been with in the past? Because he wasn't all chiseled abs and dancing pecs? Sure, he was a bit softer around the edges than every other guy I'd been with, but sinking into that hug? I had never felt so warm and safe.

I was about to say as much when Ethan came around the corner and rested his elbow on the desk. "Hey, Julie, how's it goin'?" He picked a pen up off my desk, clicked it a couple of times, and put it down again. He had on new cologne. I liked it.

"Good, thanks. You?" I grabbed the pen and moved it out of his reach.

"I'm excellent, thank you. Ready for the big presentation. Have you seen the PowerPoint Quinn made? It's amazing."

Quinn grinned. "Well, I did come up with the concept. I wanted to make sure it was presented properly."

"Good luck, you're going to do great," I said, walking around my desk to give Quinn a hug.

"Where's mine?" Ethan held his arms open and my mind immediately went into the gutter.

"Hey!" Marc boomed as he walked around the corner, scaring the crap out of me. I lowered my head to hide the heat that was surely radiating off my face. "Are you guys ready? The clients should be here any minute," he said as he ushered them into the boardroom.

"I guess I'll have to get my hug another time," Ethan said quietly before he turned to leave.

He must not have a girlfriend anymore, I thought and my stomach buzzed. I then remembered my sobriety goal.

Crap. This was going to be a long six months.

Chapter Sixteen

"I'm sorry, we're doing what?" My mouth gaped as I tried to reconcile what I'd anticipated with what actually appeared to be happening. Our next activity was going to be a surprise, Luke had said. "Wear sweats."

Not having any "sweats," I decided on a cute pair of navy LuLu Lemon knockoffs and a loose-fitting cream-coloured tunic, thinking we were maybe going to go to a spa or something less enjoyable like an indoor sporting event. I was not even close to being prepared for what came out of his mouth.

"Dodgeball!" He grinned so wide it took up three quarters of his face.

"No, we are most definitely not," I said, my arms crossed, refusing to exit his truck, which was currently sitting in an elementary school parking lot.

"C'mon." He nudged me with his elbow. "My buddy's a wedding photographer and he said he'd give us a deal if we subbed on his team tonight. They're short two players."

"First of all, I can't play dodgeball in what I'm wearing," I said. "And secondly, I can't play dodgeball period. I still have nightmares from elementary school. Anytime I see a kid playing with a red ball, I almost have a panic attack."

"Really?" He looked concerned.

"No." I sighed. "But I do intensely hate dodgeball." How could I not when the two times I'd actually played dodgeball as a kid were spent guarding an anxious, bullied Ben while the other kids pelted him with the sting of rubber. "Besides," I said, "I don't want to look stupid in front of all of your friends."

Luke's grin faltered and his eyes softened. "Totally fine. Of course we don't have to play if you don't want to. Sorry, I should have asked before I planned the surprise. I love dodgeball; I always have a ton of fun."

"You play? Like regularly?" I asked, instantly regretting the note of surprise in my voice.

"Look, Julie," he said and I winced. "I know I'm not super buff, but I still play sports. And don't look too shocked but" he—held up his hand—"I'm actually *good* at some of them. I used to play on this team every week, but I took some time off to plan the wedding. I know how much it being a success means to you and I wanted to give it my best effort."

"I didn't—" I started, but what could I say? He was right.

"I'm sorry," I said softly. "That was really unfair and judgmental."

He nodded. "It was," he said. "But I forgive you."

"Really?" I looked up and was relieved to see sincerity.

He sighed. "I'm not going to lie and say it doesn't sting. I just like to think I have a lot more to offer than whether or not you can see my pecs through my shirt."

I nodded. "Thank you for calling me out," I said. "Most people don't, and it's not an excuse, but it has allowed me to get away with being an insensitive jerk for the vast majority of my life."

He shrugged. "Not caring what other people think is hard, but it's more important to me to make sure my daughter grows up not trying to achieve someone else's idea of beauty. It can be very damaging." He gave me a look that said I might do well taking his advice.

"Will you teach me?" I asked, shifting in my seat so I could look him in the eyes.

"To not be an insensitive jerk?" he asked, eyes twinkling.

"No." I laughed. "Well, yes, but also, will you teach me how to play dodgeball?"

"Really?" he asked, his face now glowing with excitement.

It was my turn to shrug. "Maybe I will look stupid, but maybe it will also be fun. At the very least, we'll save Kate and Ben money on the photographer." I smirked.

"Yes!" He undid his seatbelt with the joy of a kid who had just been told he was going to Disneyland. "You won't regret it."

It turned out Luke was right. I had a blast playing dodgeball. After a brief period of panic because I didn't know what I was doing, I relaxed into the game and started having fun. The balls were not the hard, piercing rubber I remembered from my childhood. They were foam and soft and didn't leave a stinging bruise when they hit you smack in the thigh. I know this because it happened often.

Luke's friends were all amazing and kind, cheering me on when I had a ball to throw, yelling out things like "Good try" and "You'll get 'em next time" when I was only able to throw it about a foot in front of me. And Luke? Well, he was right. Not only could he play dodgeball, but he was exceptionally good at it. He ran and dove and threw and caught balls like he was born to play the game. It was so impressive that I got hit a couple of times because I couldn't stop watching him.

By the end of the night, I was sweaty and exhausted and no better than when I started, but I felt great. I was buzzing with adrenaline, a high I hadn't felt since I'd stopped drinking. I loved it.

"You played so great!" Luke cheered as I joined the group in the lobby where everyone was putting on their winter boots and coats.

"I didn't, but thank you. You sure did though." I looked up at him and smiled. "And you were right; it was a lot of fun."

I wonder if his beard is soft or prickly.

Where on earth did that come from? I cleared my throat and bent over to slip on my boots, trying to hide my reddening face. What the hell? Was I having hot flashes already? That didn't seem fair.

"Come back any time, Julie," Kerry, the photographer, said as he passed us on his way to the door. "See you at the wedding!"

I straightened up and waved. "See you!"

"I'm glad you had fun," Luke said as he held open the door.

"Me too. Thanks for encouraging me to try something new." I ducked under his outstretched arm.

As we walked towards his truck, I wondered if I was getting soft in my old age. I was not usually one to do things I didn't enjoy just to make another person happy. Unless that person was Kate or Ben. Usually, my own happiness was the only thing I was ever concerned with.

The weird thing was when Luke's eyes had lit up, when excitement had replaced the pain I had caused, I had felt happier too. For the first time in a long time, I cared more about someone else's feelings than I did about my own.

I wonder what changed.

Chapter Seventeen

"You look so tanned!" I grabbed Kate and pulled her into a tight hug as I walked into their apartment, almost tripping over a box. Another reason I hadn't seen much of Kate and Ben lately was because they'd sneaked away on a last-minute trip to Mexico. They had smartly decided to go on their honeymoon before the wedding so they could spend it somewhere hot while Saskatchewan was in the middle of its tundra-like winter.

"Sorry," she said, kicking a roll of packing tape into the corner. "Deciding to move into a house six months before getting married wasn't the smartest decision we've ever made. Thank goodness for you and Luke. If the two of you weren't doing all the wedding planning, we probably wouldn't be getting married at all. This move is taking over our lives." She sighed.

"And right in the middle of winter, no less." I stamped the snow off my boots and handed her my heavy coat. "It's freezing outside."

Kate led me through the maze of boxes. "Coffee?"

"Please." I followed her into the kitchen. "So, how was Mexico? Tell me everything! Except the sex parts, please leave those out. In my mind you slept in separate beds."

"It was so amazing!" She pulled out her phone and scrolled through her pictures: Kate, lean and tan in her cute polka dot bikini. Ben, the whitest white man who ever lived.

"Did Ben get any sun at all?" I asked. "He looks like he stayed inside all day."

"Skin cancer is a real thing, Julie," Ben said as he popped his head over a stack of boxes, startling me.

"I thought you weren't going to be here." I bounded towards his box fort in the living room and gave him a hug.

"I guess you're going to have to talk shit about me another time." He pulled back and grinned. "How's it going? How's Luke? How's the planning? Luke told me you've been having a lot of fun together."

"I'm good. Luke's good. The planning is good." I smiled, pleased that Luke had also been having fun.

"I don't know why you and Luke don't date," Kate called from the kitchen where she was making our coffee. "He's fun and smart and nice. You get along so well."

I shrugged. "We're becoming good friends. I don't want to ruin that." I picked up the mug of coffee Kate placed in front of me and wrapped my fingers around it, trying to warm them up.

"He told me what happened to his wife," I said, chest tightening. "Sounds like she was an amazing woman."

"Theresa?" Ben picked up his mug of tea and blew on it. "Yeah, she was pretty great. Luke went through a really tough time after she passed."

"You knew her?" My chest tightened just a bit more,

this time with regret. The longer I went without a drink the more I realized how little I knew about my brother. He had always been there for me—driving me home when I'd had too much to drink, bringing me take-out when I was too hungover to get off the couch, coming home early from university when I needed him the most. Would it have been too much to have asked him how he was doing? To have asked him what he had given up?

"I met her a couple of times when I visited Luke in Toronto; once right before Hannah was born. She was glowing." He smiled as his thoughts took him back. "But then she always was. She was a kind, beautiful person. She and Luke were a perfect match."

"Do you think he'll ever date again?" I asked, my heart breaking for Luke and his sweet little girl.

"I know he will," Ben said, nodding. "Luke is a strong man with a lot of love to give. I'm sure Theresa will always be with him, but I'm also sure there's room in his big heart for someone else." He looked at me knowingly.

I nodded, knowing what he was getting at but also knowing that I was a far cry from being someone who would even come close to being that perfect of a match.

"I'm glad you asked him to help me plan the wedding," I said, surprising myself. "He's doing a great job."

"So are you, Julie," Kate said. "Don't discount all the hard work you're putting in. We wouldn't put our wedding into the hands of just anyone."

I shrugged, unsure.

"We trust you both, Julie," Ben said. "We know the wedding is going to be great."

"Well, good," I said, pasting a confident smile on my face. "Now, tell me more about your pre-wedding honeymoon! That's why I came over here. I don't want to talk about me."

They happily obliged, and while they talked about the weather and the food and the people they met and the adventures they went on, I thought about Luke. When I'd first told him I wasn't interested in dating him, it was because I thought he was too cheerful. And while I did still think that sometimes, I'd also learned he was so much more. He *was* fun and smart and nice, just like Kate had said. Why couldn't fun and smart and nice be my type?

In the past, my type had been based on looks alone. If he fit into my idea of attractiveness—pretty face, toned body—I would swipe right. If he didn't, I swiped left. I never read online profiles. It didn't matter if the men were fun or smart. Who cared if they could carry on a conversation? If I kept my searches to looks over substance, there was little possibility of me wanting to see them again.

"Julie!"

"What?" I jumped.

"Are you paying attention to anything we're saying?" Ben was standing in front of me with his arms crossed like he'd been standing there for a while.

"Of course I am," I said in what I hoped was a convincing tone.

"What did I just say?" Kate's eyes were narrowed.

"Um…something about Mexico? How it was hot?" I tried.

"Wrong." Ben frowned.

I sighed. "I'm sorry. Talking about Luke just got me thinking."

Kate perked right up again, my inattentiveness forgiven. "And?"

"And nothing. We're still just friends."

"Fine," she said. "Then you won't mind if we invite him for Christmas Eve game night this year."

"Of course not," I said. "Why would I mind?"

"Great!" she said, a big smile on her face. "Hannah is spending Christmas Eve at her grandma's so we didn't want him to be alone."

"Very thoughtful," I said.

"And?" Ben nudged her gently.

"And what?" I raised an eyebrow.

"And we've also invited Marnie," Kate blurted. "Sorry, I know you don't like her, but we thought since we were inviting you two, and you're both in the wedding, and Ben wanted to invite his groomswoman Sherri, who is in town visiting her cousins, we should probably invite Marnie as well." She took a deep breath, refilling her lungs after her ramble.

"Marnie was much easier to deal with when I was drunk," I sulked. "But of course it's okay. It's your party. And she is family. And I'm actually very excited to finally meet Sherri."

"So, it's settled then?" Kate looked at me and then at Ben and then back at me. "We're okay? Christmas Eve game night is going to be very fun and you won't ruin it by being mean?"

I laughed. "Don't worry; I won't ruin Christmas Eve

game night, I know how much it means to you." I glanced at Ben and he gave me a grateful smile. "Who knows, maybe Marnie and I will become friends."

"While welcome, I find that unlikely," Kate said.

"As unlikely as me playing dodgeball?" I leaned forward, hands on my knees, like I was ready to dish some hot gossip.

"What?" Kate exclaimed, leaning forward to meet me. "I want to hear everything. And please tell me someone took pictures."

Chapter Eighteen

It had started snowing Christmas Eve morning, and by the time games night rolled around, it was still going strong. I pulled open the door of my apartment building and stepped out into a snow drift that had piled up against it, gasping when a chunk of snow tipped into my knee-high boots and slid down my leg.

"Why do I live here?" I muttered as I kicked my way through the drifts to the parking lot. Or, at least, I thought it was the parking lot. I couldn't tell because all the cars were covered in about four feet of snow. There was no way I was getting my car out without a bulldozer. I didn't even own a shovel.

"For shit's sake," I said out loud and pulled my phone from my purse.

Can you pick me up? I texted Luke. *By the looks of things, my car isn't coming out of hibernation until summer.*

Luke had a garage and, presumably, a shovel, so I knew he wouldn't be having the same issue as me.

Bet you wish you'd gotten snow tires like I suggested, he texted back.

Snow tires wouldn't help this situation. I can't even see my tires.

On my way.

I trudged back to the front of the building so I could wait in the warm lobby. When his large silver Chevy truck (with snow tires) pulled up, it looked like it could cut through a mountain. I knew I had made the right decision.

He hopped down from the driver's side and came over to help me carry my bag of snacks and non-alcoholic beverages. After he set it in the backseat, he opened my door for me like a gentleman.

"Well, how chivalrous." I fanned my face with my hand. "You're going to make me blush, kind sir."

He bowed. "M'lady," he said, which earned him a laugh. "I know you sometimes need a boost. And you've got some very inappropriately high heels on those boots. I didn't want you to fall on your face on Christmas Eve."

"Thanks," I said when I was all settled and he had jumped back into the driver's seat.

"Of course," he said. "So, what games did you bring?"

"I don't like games, so none. I don't own any."

"I'm sorry, what?" He turned to me, an astonished look on his face.

"Eyes on the road, please!" I yelled as he swerved out of, and then back into, a well-formed snow rut.

"You don't like games?" he asked like I'd just told him I didn't like breathing.

I groaned like I'd heard this a hundred times. (I had.) "I don't like games. I know, 'who doesn't like games?'" I mocked. "Me, I don't like games."

"Why? Games are fun. Is that why you didn't know what you liked to do for fun? Because you don't actually like fun?" he asked, trying to both keep his eyes on the road and let me know how utterly bewildered he was by gesturing wildly. "I can't believe I didn't know this. I was going to take you to a games cafe for our next meeting."

"Well, I'm glad you're learning this now because I wouldn't have liked it." I dodged one of his flailing arms. "Take your next right."

He turned down the street, his giant tires cutting through the snow like it was cotton candy. "And yet...." he trailed off.

"And yet?"

"And yet, we're on our way to a *games night*."

I nodded. "Yes."

"Please explain."

He pulled over in front of Kate and Ben's new place and turned towards me, giving me his full attention.

I thumped my head back against the seat. "It's not a big deal. When Ben and I were kids, we always had Christmas Eve games night with our parents. As you know, our mom and dad weren't the kind of parents who spent every second of their lives entertaining their children, so it was always something we looked forward to—spending time together as a family, drinking hot chocolate and listening to Christmas carols. It was basically the beginning of every Hallmark Christmas movie. Honestly, I used to love games, just for that reason."

"Wait." He held up his hand. "You watch Hallmark Christmas movies?"

"Not relevant to the story."

"Fine." He laughed. "Please continue."

I cleared my throat. "The guy I told you about—Todd—he liked games nights. We would go over to his friend's place or, more often, we would host." I twirled a strand of hair around my finger absently. "Now, to be clear, the games I used to like, the games my family used to play, were fun. Games like Trivial Pursuit, or Pictionary or Monopoly, ones that didn't take a lot of strategy; where you could still laugh and talk and enjoy yourself, you know?"

Luke nodded.

"Todd and his friends liked strategy games. Like Risk and Settlers of Catan. I am not good at those kinds of games. I'm not even adequate. I don't know what it is, but my brain doesn't work like that. I can remember who pitched for the Yankees in 1992, and I can draw a mean 'We wish you a merry Christmas,' but I cannot strategically conquer anything to save my life."

"So it wasn't fun for you because you weren't very good?"

I looked down. "No. I don't care if I'm not good at something. I can still have fun. You've heard me sing along to songs on the radio."

He laughed. "Fair point."

"It wasn't fun because Todd was very competitive. And he wouldn't accept that I wasn't good at them. We were often partners, and when I made a move he didn't agree with, or if I asked questions, he would get frustrated.

"At the beginning he would laugh it off, but by the end of the night he would be angry, often saying things about me and my intelligence level that…well, they weren't very kind." My voice cracked and I swallowed hard. I hadn't talked about this in so long I'd failed to realize how much it still affected me.

Luke gently put his hand on my leg. "Like, in front of people? He would belittle you in front of people?"

I nodded, not trusting myself to speak. Trying to keep my emotions buried where they belonged. But also, strangely, wondering why my leg was tingling where it met with Luke's palm.

He shook his head. "Man, this guy." His hand closed into a fist, leaving a warm spot on my thigh. "No wonder you don't like games. What a jerk." His face had contorted into what I'm sure was supposed to be a scowl but on Luke's face still looked pretty pleasant.

"Yeah, so, that's why I don't like games," I said in a tone that made it clear that the story was over, hastily undoing my seatbelt, ready to remove myself from this bubble of vulnerability.

"And you still come to Christmas Eve games night…" he started.

"…because of Ben. He loves it and it would break his heart if I stopped coming." I glanced at Luke, who was still strapped into his seatbelt, unmoving.

"What are you thinking?" I asked, hoping I hadn't upset him again.

Luke finally undid his seatbelt and opened the door. "That I'd really like to find this Todd guy and punch him in the throat, but that's not very Christmassy so I was going to keep it to myself."

A warm glow surrounded me as Luke closed the truck door and stepped in front to tread a path for me through the snow. I hadn't expected him to be so angry on my behalf. Was it weird that I liked it?

We walked up the steps to the house and the door flew open, slamming against the outside wall.

"What the hell?" I turned just as Luke pulled me back so I didn't get knocked unconscious.

"Julesie, oh my God," Marnie slurred as she stepped out into the snow in her bare feet. Her phone, always in hand, slipped out of her grasp and fell to the ground. "I'm so excited to hang out with you tonight!"

"Julesie?" Luke mouthed and I shrugged, picking up her phone and wiping off the snow with my mitts.

Now, I'm obviously not one to judge someone who has dipped into the sauce a bit too aggressively, but holy crap, was I ever this ridiculous? The spaghetti straps of her (actually quite adorable) red slip dress slid down her bare, goosebump-covered arms as she tugged on the elastic waistband of her sparkly black tights. I reached up and pulled a piece of tape off what appeared to be a piece of Christmas garland she had wrapped around her neck.

Her petite frame was gently swaying back and forth as if dancing to a playlist that only she could hear and her half-closed eyes were focused on my face, waiting for me to respond before she moved aside to let us in.

"Yeah, me too," I said, knowing from experience that drunks often aren't able to pick up on sarcasm.

She stepped aside and let us into the house, the warmth so comforting that I actually sighed with contentment. I took off my puffy coat and hung it on a wooden hook, smoothing my hands over my newly purchased cream-coloured sweater dress. I might not have looked as young and sultry as Marnie, but I was comfortable and cozy and, lately, that was all that really mattered to me.

Marnie squealed. "OMG, I love your dress! You look amazing." She put her hand on my shoulder, leaned in and loudly whispered, "Kate told me you were having problems finding something that fit. I'm so glad you did."

I moved back and wiped her saliva from my cheek, a poke of irritation jabbing my stomach. "Thanks. Me too."

"Oh my God, we have to take a selfie!" she trilled, looking around for her phone. I handed it to her and she held it up at the perfect angle and posed, red lips pursed, blue eyes shining, not noticing that half my head was cut out of the shot.

"And who's this hottie?" She looked at Luke like she'd just noticed him, eyelashes lowered, hand out like she was waiting for him to kiss it. "I'm Marnie."

"Nice to meet you, I'm Luke." He took her hand and lightly shook it, pleasant as always.

She leaned in and looked up, her chin almost touching his chest. "Do you have a girlfriend, Luke?"

"How do you know I'm not his girlfriend?" I crossed my arms and raised my eyebrow. I mean, obviously I wasn't, but wasn't she being a bit presumptuous?

"Pfft, you never have a boyfriend." She looked at Luke and shook her head, her thick hair brushing across her shoulders. "She never has a boyfriend."

I laughed, pretending that what she'd said hadn't stung. *By choice, Marnie*, I thought.

"Well?" She stared at Luke, waiting.

Luke looked at me and then back at her, discomfort creeping into his normally relaxed features. "I don't have a girlfriend."

"Let's be game partners then!" she screamed. "Come on, it'll be so fun. You drink, right? Just because Julie's boring doesn't mean you can't have fun."

"We're actually—" I started and then saw Luke's face. He was smiling. He actually looked charmed. And honestly? Who wouldn't be. Just because I disliked Marnie didn't mean everyone had to. She was youthful and beautiful and bubbly. A tiny package of fun. And she knew exactly how to hold a man's attention. Something we used to have in common.

"You're actually what?" Marnie pulled on Luke's arm and he turned to me, eyes questioning.

I knew if I said we were supposed to be game partners that he'd decline her request. But who was I to decide for him? He very well might have more fun with her. He was a great guy; he deserved a woman's attention. Maybe Marnie would be his perfect teammate.

"We were actually just talking about that in the truck," I lied. "Seeing as we're such good friends we thought it would probably be unfair to be on the same team because we know each other so well. Of course you should be partners."

Something flickered across Luke's face. Disappointment maybe? I was probably imagining it. His eyes met mine, searching. I smiled again and nodded as Marnie pulled him into the kitchen and I followed, trying to look happy, trying to remember this night wasn't for me.

"Hey Jules." Ben got up from his place at the kitchen table and wrapped me in a hug. "Merry Christmas." I held him tight, comforted by his strength. He had come so far in the past couple of years. Since he and Kate had gotten together, he had grown from a quiet man—always standing off on the sidelines, waiting for joy to find him—to a man from whom joy radiated on an almost continual basis. Tears of pride filled my eyes.

He pulled back, his smile turning to concern. "What's wrong? Are you okay? Do you want to go talk?" And then, quieter. "Did you...?"

I shook my head. "Don't worry; I didn't fall off the wagon. It's just the holidays, you know? I get emotional."

"No, you don't." His eyebrow rose accusingly.

"Well, I do now, okay?"

His dubious expression dissolved into a grin as Kate walked into the room, joined by a tall, friendly looking woman with a warm smile. Her dirty-blonde hair was tied back with a festive Christmas ribbon that matched the ribbon tied around the black puppy on her brightly coloured Christmas sweater. If she was indeed older than us, she sure didn't look it. Rather than pushing fifty like Ben had said, I would have guessed late thirties.

"Julie, you're here!" Kate bounced up to me and wrapped her arms around my neck in a fake-out hug so she could whisper in my ear, "I'm sorry about Marnie, she was half-trashed when she got here." She pulled away and gestured to the woman she'd entered the kitchen with. "This is Sherri; I've been giving her the tour of our new place."

I leaned forward and stuck out my hand. "I'm—"

"Julie of course," she said as she pulled me in for a hug instead. "I've heard so much about you, I feel like I've known you as long as I've known Ben."

"Oh," I said into her shoulder, not sure what that meant. Had Ben told her why he'd left university so early? I pulled away and forced a smile. "I'm glad we finally get to meet in person."

"You look gorgeous," Kate whispered as she linked her arm through mine. "I always look like a scrub compared to you."

"Untrue, you look great!" I exclaimed, slightly annoyed. For as long as I could remember, Kate had always played the role of "less attractive best friend," and while I used to be flattered, it had recently started to bother me. I now wanted to be more than someone's pretty friend. Especially considering, now that my confidence wasn't amplified by booze, I was finding it increasingly difficult to see myself that way.

"Enough with the hugs already!" Marnie yelled from the table. "Let's play some games!"

And so we played games. I was paired with Sherri, who was better than me at drawing, but I carried the team during Trivial Pursuit. We would have won if Ben wasn't a genius. Luke could also hold his own, but Marnie kept yelling things out before he had a chance to answer, and while she might have been cute, she definitely was not the smartest person in the room.

After they were asked the question, "Which famous spouse was wrongly credited with breaking up the Fab

Four?" she jumped up and yelled, "Taylor Swift!" Luke quit trying and decided to just enjoy the show.

I found it fascinating that, regardless of how badly they were losing, he still seemed to be having fun. No matter what happened, no matter what ridiculous thing burst from Marnie's mouth, he didn't stop laughing, his smile so bright it lit up the room.

And because he was having so much fun I started having fun too. I forgot how miserable I used to feel when I got things wrong. Luke took losing so well and had such a good time doing it that everyone else had fun watching him. His absolute joy at everything that happened was contagious. Even when my answers were incorrect—dread creeping in, embarrassment flushing my face—all I had to do was look his way and he would throw me a wink and a smile; the warmth in his expression instantly evaporating my self-doubt. I hadn't had so much fun playing games since I was a kid.

And then we were done. And things were wrapping up. And Sherri was asking for her coat.

"See you tomorrow," I said to Ben after giving him a tight goodbye hug. We may not have done much else as a family anymore, but we still met at our parents' place every Christmas morning to open gifts. And it was still something I very much looked forward to.

Luke and Marnie were in the living room, her head resting on his shoulder, her eyes fluttering as she tried to stay awake. My chest tightened with an unexpected twinge of jealousy.

Why wasn't I the one sitting there, my head on his

shoulder, winding down? Why hadn't I fought harder to be his partner? What had I been afraid of?

The longer I watched them softly talking the lonelier I felt. The more I thought about how much fun Luke had been having the more I wished he had been having that much fun with me. I felt like I'd lost a connection Marnie had gained. Because they did look like they had a connection. And if that was the case, shouldn't I have been happy for Luke? Shouldn't I have felt something other than disappointed?

I sighed and turned away, not wanting to intrude. What was wrong with me? It was almost like I'd lost something. Like something inside me was missing. But how could I be missing something that I'd never had in the first place?

Present Day

Hi Luke,

You'll never in a million years guess what I did today. I walked around Wascana Lake! On purpose! It was so gorgeous out that I wanted to do something outside and I thought to myself, *What would Luke do?* I figured you would make me walk around the lake with you so I decided to do it myself. I thought about you a lot. On my walk I thought about what I would say to you if you were there. I thought about what we would talk about. I think you would have enjoyed the conversation.

After the walk, I went to Bar Willow and sat on the patio and had an iced virgin Margarita. It turns out they're much better in the hot summer when most normal people drink them. Who knew? (Me, I knew.)

I miss you a lot. When are you coming home?

Love, Julie

Chapter Nineteen

Six Months Ago

It had been over seven months since I'd stopped drinking. Again. It had also been over seven months since I'd made my one-year celibacy proclamation. And I was getting antsy. I hadn't gone this long without sex in decades and I did not like it.

Sure, I enjoyed getting up in the morning without finding some random on my living room couch asking me what I was going to make him for breakfast, scowling when I said, "Nothing" and "Please get the fuck out." I knew my year-long sex break was definitely for the best, but now I couldn't tell which I craved more, booze or men.

"You're doing a very brave thing," Quinn said as we sat down with our lunch on a Friday afternoon. "Just think, in less than five months you'll be free to enter into a relationship with whoever you want."

I laughed, almost spitting my fried rice onto the table. "I don't want the relationship part; all I want is the sex part. Finding my soulmate is not what I'm craving right now."

I scooped a bunch of rice up with my fork and stabbed a piece of breaded chicken.

"Nor should you be," Quinn said as she peeled the foil back on her burrito. "I was just saying that maybe one day your 'only sex'"—she air-quoted—"will turn into something more."

"Doubtful." I took a sip of my green tea.

"What's doubtful?" Ethan walked in and plopped himself down on a chair across from us. At some point we had all become lunchtime buddies, the three of us taking a late lunch so we could hang in the kitchen and chat and be inappropriate without anyone else listening.

"Julie ending up in a relationship," Quinn said and I kicked her under the table.

"Ouch, what?" she said, oblivious.

"Oh, sorry, was that your leg?" I caught her eye and gave her my "shut it" look, which she shrugged off as usual.

The side of Ethan's mouth tugged up in a half grin. "I find that hard to believe."

Did I just blush?

I opened my mouth to say something sarcastic and a giggle popped out, which I promptly covered up with the back of my hand. Good Lord, what was wrong with me? I was turning into Marnie. And with that thought, I immediately recovered, arranged my features back into their usual cynical places, and rolled my eyes.

"Speaking of dates," Ethan said, "do either of you want to go to Avenue after work? They have a new cocktail I want to try."

"I can't," Quinn said as she cleared up her lunch dishes.

"I have a date with my washer and dryer. I ran out of clean clothes this morning."

Ethan looked at me, his eyebrow raised in a sexy question mark. "I know you don't drink, but they have some tasty mocktails there as well."

"Who else is going?" I wasn't sure if I was in the mood to try to be nice to people.

"Just me," he said. "The rest of the office isn't really a cocktail kind of crowd."

"So, just me and you?" I asked and then glanced at Quinn, who shrugged.

"Yeah," Ethan said. "So, did you want to go or are you going to break my heart?" He clasped his hands onto his chest dramatically.

I thought about it for half a second and then nodded. "Sure, I'll go."

What was the harm in just us going out? The fact that he had asked me and Quinn to go must mean he no longer had a girlfriend or he would have gone with her. And he looked so pathetic waiting for me to answer. Like I'd actually break his heart if I said no. "I'll meet you there though. I have a couple of errands to run after work."

"Great!" He beamed and dug into his disgusting-looking tofu salad. "It's a date."

All right then, game on.

Avenue was packed when I got there, of course, because it always is, and I was late, of course, because I always am. As I walked in the door, the warm air immediately relaxed my shoulders, previously hunched due to trying to push my way through the frigid gale-force winds Mother Nature had offered up as a mid-January blizzard surprise. The tangy smell of garlic made my stomach growl; I was starving.

I looked around the cozy wood-paneled dining area, my eyes touching on the tables full of cocktails that the restaurant was famous for. *I could sure use a cocktail,* I thought but quickly pushed it away. Just because I couldn't drink didn't mean we couldn't have fun. I liked Ethan. Well, I liked to look at Ethan. The truth was Quinn usually carried the lunchtime conversation. I wasn't sure if he and I had anything in common other than our presumably mutual attraction. I guessed I would find out.

I peeked at my reflection in the mirror and ran my fingers through my hair. I'd brush-curled a few pieces on the side and the ringlets perfectly framed my face. Despite the wind, they'd held up pretty well.

I scanned the room and found Ethan sitting at a table in the corner. He hadn't seen me yet so I indulged in some blatant staring. When we hung out at work, I only allowed myself fleeting glances so I wouldn't be so obvious.

My goodness, he was gorgeous: young and blemish free. His dark blond hair framed a strong jaw with just a hint of stubble. Even from a distance I could see the outline of his toned arms under his slim-fitting long-sleeved T-shirt. A shiver fluttered through me, starting at my stomach and ending at my toes. This should be an interesting night.

"For how many?" The hostess walked up, menus in hand.

"I'm with him." I pointed at Ethan.

"Lucky." She winked.

Ethan stood as I arrived at the table. "You made it!" he said and walked over to give me a hug. I momentarily stepped back. We'd never hugged before, was this weird? He didn't seem to notice and drew me in. I'd never been this close to him. He smelled like mint mixed with the spicy scent of his cologne. He was so tall that my face pressed into his shoulder and I could feel the solid outline of a deltoid though the soft fabric of his shirt. Another shiver shot through me, stronger this time. It had been so long since I'd felt this kind of sexual attraction that I almost didn't know what to do with myself.

"You look nice," he said as I took off my coat and hung it on a hook beside the table. I was wearing the same thing he'd seen me wearing at the office, but sure, I'd take the compliment.

"Thanks." I smiled and sat down. "You're not so shabby yourself." *Shabby? Am I British now?*

He smiled and ducked his head with false modesty. He was obviously the kind of guy who heard similar sentiments all the time. Probably not sentiments that included the word "shabby," but who's to say, really?

"Have you been here before?" He handed me a menu and pointed out the mocktails at the bottom. "They have great food too, are you hungry? Maybe we should get something to eat."

"I have been here, but not for a while. I can't say I've tried their food before though, which is pretty sad." I glanced at the prices, knowing that on my salary I couldn't afford much. I was very hungry, however. Maybe just something small. My stomach, as if trying to convince me, growled loudly.

"Was that your stomach?" Ethan said, laughing, and I blushed. "Wow, you are hungry. How about I treat?"

"Oh, no, that's fine, thanks." Maybe we would get some free bread.

He leaned forward conspiratorially. "Don't take this the wrong way, but I know you probably don't make much as an admin assistant; let me treat. You deserve it for working so hard."

Well, if he insisted. "Sure." I smiled. "That would be really nice."

The server came by and set two waters on our table. I ordered a cranberry and soda even though my mouth watered when Ethan ordered a Cherry Smash cocktail.

"So," he said after the server left, "you don't have to tell me if you don't want to but—"

"Why don't I drink?" I knew it had to come up at some point.

"Yeah. I feel like we know each other well enough now that you could tell me." He put his menu down. "If you want," he added.

And there was the question. Did I feel comfortable telling Ethan why I didn't drink? Did I feel comfortable telling him I was an alcoholic? That I used to drink to excess and make poor choices and swipe through Tinder like I was playing Russian roulette? That it had gotten so bad that I couldn't get through the day without the background buzz of alcohol numbing my thoughts and feelings to the point where I just stopped feeling anything at all?

I decided I didn't.

"Just for health reasons," I said. "I don't need the extra calories."

"Wow, respect." He took a sip of water. "It's nice knowing someone who doesn't like putting trash in their bodies. It's pretty rare, actually."

"Totally." I sipped my own water.

"I mean I like drinking for sure, but other than that, I eat really healthy. My body is a temple, you know?" He patted his abs like he'd just eaten a good meal.

I raised my eyebrow. Was he joking? I seriously couldn't tell. But who said that out loud?

"Well, you know what I mean." He leaned in. "Obviously you take pretty good care of yourself."

I smiled. I was having a hard time reconciling the fact that I was super attracted to what he looked like but not really to what was coming out of his mouth. Maybe he would eventually stop talking.

He didn't.

"I know you totally get it, but people don't realize how much work this takes. It's not like I can just eat anything I want." He pointed at his stomach and then flattened his hand across his shirt, revealing very little, if any, body fat underneath. "How much do you work out?"

Oh, good. It was going to be one of those nights. I was beginning to regret accepting his dinner offer. Free meal or no free meal, the only thing I hated more than exercising was talking about exercising.

"Oh, about zero times a week," I said.

"Damn, girl!" He reached out to give me a high five

and I returned it, hating myself. "You're so lucky; you must have a super-fast metabolism."

"Sure," I said, desperate for the server to come take our order. I honestly didn't remember our lunchtime hangouts being so painful. I missed Quinn.

"That's so dope."

So dope.

For the next ten minutes he talked about working out and how much fun working out was and how he would probably die if he didn't work out. He talked about the endorphin rush he got after a "solid set" but how he didn't want to get "too jacked" because huge muscles were sometimes "a turnoff for the ladies."

When the server finally came around, I ordered a plain salad with oil and vinegar and a chicken breast with steamed veggies, even though I really wanted the beef Wellington. I didn't want Ethan to run away in horror. He was paying, after all.

"I saw you the other day," Ethan said after he handed the server our menus.

"Oh yeah?" I sipped my cranberry and soda, looking up through my eyelashes.

"Yeah, at 13th Avenue Coffee House. You were sitting in the corner with some pudgy guy."

I looked up with a start. Pudgy guy? That was rude.

"What?" he said, finally noticing my expression.

"That's not very nice."

"What? Pudgy?" He laughed. "I was just joking around."

"It didn't sound like it to me. It sounded mean. Luke is a great person."

"Is he your boyfriend?"

"No. He's not my boyfriend. We're good friends though. And calling him pudgy is offensive."

"Aw, come on," he said, "it's just like we were talking about. Some people kind of coast through life, not trying hard, not wanting to do things that are challenging. It just seems like whatever his name is—"

"Luke."

"Right, Luke. It just seems like Luke is probably one of those people."

"Luke is *not* one of those people." I'd had about enough of this bullshit. Spewing crap about people in general being lazy was one thing; talking about someone specific was another, especially when that someone was a person I cared about.

"Luke is one of the most amazing, kind, and hard-working people I know. And just because he doesn't spend his life in a gym and look like a carbon copy of every other bro-dude who works out excessively doesn't mean he isn't worth something."

"Shit, sorry. I didn't know you guys were so close," he said, looking genuinely, and rightly, ashamed.

"You know what though?" I continued, not caring how sorry he was. "Even if we weren't close, it's not a very nice thing to say. There are so many people in this world who are beautiful in many different ways, and if people like you would just open your eyes every once in a while, what people looked like wouldn't matter so much."

I sat back in silent shock. I couldn't believe I'd said that. I'd never stood up for anything other than last call.

"Okay, okay." He held his hands up in defence. "Sorry. I was just making an observation; I didn't mean to upset you. I thought we felt the same way about things. That's always been the vibe I've gotten off of you."

I took a deep breath. "Well, that's on me then," I said. "To be perfectly honest, what you said was pretty bang on to how I used to feel. It's only been recently that I've started to see things differently. I've been seeing a lot of things differently since I stopped drinking."

"Okay, cool. That's cool," he said as the server placed our meals in front of us. He leaned closer after she walked away. "Are we cool?"

"Sure, we're cool." I dug into my boring-looking meal, wishing I had taken my own advice and ordered what I'd wanted.

He grinned and then dug into his equally boring-looking meal. Why bother coming here if you weren't going to order any of the delicious food off the menu? What a waste.

We ate the rest of our meal mostly in silence. Chatting about work once or twice, not really hitting anything too deep. It was awkward, but at least we weren't talking about working out.

When the server came by with the dessert menu, I grabbed it before Ethan could finish shaking his head. I was still hungry, and after sitting through one of the most awkward dinners of my life, I sure as hell wasn't going to pass up a free dessert.

Chapter Twenty

"You went on a date with Ethan?" Luke grabbed a handful of ketchup chips from the plastic bowl resting precariously on a pillow between us on the couch. "That guy you work with?"

"It wasn't a date." I grabbed a single chip from his hand and stuck it in my mouth. "It was just dinner. As friends. Colleagues."

"You know there's a full bowl of chips right there." He pointed at the bowl between us.

"I like yours better." I grabbed another one out of his hand.

I had just finished telling him about the weird and awkward dinner that had ended just under an hour ago, minus the part where Ethan called Luke pudgy. Hannah was at another sleepover and Luke had texted to see if I wanted to come over and go through some wedding decor options. I had jumped at the chance to end my non-date as soon as I possibly could.

"Are you really still hungry?" he asked as he brushed my chip crumbs from his lap.

"I had a plain chicken breast, steamed vegetables and a

tiny sticky toffee pudding," I said as emphatically as I could with my mouth full. "Of course I'm still hungry."

"Because your body is a temple."

"Exactly."

"Okay"—he grabbed his laptop that had been sitting off to the side—"let's talk decor." He moved the chips and pillow, scooted in closer so our thighs were touching and set the laptop on both of them so I could see.

"You're warm," I said as I snuggled in. "I like it."

"So, are you into this Ethan guy?" He clicked through his tabs, trying to find the Pinterest collection Kate had sent us.

I looked at him sideways. "He wouldn't be the first person I'd choose to go out for dinner with again, but he's okay. He's fun to work with. I wouldn't say I was into him though."

Luke kept scrolling, seemingly randomly, eyes down. "So you're not attracted to him?"

"I didn't say that."

He looked up, head to one side. "Explain please." He closed the lid on his laptop halfway.

"There's a difference between finding someone attractive and being into them." I opened the lid on his laptop.

"Meaning?" He closed it again.

I sighed. "Meaning I could still be attracted to someone, and act on it, without wanting to take it any further than, you know, sex."

"You mean you could have sex with someone without feeling anything for them but sexual attraction?"

I narrowed my eyes. "Yes. Is that a problem? And before you say yes, think about what your answer would be if one of your man friends said the same thing." I jabbed my finger at him.

"Whoa." He grabbed my finger and pulled it down. "I wasn't judging. I was just asking. I've always been curious about relationship dynamics." He gave my hand a squeeze and then rested his on top.

I scoffed, pretending I wasn't acutely aware that his hand was on top of mine.

"What?" He tipped his head again. "Why the snort?"

"Nothing. I just find it funny you said 'relationship.' Like I told you before, I haven't had much luck in the relationship department."

"I predict, now that you're sober, you'll have more luck."

I smiled. "Thanks."

Luke put his laptop to the side and gave me his full attention. "I truly believe you deserve happiness, Julie.

No one had ever said that to me before. And all I could do was nod. And it wasn't because I didn't believe he thought that; it was because I didn't agree.

Was it now that I finally told him? Was I ready to take that risk? Being friends with Luke had contributed a lot to helping me stay sober; to getting my life back on track. What would happen if I lost that?

Suddenly, it felt like the joyful energy had been sucked from the room. A different kind of energy, heavy and sad, seemed to be escaping from a small hole in the wall I had so carefully built. I opened my mouth to speak, but nothing came out. I tried again, voice low, almost a whisper.

"I used to be a really shitty person," I said, eyes down.

"I don't believe that." He lifted my chin with the crook of his finger and held my eyes with his.

I removed his hand from my face and placed it in his lap. "I have to say this, let me say this."

He nodded, solemn, ready to hear what I had to say.

And then I was lost, inside my memories, inside the guilt and shame and self-hatred that had fuelled my alcoholism for decades. Waking up with the heaviness of knowing I had, once again, done something I would never have done when I was sober.

"One of the reasons why I would get so drunk is because I could do things without thinking. I could do a lot of shitty things without caring about the repercussions," I finally said. "I wouldn't care about the friend who threw me a party, spent a ton of money on food and booze, and then watched as I left for the club with my friends," I said in a daze. "I wouldn't care about the girlfriend who was sitting at home waiting for her boyfriend who was, at that moment, passed out in my bed. I wouldn't care about things I'd say and then forget; about people I'd hurt in the process."

I flashed back to the evenings before I would go out. Smoothing shaving cream on my legs, knowing there was always the chance I would get so trashed that I would hook up with someone who was equally as trashed. I didn't care about their situation. I knew I wouldn't feel guilty if I had enough booze coursing through my veins.

Until the next day. Until I'd wake up. That's when the guilt would rage. The shame sitting in the pit of my stomach and then rising to tighten my chest, pulsing around the never-slowing beat of my hungover heart. It was then that I hated myself the most.

"Do you know what it's like to have to quit a job because you've slept with basically everyone you've worked with?" I said solemnly, snapping back to reality. "To be literally sick with worry the next day because you know you had sex with someone but you don't remember how it started, and you don't know who knows, and you don't know if the person you slept with is even going to remember?"

He shook his head. Of course he didn't. He was an amazing person. Doing even one of those things wouldn't have even crossed his mind. But when I looked into his eyes, instead of seeing what I expected, instead of seeing judgment, I saw tenderness. I saw kindness. And I knew how important his friendship truly was to me.

"It feels horrible," I whispered, emotion finally cracking my stoic façade. His compassionate gaze gave me permission to be openly flawed. "And as much as I would be terrified of being found out, as much as I would dread the whispers and sneers, I secretly wanted it to happen. I wanted to be mortified. To feel pain. And do you know why? Because I fucking deserved it. And even though I would feel ashamed, at least I would feel something." Tears filled my eyes and I stopped to take a sip of water.

"Did it ever happen?" he asked gently. "Did anyone ever confront you?"

"No," I said. "No one ever did. Or, I guess, no one ever has. Yet. But now, now when I become overwhelmed with guilt and shame, I have to deal with it. I can't have a drink—or seven—and push everything away and pretend it didn't happen. I have to feel my feelings and suffer through them. Because if I let them go, I won't remember why I need to be sober. And what if I forget? If I think it's okay to forgive myself, then there's nothing stopping me from drinking again." I was now full-on crying, tears running down my face.

Luke handed me a tissue from his pocket. "So, you think you don't deserve to feel better?" he asked.

"I know I don't deserve to feel better."

"Why not?" he asked.

I threw up my hands in exasperation. "Because of the things I've done." Was he even listening? How was he still sitting here so calmly? How was he not halfway out the door?

"And," I continued, "to be clear, I'm not asking for absolution. I'm telling you because I thought it might help explain why I am the way I am."

"It does actually," he said. "I've always thought you were closed off; now I know why. It makes a lot of sense. You don't think you deserve love so you close yourself off to anyone who might be wanting to give it to you." He paused and scratched his chin. "One thing I don't understand though. Why did it start? In my experience with people who drink too much, there's always something that kicks it off. Some sort of damage. Something that sparks the drinking and the destructive behaviour."

I closed my eyes. Letting my thoughts go back to when I was young. Remembering how incredibly naïve I had been.

"You likely won't believe this," I said, "but I used to be kind of a romantic. More like Kate." I smiled wistfully and Luke nodded, urging me to go on.

"I didn't rush into things back then. Sure, I'd pick up men and have some fun after the bar, but it never went further than making out on the couch. Sex was never on the table.

"One night, at a club, I ran into a guy I hadn't seen since high school. A guy I'd known had always had a crush on me. We chatted and danced; I flirted and he bought me drinks. By the end of the night, I knew I'd had too many, but I invited him back to my place anyway. The romance of meeting up and getting together after not seeing each other for a while didn't escape me."

Luke smiled as if he understood. As if he could see my youthful hopes and dreams. As if he could also believe them.

"So." I shrugged. "I broke my rule. I slept with him. All drunk and sweaty and slippery on my beige suede couch, caught up in the passion of finally giving in to what we both wanted. I fell asleep and he left shortly after, leaving a note saying he had to get up early for work." I shook my head. "I actually folded it up the next morning, thinking of where I could save it. A keepsake from the start of our relationship."

"I feel like I know where this is going," Luke said quietly.

I nodded slowly. "I came home after work to a message on my machine. It was him."

I still remember the flip in my stomach when I'd heard

his voice asking me to call him back, certain he was going to ask me on our first official date.

"When I finally got a hold of him, he told me he wanted to make sure it wasn't going to be weird if we saw each other again. 'If?' I asked him, still not fully understanding." I laughed bitterly.

"Don't be so hard on yourself," Luke said. "You had every right to think you would see each other again."

"He didn't respond at first, but after a lengthy pause, he told me he had to go. I was 'super-hot and everything' but he wasn't really looking for a relationship. Two weeks later, I found out through a mutual friend that he was dating a cute redhead he'd met at work."

It turned out he *was* looking for a relationship; just not with me.

"I mean, honestly," I continued, "it wasn't that big of a deal, these kinds of things happen all the time, to both women and men. But for some reason, I took it hard. I guess it didn't help that, over the next year or so, I heard that several more times: I was fun but not relationship material. Every time after I'd had too much to drink. After I'd invited a guy back to my place hoping he wanted more than just sex, thinking in the back of my mind that this time would mean something."

The worse I felt about myself, about the way my life was turning out, the more I drank. And the more I drank the more stupid decisions I made. I slept with men I knew and then started sleeping with ones I didn't, trying to make myself feel better, wondering how things could possibly get any worse.

And then they did.

Luke brushed back a tendril of hair that had fallen in front of my face. "People deal with rejection in all sorts of different ways," he said. "And that's okay." He squeezed my hand. "Thank you for telling me. It couldn't have been easy to go back to when it all started. We never know what's going to push us over the edge."

"That wasn't it," I said. "That wasn't what pushed me over the edge."

Chapter Twenty-One

Luke's questioning eyes searched mine, windows wide open to his heart. "What do you mean?" he asked. "What do you mean that wasn't it?"

"I was raped," I said without emotion, the only way I could get the words out.

His face fell. "No," he whispered.

I continued, my voice breaking. With the exception of Ben and, more recently, Kate, no one else had heard my story. I wondered if telling it would ever get any easier.

"It was just over twenty-two years ago; a guy I worked with. He was married. Had kids. It happened at his house at a staff Christmas party. We were both really drunk, me more so than him. He kept giving me shots and I kept taking them." I paused, struggling to continue, unsure if I could. But then Luke squeezed my hand again and I knew I was safe. I knew I could trust him.

"I don't remember much. I remember going into the bedroom to lie down, to stop the room from spinning. I guess I passed out because the next time I opened my eyes, he was there. On top of me. His heaviness making it hard to breathe. I remember struggling. I remember telling him to stop. I remember that he didn't."

At the time, I had wondered if he'd heard me, or if I had said anything at all. But now I knew. I knew I asked him to stop. I remembered the smudges of teary mascara on his pillowcase where the side of my face had been pressed. I remembered the ripped waistband on my favourite pair of underwear. I remembered the way he wouldn't meet my eyes after he was done. I knew he had heard me. He just didn't care.

Luke looked up with tears in his eyes. "I'm so sorry, Julie."

"I don't think I ever really recovered from it. I thought I had; I thought I'd moved on. But now that I'm talking about it again, I don't think I ever did. I just covered it up with a new problem. With drinking too much. I guess I've only recently begun to process it."

"I'm so sorry," he said again and squeezed my hand. "I'm so, so sorry." He reached over and gave me a hug and I leaned into his sturdy shoulder.

"You smell like apples," I said, my voice muffled by his soft flannel shirt.

"It's my fabric softener," he said quietly.

I slid down and rested my head on the pillow on his lap. "I do realize that being raped doesn't excuse all the things I've done. And I would understand if you wanted nothing more to do with me. You didn't sign up to be friends with a train wreck."

"Julie, look at me," he said and I slowly sat up and looked into his eyes, surprised to find they were full of tears. "You are not a train wreck. You had something incredibly horrible happen to you; something that was not in any way your fault. And yes, you may have made some poor decisions, but it sounds to me that most of them were made because of your choice of a coping mechanism, not because of who you are as a person."

"I can't blame everything on booze," I said, "no matter how much I want to."

"No," he said, swiping at a tear that slid down his cheek. "But you can give yourself a break. You took a bit of a circuitous route, but you're now coming out on the other side of what sounds to me like a major trauma. You are incredibly brave and resilient and strong. You have much more to offer than you think, Julie."

I sighed out a laugh. Only Luke could make me feel better about myself after I'd just vomited my tragedy all over his lap.

I laid my head back down on the pillow. Being vulnerable was exhausting.

"And you know what?" he said as he absentmindedly stroked my hair. "Those men you slept with? The ones who were taken? You didn't sleep with them by yourself. There were two participants every time. Those shitty feelings aren't just yours to own. It isn't fair for you to be holding all the guilt and shame by yourself. If anything, the guys you slept with should be taking *more* of their share. They were the ones who were in a relationship. They had more of a reason to stop."

"Well, I'm certainly not blameless." I sniffed.

"No, but you're not the only one to blame. By pretending

it didn't happen the men were essentially saying it wasn't a big deal. But it was a big deal."

"I know that." I sat up and rested my head on the back of the couch.

He turned and looked at me. "I know you know. And that's what isn't fair. If a guy is so unhappy in his relationship that he thinks it's okay to sleep with someone else, he should have the balls to deal with it. That shouldn't all rest on you. He's essentially taken his own mess and made it yours."

"Thanks," I said. "I'm glad you don't hate me."

"I could never hate you." He smiled. "And you shouldn't hate yourself either. You need to forgive yourself."

"I know."

"So, will you?"

I thought about it. "I don't know. I think so. I hope so. I hope one day I can." I turned my head and met his green eyes, dark with pain. My pain, taking it on as his own.

"I can't imagine having to deal with something like that by yourself," Luke said, barely above a whisper.

"I wasn't alone," I said, my voice cracking. "I had Ben."

Luke's eyes widened. "Is that why he left university early? He never really said and I'd always wondered."

I nodded. "I called him after it happened. He was the only one who knew." I dabbed at my eyes with the tissue. "He came home for me. He made a huge sacrifice. He's one of the reasons I need to be a better person."

"You're not a bad person, Jules," he whispered. "You deserve forgiveness. You deserve happiness."

I sighed. "Let's talk about something else. Or not talk at all. I feel like I could sleep for days."

Luke nodded and ran the back of his hand over his eyes, tears streaking its surface. "Of course," he said. "We can do whatever you want."

We sat in silence for the next few minutes, comfortably quiet in each other's company. Luke processing my secrets. Me relieved to have someone else in my circle of trust. Relieved he was still my friend.

"I guess I should probably go," I said, sitting up and stretching. "There is only so much trauma one can unleash before they overstay their welcome." I smiled, hoping to lighten the mood.

Luke grinned half-heartedly. "You know you can always talk to me, Julie. About anything."

His eyes flickered down to my lips and my stomach flipped. Did I want Luke to kiss me?

And then the doorbell rang.

"I'm so sorry, I know it's late." My ears perked up at a woman's murmur.

"I got homesick, Daddy." Hannah's tiny voice floated into the living room.

Hannah's friend's mom, I thought, and my shoulders settled.

Luke thanked the mom and closed the door, ushering Hannah into the living room as she unwrapped her sparkly pink scarf from her neck and tossed it on the chair. Her eyes lit up when she saw me and I couldn't help but feel flattered. Kids never seemed to warm to me, but Hannah was different. It was like in her seven-year-old brain she saw me how I wanted to see myself.

"Hannah, put that away, please," Luke said and then sighed as she ignored him and walked up to me.

"Hi, Julie," she said, chin tipped down, a shy smile on her face.

"Hi, Hannah, do you want me to help you put away your coat?"

"Okay." She took a couple of tentative steps forward and shrugged off her fuzzy purple coat, revealing flannel princess pajamas underneath.

"Why don't you show me where this goes and we can put it away together?"

She nodded and I stood, lifting my arm to grab her coat. My heart stuck in my throat when she, instead, slipped her small hand into mine and tugged me towards the front closet. I glanced at Luke and he smiled and nodded, giving me permission to hold her hand. Giving me permission to hold the trust of this little person he loved the most.

I hung her coat on a wire hanger and she handed me the scarf she'd tossed on the chair.

"I got homesick," she whispered, her eyes down, embarrassed.

I crouched down so I was at her level and then remembered I was in my mid-forties with no lower body strength and sat on the bench instead. "My brother used to get homesick all the time when we were kids," I said. "He didn't like sleepovers."

"What's your brother's name?"

"Ben."

Her eyes lit up. "I know Ben! You're his sister?"

I nodded, sharing in her delight.

"Why didn't Ben like sleepovers?" She reached up and touched my hair and then grinned like she had been daring herself to do it.

"He liked being at home better," I said. "That's where he felt safe."

"I feel safe here." She nodded as if she was figuring it out. "I feel safe with my dad." She grabbed my hand again and tugged me up into a standing position, pulling me back into the living room where Luke was waiting with a welcoming smile. "Are you my dad's girlfriend?"

I laughed, not sure what to say, trying to pretend my chest didn't immediately tighten at the thought. My eyes met Luke's, holding them for just a second longer than necessary.

"No, sweetheart," he said, his smile slightly forced. "Julie and I are just friends."

"Oh." She gave a little sigh and my heart broke.

"I should get going," I said as Luke gently guided Hannah towards her bedroom. "Good night, Hannah."

"Good night, Julie." She bounced over to Luke, all grins and giggles, and he held up his hand. "Five minutes?" he mouthed and my eyes darted to his lips.

I nodded and sat back down, my thoughts jumbled.

Ten minutes later, he came back into the living room and I had my coat and mitts on, ready to leave.

"You don't have to go," he said. "She'll be fine now. She just likes to be where everything is familiar."

"I know." I smiled. "But I do have to go. I'll send you the quotes I get for the wedding party favours on Monday."

He followed me to the door and watched me pull on my boots. "Can we ta—"

"I'll talk to you Monday." I cut him off as I opened the door, shutting it quickly behind me. I breathed in the frigid air, grateful for the sobering bite. How could I have even entertained the thought of kissing him? He wasn't just some guy I'd met. He was my good friend. He meant a lot to me now.

I opened my car door and slid into the icebox interior, turning it on immediately so it would warm up. Tears filled my eyes and I brushed at them angrily. Why was I suddenly so sad? This was a good thing. Not kissing Luke was a good thing. Luke and I were just friends. That was all we were meant to be.

Although his beard was kind of sexy. And his eyes sparkled like nothing I'd ever seen.

I shook my head firmly, trying to erase the intruding thoughts from my brain like it was an Etch A Sketch. More importantly, Luke deserved better. He deserved someone who wanted more. Someone who wanted to be in a relationship. Someone who could love him and Hannah with all their heart.

Someone who wouldn't end up ruining everything.

Present Day

From: Julie
Sent: July 25th 3:22 PM
To: Luke
Subject: Hot Girl Summer

Hi Luke,

It's SO hot here today. I'm glad I chose yesterday for my vigorous (JK, it was very slow) walk around the lake. Today, I would have died. I still like summer better than winter though. I don't care how much I sweat; it's better than the air hurting my face.

I miss you a lot.

Love, Julie

Chapter Twenty-Two

Five Months Ago

I'd always disliked my birthday. Every year, I'd begged my parents for a party, and every year they'd been too busy to plan one. And to be clear, the birthday parties back then were nowhere near the extravagant events of today. There were no bouncy castles. There were no petting zoos. Kids in the '80s were lucky to get a cardboard cup of mystery orange drink and a goodie bag of McDonald's coupons. And Ben and I hadn't even gotten that.

It wasn't like our parents had ignored our birthdays— we'd always received nice gifts, and my mom would usually make us our favourite meal—but not having a party had always been disappointing. As I got older, I dealt with that disappointment by telling myself I didn't care. I stopped telling people. I stopped celebrating. I treated it like any other day.

Now that I was in my forties, getting older was something I would rather not think about anyway, so not celebrating my birthday suited me just fine. The only people who knew when it was were Ben, Kate and my parents, and they were the only ones I needed to hear from to make the day special.

So, on Monday morning, after a hearty rendition of "Happy Birthday" from Kate and Ben, and a more subdued version from my parents, I headed out the door like it was any other day.

Except this particular Monday felt a bit weird. Most of me knew that going out for dinner with Ethan on Friday hadn't been a date, but part of me wondered what he had thought. What he had really wanted it to be. And all of me prayed he hadn't told anyone. The last thing I wanted was to be a hot piece of gossip at a place where I was only a temporary employee, even if my term had recently been extended for another six months.

And what about Luke? A tiny, irritating voice piped up in the back of my head and I did my best to squash it. I didn't like that I had started to think about Luke in that way. Mostly because I didn't know what to make of it. I wasn't one to have healthy feelings about a member of the opposite sex, and my poor, tired brain didn't know how to handle it. "We're just friends," I said under my breath, but apparently not as quietly as I'd thought.

"Who's just friends?" Ethan walked in the door and pulled off his woollen hat revealing hair that was slightly ruffled. Not enough to be messy; just enough to be sexy. This was more like it. These kinds of thoughts I could handle.

He walked over to my desk and ran his hand through his hair, checking it in the window to make sure everything was in place. It occurred to me that it must take a lot of work to look as perfect as he always did. I wondered how much time he spent getting ready. My thoughts went back to what Quinn had said about his Instagram posts.

"How much time does it take you to get ready in the morning?" I asked, knowing I was being blunt but also knowing Ethan liked to talk about himself.

"Hmm…." He rubbed the bottom of his chin, the rasp of rugged stubble underneath his fingers melting my judgment away. "Well, I get up at 4:30 a.m. to work out—"

"What the fuck, seriously? Every day?"

He spread his arms, looked down at his chest and then back at me with a look that said, "Obviously," and then continued: "I usually work out for about an hour or so, then around twenty minutes to shower—more if I use a leave-in conditioner—about thirty minutes to get ready after that. Then I get dressed—"

"What? Sorry to keep interrupting, but you take thirty minutes to get ready *before* you get dressed?"

"I have a very intense skin care regimen." He seemed bewildered that he had to say this to me. "Don't you?"

"I mean, I use moisturizer," I said, embarrassed for some reason. Should I have had a more intense skin care regimen?

He shook his head. "I started moisturizing when I was fourteen. We're in our thirties Julie…well, I am anyways. We need to take care of our skin. Instagram may have filters to cover up wrinkles, but life doesn't." He nodded solemnly.

I unconsciously brought my hand to my face. I had been noticing more fine lines lately. *Maybe I should be investing in something more expensive,* I thought.

"So, all in all," he finished, "after getting dressed and

then making and drinking my protein shake and packing my cooler full of small meals and healthy snacks for the day, I'd say it takes me about three hours to get ready." He flashed a brilliant grin.

"Three hours. Every day." I barely got up an hour before I had to arrive at work. If it wasn't for the thirty minutes I took to style my hair and swipe on some make-up, I could probably get away with showering the night before and starting my car from the warmth of my bed. I couldn't imagine getting up that early. Four-thirty a.m. was usually when Old Julie was finally getting home.

"It's worth it," he said. "If you want to look good and stay young, you have to work at it. Most people think I'm still in my twenties." He grinned.

I nodded. It was true, I'd thought that when I first met him.

"I mean, obviously Botox helps," he said.

"Botox? You get Botox?"

"Of course I do. Like I said, I'm in my *thirties*, Julie. You've never gotten it before?"

Should I be getting Botox too? "I probably can't afford it," I said, certain that I couldn't.

He sighed. "Julie, you need to start investing in your future face. It might be expensive, but it's worth it."

"Like, how expensive?" I lightly touched the skin around my eyes. I'd always been told I looked younger than my age, but lately I'd started to question it.

"I get a Botox shot, here, here and here." He pointed to the spot between his eyebrows, his forehead and around his mouth. "Once every four months or so. That's about $300."

"Plus, how much do you spend on your 'aggressive skin care regimen'?'" I air quoted.

"About $100."

"A month?"

He nodded.

"That definitely wouldn't fit into my current budget."

"Like I said, it's worth it to look good. I mean, you're still smoking hot." He leaned closer and squinted. "But Botox would probably shave about ten years off your face. Didn't you use sunscreen when you were a kid?"

I opened my mouth but was too shocked to say anything. What the actual hell? I couldn't afford to drop over $100 a month on my face. And, even if I could, did I want to?

"Let me know if you decide to get a shot or two. I know a good place." Ethan knocked on my desk a couple of times, signalling the end of the conversation. "See ya." He turned back suddenly. "Oh, I forgot, Quinn's birthday is coming up in a couple months; we should plan a party or something."

"By 'we' you mean 'me,' right?"

He laughed. "Yeah, you're so good at that kind of stuff. Let me know if you need help."

He walked away with a bounce in his step. As if he hadn't just dropped the "you need Botox" bomb on my desk, ignoring the explosion, ignoring the shrapnel of self-doubt piercing holes all over my aging skin. *Happy birthday to me.*

"Asshole," I said under my breath as I rubbed the spot between my eyebrows, willing the divot I knew was there to go away. "What does he know anyways?"

It had been several months since I'd been to Group and as I walked into the room, I realized how much I had missed it. I hadn't been back since Corie had suggested I'd fallen off the wagon at Ben and Kate's engagement party in an effort to get attention. Initially I was too angry to return; then I kept telling myself I was too busy, but now I was just ashamed about being such a jerk.

I had also let it slip to Ben that I hadn't been for a while and the fear on his face had forced me to reconsider.

"I thought it was really helping you," he'd said.

"It was." I'd nodded. "But maybe I can do it myself now?" My voice unintentionally lifted. Even I didn't believe that.

"You know," Ben said, "I feel less anxious when I take my medication, but that doesn't necessarily mean I should stop taking it. You know what I mean?"

I did.

"And maybe someday I will stop taking it," he continued. "And maybe someday you will be able to do this yourself. But do you think that day is today?"

I didn't.

So, I sucked it up, swallowed my pride, and went back to Group. Both because of Ben's gentle nudges and also because that's where I knew I belonged. It had taken me a while to fully admit it, but I knew Corie had been right. It was amazing what happened when I surrounded myself with healthy friends instead of drunken randoms.

"Julie!" Corie waved from the coffee and treats table, taking donuts and muffins out of a large pink box. "We've missed you."

I gave her a tentative smile, trying to gauge if we were okay, trying to tell her with my eyes that I was sorry.

She smiled back and nodded almost imperceptibly and I knew I'd been forgiven.

I breathed out a sigh of relief and waved at Jess, who was already sitting in the circle of chairs. "Where's Jenn?" I asked as I sat down beside her.

Her smile dimmed and her eyes settled in her lap. "She's in the hospital," she said, barely above a whisper.

My stomach sank. "What happened?"

Jess sighed and pulled a Kleenex from her sleeve. "She relapsed. Her boyfriend left her and she drowned her sorrows with a bottle of vodka. She drank so much they had to pump her stomach. Who knows where she would be now if she hadn't finally texted me an S.O.S." Jess balled up the Kleenex in her fist and punched her thigh. "I'm so mad at her. She was doing so well. Both of us had gotten to two years." She looked at me. "How could she have done this? How could she have ruined all her hard work? And what if she'd died? I'd be alone. How selfish is that?" She threw up her arms and then burst into tears.

I moved my chair closer and wrapped her in my arms, letting her bury her head into my shoulder. As she had been talking, the rest of the group had quietly come in and sat down. We were all ready to be there for her. And, of course, for Jenn when she came back.

"People make mistakes," I said as I smoothed Jess's hair. "I've made plenty. And, yes, I know it seems selfish, but Jenn's mistakes aren't a reflection of you or your friendship. They're only a reflection of what's going on with her. And there are probably a lot of things she's not even aware she's dealing with yet."

Jess lifted her face up and sniffed. "I know."

"And she likely feels just as bad as you do about this. More than likely, much worse. She'll need your support more than ever right now."

Jess wiped her eyes with the back of her sleeve and nodded. "Thanks, Julie. I know in my head that she needs me to be there for her, but my heart breaks when I think of all the time she's wasted. She's going to have to start back at the very beginning."

I squeezed her hand. "Time spent learning is never wasted. As long as she learned something, a mistake is never a failure. And that's how you can help. Help her focus on that. Because, knowing from experience, she's going to be in a pretty low place and will definitely need some encouragement." Good Lord, I sounded like Luke. Where was all this coming from? Since when did I care this much about other people?

I then realized the whole group was surrounding us, all of them nodding their assent and murmuring words of encouragement. I slipped away from Jess, allowing others to take my place.

I was stunned at my behaviour, shocked at the encouraging words that had come out of my mouth, but pleasantly surprised to know I might have helped someone. To know I might have made a difference.

Corie walked over and put her hand on my shoulder. "I'm glad you came back."

I lowered my eyes and smiled sheepishly. "I'm sorry

about how I behaved last time I was here. I didn't want to admit that what you were saying was probably true." I shook my head. "You must think I'm a terrible person."

"Of course I don't." She tipped her head so she could meet my eyes.

"Well, I do."

"I know you do," she said. "Because you're an alcoholic."

I nodded. "And alcoholics are terrible people." The truth stung.

"Oh my gosh, Julie, that's not what I meant at all." Corie's hand fluttered up to her chest, her eyes wide. "Alcoholics are *not* terrible people. But they are prone to think they are. There are numerous studies out there that show that people who struggle with addiction are much more likely to have lower self-worth; to be more self-critical; to see themselves in a negative light—especially women. I did my thesis on this actually."

"Really?" I didn't know what else to say. How had she gotten so deep inside my head?

"How did you see yourself in what just happened?" She gestured towards the group rallying around Jess.

I thought about it. "I don't know. I think I was channelling a friend of mine." I laughed. "I tried to think of what he would do. Of what he would say. And then I did that."

"See?" Her eyebrows rose. "That's where self-perception comes in." She took my hands in hers. "This is what I saw: I saw how you comforted Jess, how you pulled that group together, that was all you. You did all of that by yourself. Did you believe the things you said?"

"Sure." I nodded slowly and then with a bit more conviction. "Yes, I did believe them."

"You've come a long way since you first started here," she said, smiling. "I hope you realize that. I know it's not going to happen overnight, but I hope you start believing those things for yourself."

I nodded again. I hadn't thought about it, but she was right. I had come a long way. Seven months ago, when I'd first come to Group, I hadn't wanted to be there. But now I not only knew I needed other people in my corner, I wanted them there. I was grateful for the help and support. And, strangely, I wanted to be there for other people who were on their own journeys.

I guess at forty-five I was finally growing up. Or maybe I was finally ready to start trusting people again. Whatever it was, it felt good. And also a bit terrifying. My track record on choosing people to trust had been less than stellar. The difference now, though, was that I was going down this path with a clear head and a stronger heart; stronger because of the people I was surrounding myself with.

I couldn't wait to tell Luke.

Chapter Twenty-Three

"Do you think I need Botox?"

Luke had picked me up from work so we could check out some venues for the Stag and Doe. Neither Kate nor Ben wanted a big party or lots of drinking, but they wanted to do something fun, which, unhelpfully, was the only direction they'd given us.

"What?" Luke looked at me and then started laughing. "Seriously? Why on earth would you want to get Botox? You're basically injecting poison into your face."

"Because of my wrinkles." My hand involuntarily went up to my lips.

We pulled up to the front of Escape Manor, an escape room Ben had always wanted to try, and Luke put his truck into park. "What wrinkles?" He looked at my face, which was now somewhat visible due to the glow from the streetlight we had parked under.

Even though his face was in the shadow, I couldn't help but notice his eyes lingering on my lips, so I put my hand back in my lap.

"You know"—I gestured to my face—"I'm in my

mid-forties. I have wrinkles. Maybe I should take better care of my skin."

He took his seatbelt off and turned his body towards me. "Julie," he said. "Don't take this the wrong way, but that's the stupidest thing I've ever heard."

I laughed. "How could I possibly take that the wrong way?"

But he didn't laugh. He was dead serious. "You're beautiful, Julie, both inside and out. Whoever got it into your head that you need Botox, or anything else for that matter, doesn't know what they're talking about. Don't change anything about yourself. You're perfect just the way you are."

He reached up and slipped a tendril of hair behind my ear. He was so close I could feel the warmth of his breath on my cheek. My face flushed as I remembered thinking about kissing him the last time we were at his place. Did he want to kiss me now? I had no idea what to think. No idea what to do. So, in true Julie fashion, I bailed.

"Well! We're here!" I exclaimed, undoing my seatbelt and opening the passenger side door, letting a burst of cold air into the truck's cab. I pretended not to notice Luke's look of confusion as I basically tucked and rolled out of the car.

"Have I ever told you how much I dislike escape rooms?" I scrunched up my nose as Luke caught up to me at the door of Escape Manor.

"Only twenty times on the way here," he said.

"They're so dumb," I whined.

He chuckled. "Have you ever noticed that you call everything you find challenging dumb?"

"No, I don't."

"What do you think about running?" he asked.

"Running is dumb."

"And math?"

"Also dumb."

He raised his eyebrow.

"Merely a coincidence." I looped my arm through his. "Now, let's check this place out so we can find something wrong with it and take it off our list."

Our visit to the escape room was short and sweet. They were fully booked the night Ben and Kate had chosen for their party. You had to book well in advance for weekends, the guy had said while I pretended to look disappointed.

"Ugh, I hate winter," I muttered as we exited Escape Manor and I almost successfully dodged a snow drift.

"Did you just say you hated winter?" Luke stepped outside behind me and we walked towards his truck.

I stuffed my hands into my pockets, lifting my shoulders up so my face disappeared into my scarf. "Yes, I absolutely did. I hate winter. It's cold and it's snowy and it's slippery and there is nothing at all good about it," I grumbled. "Please don't tell me you like winter."

"I love winter, actually." He grinned.

"Well, we obviously can't be friends anymore," I said, briskly walking towards his truck. "That's disgusting."

"Wait," he said and I ignored him. "Wait!"

I stopped and turned. "What? I'm freezing!"

"Are you?" He raised an eyebrow. "It's actually not that cold tonight. And you're wearing seven layers of clothing."

I stood still and thought for a second. I guess I wasn't

freezing. I was just reacting out of habit. It really wasn't that bad out.

"Come here." He pulled me over to the side of the parking lot that overlooked a field, the clean, white snow pristine and untouched. "Listen—"

"To what?" I cut him off.

"Shhh…just listen." He grabbed my hand and squeezed.

I listened, very aware of his hand holding mine. Feeling the warmth, despite the thickness of my mitts. I didn't hear anything.

He took a deep breath of the cool, fresh air with just a hint of wood smoke and sighed. "This is why I love winter. This silence."

"I like hot better than silence," I whispered.

"Summer is great too," he said. "But it's different. Summer has a joyful vibe: the buzz of the frenetic pace as we try to squeeze out every last drop. But winter? Winter is peace. Winter is heavy and soundless and restorative; the snow covering up the plants and grass and trees while they rest. Letting us breathe while we heal.

"Look at this." He gestured out into the field, the glow from the streetlamps making the falling snow sparkle like Christmas lights. "If you switch your perspective a bit, if you stop looking at the snow as a burden, it starts to become something beautiful and necessary; it becomes something that covers up the noise. Something that gives us permission to slow down and stay inside and curl up under a cozy blanket and watch TV or read a book all day and not feel guilty. It becomes something we all need."

I looked up at him, at his tranquil expression, and

then looked back at the field and I could see it. I could see winter through his eyes. The calmness. The quiet. The peace. How did he keep doing this? Without fail, he would take something I didn't like—whether it be dodgeball or winter or even what I thought about myself—and he would turn it into something else. Something beautiful. It was like a superpower. One I could never hope to possess. I looked back to say something to that effect and found myself looking right into his eyes, his face dangerously close to mine.

"Julie," he said softly, but I cut him off. Not wanting to hear what he had to say. Not wanting to feel what I was feeling. Resisting the part of me that was starting to open. Closing it back up tight. I knew I was getting better, but I still had a long way to go. He shouldn't be with someone like me. And I wouldn't let either of us take that chance.

"Turns out, I am pretty cold." I shivered, part of it exaggerated, part of it real. But it wasn't because of the cold.

"Sure." He smiled, the sparkle in his eyes dimming. "Let's go check out Sparky's. I have a good feeling about karaoke."

"If you request 'Living on a Prayer,' I'm out." I jumped into the truck and closed the door.

"But we have to test out the equipment to make sure it works," he said as he slid in. "If it doesn't hold up for an epic Bon Jovi ballad then why even bother?"

"Exactly," I said and he laughed.

My shoulders lowered in relief. Good. Things were back to normal.

"I almost ruined it," I said to Quinn as we sat down at one of the empty high-top tables at a bustling Vic's Tavern. Ben and Kate had both been too busy for our monthly lunches so I'd swapped both of them out for Quinn, and we'd swapped the lunches out for weekend brunch, easily making the transition from "work" friends to "hanging out" friends.

I pulled out my phone and brought up the brunch menu. "And if I had ruined it, I don't know what I would have done. Luke is my good friend. He's been my go-to guy now that Ben and Kate are always so busy. And, let's be honest, he's been doing all the heavy lifting with the wedding planning. If I'd slipped up, everything would be over, the wedding would be a disaster and my plan to prove that *I* wasn't a disaster would be ruined."

"Why do you think giving in to whatever it was that was happening would be a slip-up?" she asked. "Why would it ruin everything? Do you have feelings for him?"

"Like more-than-friend feelings?" I sipped my water, trying to hide the flush that had brightened my face.

She rolled her eyes. "Yes, more-than-friend feelings. You hang out with him all the time; he's all you ever talk about, what's wrong with falling for your friend?"

The server picked that point, the perfect point in my opinion, to come and take our order.

"Anything to drink, ladies?" he asked as he put down a couple of cardboard coasters. "Our bottomless mimosas are on special today."

"I'll just have a coffee." I sighed. "I miss day drinking," I said to Quinn. Although I did appreciate how long my weekends seemed now that I didn't have to have three-hour naps in the afternoon.

"I'll have the same," Quinn said, shooting me a supportive smile. "And the crab Bennie, please. With pan fries."

"Same," I said.

"Great." The server put his pencil and notepad back in his apron. "I'll be right back with your coffees."

"So, what are you up to for the rest of the day?" I swirled my water with my soggy paper straw, hoping Quinn had forgotten what we were talking about.

She hadn't.

"The only plans I have are waiting for you to answer my question." She laced her fingers together and propped her chin on them, eyes locked on mine.

I sighed. "I don't know, okay? I don't know what I feel for Luke. I care for him as a friend, I know that. But do I feel anything more? Maybe? Honestly, it's been so long since I've felt something real that I don't remember what it feels like."

"How do you feel when you're around him?"

"I don't know." I thought about it. "Good. Happy." I thought some more and then surprised myself. "Safe." Luke did make me feel safe; something I hadn't felt in so long. When he'd held my hand in the parking lot of the escape room, it was the safest I'd felt in a very long time.

"And are you attracted to him? Physically?" Quinn continued.

Was I? I didn't know. I took a deep breath and conjured his face in my mind. I didn't have to try very hard. His warm smile was always there, comfortably living in the background of my thoughts. He wasn't the type I usually went for; it was true. He wasn't built like Ethan; he wasn't a pretty boy. But his eyes were so soft and kind and their sparkle made me shiver, even when it wasn't cold. His auburn hair, curling around his ears. His strength, his compassion, his humour. His full beard adding a ruggedness that I was, admittedly, starting to find sexy.

"I think I am," I said on an exhale.

"Why is that bad?" Quinn asked as the server set down our coffees. We both shook our heads when he asked if we wanted milk or cream.

"Because I'm happy right now just being friends. I don't want this to change."

"And?" Quinn probed, somehow knowing I wasn't being completely honest with my reservations.

I sighed. "What if I wreck it? He was once married to an amazing woman; I feel like it would be a step down to start something with someone like me. What if I fall off the wagon? What if I have to start all over?" I said, thinking of Jenn. I sipped my coffee and it burned my tongue. This brunch was turning out to be way less fun than I thought it would be.

"And what if you don't?" Quinn blew on her coffee and sipped.

"He has a daughter," I said. "This isn't just him and me. Whatever we do, whatever happens with us, it will affect her as well. So, I have to be sure. *We* have to be sure. And I'm not. I'm not sure." I picked at my cardboard coaster, ready for this conversation to be over.

Quinn looked skeptical but stayed silent.

"I honestly think it's best to stay friends," I said, a note of finality in my voice. "Whatever I want, whatever I'm feeling, whatever he's feeling, we can push past it. We'll get through it. And before you know it, I won't even remember I felt anything other than friendship." I nodded my head affirmatively, trying to convince myself.

"If you say so." Quinn clapped her hands as the server put down our food. "This looks amazing! Well done, young man."

"Enjoy," he said, bowing towards the table and then walking away.

"I feel like he's too young to be serving alcohol." Quinn popped a pan fry in her mouth. "Although the older I get, the more I think everyone in their twenties looks like they're twelve."

"Speaking of getting older," I said, lifting my forkful of egg and imitation crab, I hear your birthday is coming up, the big three-five. How about a work party at my place to celebrate? I know my apartment isn't the greatest, but I think hosting a party would be the kick in the pants I need to fix it up a bit. I can't promise you anything fancy—I do still have a limited budget—but I can promise I won't invite Marc."

"Sold." She licked ketchup off her fingers. "I may have to get super trashed though."

"I wouldn't expect anything less."

Present Day

From: Julie
Sent: July 26th 4:20 AM
To: Luke
Subject: Can't sleep

Hi Luke,

You know how when you're really tired all day and then you try to sleep at night and you can't because all you do is think about all the things you've done in your past that you regret? That's me right now. And you know what I've figured out? Despite all the shitty things I've done in my past, despite all of the people I've hurt, the person I regret hurting the most is you. The thing I regret most in my life is when I hurt you. And that's something I will never forgive myself for.

Love, Julie

Chapter Twenty-Four

Four Months Ago

The second Sunday in March was rainy and gloomy, a perfect day to spend inside at Luke's place, cozy and warm, finalizing centrepieces and gifts for the guests. March was typically still winter in Regina, but every once in a while, it rained, and everyone got excited that spring was on its way. Sadly, not only was everyone usually wrong, but as an added punch to the gut, the rain would freeze under the newly fallen snow a few days later, and bedlam would ensue. I was planning on staying off the streets for at least a week after I got home.

Hannah's grandma Janet was busy, and Luke felt like he'd been neglecting his daughter lately, so she was sitting at the table with us crafting something out of colourful construction paper while Luke and I were buried in our laptops.

"Sorry," Luke had mouthed when I'd walked in and Hannah had barrelled into me for what was turning into our normal intensive hug greeting.

I shook my head and smiled. "No problem," I mouthed

back. I actually loved hanging out with Hannah. For someone who never really liked being around kids, I was finding that this joyful little girl was growing on me. With the exception of my dog friend Marty, no one in my life was happier to see me than she was. I could get used to that kind of welcome.

As Luke and I worked, showing each other centrepiece ideas, arguing about how much to spend. I checked his face, his tone, and his words for signs of acknowledgment of the escape room parking lot almost-kiss. It had been over two weeks and neither of us had said anything about it, and he hadn't been acting any differently, so part of me thought that maybe I had imagined it. Had he wanted to kiss me? Maybe he'd just gotten lost in the moment like I had. Maybe there hadn't been anything there.

"What are you making?" I asked Hannah, watching her cut paper of different colours into rectangles and neatly folding them over.

"Place cards for the wedding," she said without looking up. "I Googled 'things you need for a wedding' and this was one of the things. You don't have place cards yet, do you?" She grinned, her large green eyes wide, sparkling just like her dad's.

Luke's face tightened with barely disguised panic. "Hannah—" he started.

"What a great idea!" I finished. "Ben and Kate will be thrilled to have something so heartfelt and handmade. What a kind gift."

Luke shot me a questing look and I shrugged. Construction paper place cards might not be *exactly* what

Kate wanted, but it was worth it to see the glow on Hannah's proud face.

My thoughts were interrupted by the intense stare of a seven-year-old.

"Can I help you?" I laughed and she smiled shyly.

"How did you get to be so pretty?" she said, serious like only a child can be about such things.

"The same way you got to be so pretty." I gently tugged on one of her red curls and tucked it behind her ear. "We were born that way."

Hannah's eyes dimmed and the corners of her mouth tugged down, a reaction I was not expecting. "No, I mean pretty like you. I want to be pretty like you. I don't want to look like me anymore." Her small voice cracked and her eyes filled with tears.

Luke got up and crouched by her side. "What do you mean, sweetie? Why don't you want to look like you?"

She heaved a sigh too large to have come from such a little girl. "All the popular girls at school have long blonde hair like Julie, not like me. I hate my hair. I hate my freckles. Can I get my hair dyed for my birthday?" She looked up at her dad, eyes pleading.

"Hannah, you're seven years old, that's too young to dye your hair. And besides, that would make me really sad. I love your red hair. You got that from me."

"Amelia's mom lets her older sister get her hair dyed. And straightened. She posts pictures of her on Facebook and gets thousands of likes every day. Thousands, Dad."

What the fuck? How on earth was a seven-year-old worried about how many likes her classmate's mom got on Facebook? "Are you on Facebook, Hannah?" I asked gently.

"No, Facebook is for old people."

Cool.

"I'm sorry, Daddy, don't be mad." She lifted her head, tears in her eyes. "I just want to be pretty."

"Sweetheart." He crouched back down again and pulled her into a tight hug. "You are pretty. You're my beautiful little girl. You shouldn't be worrying about this kind of thing yet. How are you worrying about this already?" He directed the last question at me, eyes glistening.

She pulled away. "You have to say that, you're my dad."

Luke sat on the ground, his face a mixture of anger and defeat, and my heart broke. I knew all he wanted to do was protect her. But I also knew from experience that, no matter how hard he tried, he couldn't protect her from everything.

"Hannah." I held her small hand in mine. "I wish I could tell you that things will get easier when you get older, but I can't." Luke held out his hands as if to beg me to stop making it worse. "What I can tell you though," I continued, ignoring Luke, "is that when you get older— hopefully younger than I was when I discovered this— you will learn that what someone looks like isn't the most important thing."

"I know." She sighed dramatically. "It's what's on the inside that counts." She rolled her eyes.

"I know it sounds stupid, but it's true." I looked up at Luke, hoping I wasn't permanently damaging his child. "It's easy to look like everyone else. But to be yourself? To look like yourself and do your hair like you want and dress like you want, that takes courage. And I'm not going to lie, that's a kind of courage I haven't always had."

"Really?" She sounded shocked. "But you're perfect."

I laughed a humourless laugh. "Thank you, but I'm definitely not that."

She nodded but still looked slightly confused. I didn't know if I should continue with my Ted Talk, but I was already this far, so I might as well either hit the point home or completely lose her.

I put my hands on her shoulders and looked her straight in her eyes. "Hannah, you are so smart and so funny. You're kind and thoughtful. You care about your family and friends. You love animals. You're full of curiosity and creativity. You have beauty inside that makes you shine. And even though you might not think so, even though you might not look exactly like the popular girls at school, you're beautiful outside as well. You're the whole package, and that, my dear, is exceptionally rare."

She wiped her eyes and gave me a tight hug, which I returned. "Can I watch TV, Dad?" She jumped off her chair, tears forgotten.

"Sure," Luke said. "But only for thirty minutes and then it's time for bed."

I watched as she slid out of the kitchen on her fuzzy socks and then I promptly burst into silent tears.

"Not you too!" Luke sat down in Hannah's empty chair and rested his hand on my shoulder. "Why are you crying? You did so great. Everything you said was perfect. I would never have thought of the things you said. You're really good with her, you know."

He handed me a Kleenex and I blew my nose. "It's so unfair that she has to deal with these things so early. When I was her age, I had no idea what women had to deal with. I was still mindlessly playing with Barbies and My Little Ponies, blissfully naïve."

"To be fair, Barbie doesn't really portray the healthiest body image." Luke grinned.

"True," I said. "But I never thought about it that way. I never realized how hard it must be for little girls in the age of internet and social media. We were so lucky not to have had to deal with that sort of thing."

Luke sat back. "It's tough. Parents today are dealing with different things than our parents had to deal with."

"What can we do about it?" I asked, hoping he had a magic answer. "How can we make it better? Take all their phones and iPads away forever?"

He shrugged. "I have no idea. I think the only thing we can do is be there for them. If we took their iPads away, they would find someone else's iPad to look at. We just need to listen to them and do the best we can to be good examples. Kids see and hear everything. We need to be good role models for them and be on our best behaviour whenever they're around."

"You're a good dad." I smiled.

"Thanks," he said. "That's honestly all I want to be."

It was just under a month until Quinn's birthday party and I had done literally nothing to plan for it. I had barely mentioned it to anyone and I was feeling like a terrible friend. I'd been so busy planning the wedding with Luke that I hadn't had time to plan anything else.

Thankfully, we had finally determined what we were going to do for the Stag and Doe—Kate and Ben had decided that karaoke was a great choice after the escape room fell through—and we had almost wrapped up planning the decor for the wedding itself.

We had decided to go simple: round tables with white tablecloths and white chair covers tied back with rose-coloured satin bows. Bouquets of Gerbera daisies would be bound together with single silk ribbons, sitting snugly in tasteful glass vases I was going to pick up at the dollar store. It turned out we hadn't needed Marnie's mom to do the flowers after all.

Today was going to be the day though. Today I would figure out the details of Quinn's party and finally send an invite to the rest of the office.

"How's the party planning coming?" Ethan dropped a package on my desk with a thud. "This needs to be shipped out."

"I'm working on the invite right now," I lied.

"We should get a cake or something. And Jell-O shots. And maybe play a couple of games?"

"Sounds fun," I said. "Did you want to organize any of that?"

He looked puzzled. "Aren't you organizing the party?"

"Sure, but didn't you say you would help with anything I needed?"

"Did I?" He shrugged. "Isn't that just something you say though? To be polite?"

"It is if you want to help."

"Oh. Well, I just thought—"

"That I'd organize everything because I'm a woman?"

"No!" he said quickly, fear exploding on his face. "I would never think something like that. I'll totally help. If you need it."

"Great." I stood up and handed him a yellow sticky note. "You can help with the invite then. My address is on here, along with the time and date of the party. Invite anyone you want at the office, except Marc. The last thing I want is for him to start offering all the women free massages. I'm also still mad at him about Marty."

At the sound of his name, Marty trotted into the lobby, his nails click-clacking joyfully on the stone tile. Marc had recently decided that keeping Marty so his ex-wife couldn't have him was no longer worth the responsibility of looking after a dog. And now that his ex wasn't allowed to have animals in her new apartment building, he was planning on putting an ad up on Facebook Marketplace and giving poor Marty away to a stranger. I was not pleased, to say the least.

Ethan hesitantly took the sticky note with my address on it. "But Marc is my boss. He'll know if I don't invite him."

"I'm sure you'll think of something." I sat back down. "I really appreciate it."

Ethan looked around, possibly expecting someone else to pop out and take this challenging task off his hands. I watched as the features on his face comically went from confusion to reluctance to acceptance. "Happy to help," he finally said. And then he added, "You're cute when you're bossy."

"Assertive," I corrected.

"Assertive." He nodded. "I'll send the invites out before

noon. Oh wait." He stopped and turned back. "Should I tell people to bring their significant others or...."

"Let's just keep it to staff," I said. "It's more fun when we don't have to worry about people who don't know our inside jokes."

"Right." He winked. "Makes sense. Looking forward to it."

"Me too." I stood up and put on my coat. "Thanks for your help. If anyone is looking for me, I'm going to take Marty for a walk on my break."

Whatever Ethan said in response was drowned out by Marty's extreme excitement over hearing his favourite words. After circling the lobby five times in a blur of fur, he completed his acrobatic entertainment by jumping into my arms as I knelt down to put on his leash.

"I'm going to miss you so much, little guy," I said, kissing him on the top of his wriggly head.

Luke had taken a day off, and seeing as he had some errands to run downtown, we had planned on meeting for a morning walk at the park a few blocks from the agency. I rounded the corner and there he was, hands in his pockets, smiling the warm smile I never tired of seeing.

"Why so glum?" he asked as I walked up to meet him. He stood up after scratching Marty behind the ears and we settled naturally into our walk, side by side, comfortably familiar.

"I'm just bummed about Marty leaving," I said. "I love him so much, which, believe me, is something I never thought I'd hear coming out of my mouth. I'm not really a dog person."

"Seems like you are," he said. I had texted Luke immediately after I'd found out about Marc giving Marty away, and many times since then, expressing my outrage.

"I'm less of a dog person and more of a Marty person," I said. "How can you not be? He's so cute and chill. Plus, he likes me. Most dogs don't."

"Maybe Marty sees something in you that other dogs don't see," Luke said, kicking a chunk of snow off the path.

I shrugged. "Maybe."

"Have you ever thought about taking him yourself?"

I had, surprisingly. But I couldn't take care of a dog. I could barely take care of myself. I told Luke as much.

"Julie," he said, glancing my way as we followed the path around a corner, "as usual, you're not giving yourself enough credit; I don't think you realize how far you've come. You're a different person since I first met you at that meeting."

"Ugh, don't remind me." We both stopped and waited while Marty snuffled in the snow, looking for a place to do his business.

"Look at me," he said, so I did. "I know you don't see this, but coming from someone who can see you without your biased lens, you are a kind and loving person. The way you talk about Ben and Kate. The way you are with Hannah. The way your face lights up when you tell me one of the seemingly hundreds of stories you have about Marty."

I laughed. I did like a good Marty story.

"I think you have a lot to offer this little dog." Luke gestured to Marty as the dog back-kicked snow in the exact opposite direction to where he had peed. "Way more than a complete stranger would. Don't you?"

I gently tugged on Marty's leash and we continued walking. Could I take care of Marty? I did feel like I'd gotten better in the last eight months. I still had a lot of work to do, but I had definitely grown from the selfish partier that I used to be. It would be nice to have a dog to keep me company. And, best of all, I could bring him to work during the day so he wouldn't have to be home alone.

"If I went on holidays, could you and Hannah take care of him?" I looked up at Luke, allowing the buzz of anticipatory excitement to start bubbling up in my chest.

"If you ever do go on an actual holiday then, yes, Hannah would be thrilled to have a dog to take care of." He smiled a smile of victory. He knew he had me.

"Marty," I said, tears filling my eyes, "guess who's going to be your new—"

"Mom!" Luke exclaimed.

I stopped abruptly. "Hard no."

"Dog mom?" Luke tried.

"Again, no," I said but couldn't stop smiling at the thought of it.

Luke smiled back and looped his arm through mine. "We'll work on it."

"When did you start feeling like an adult?" I was sitting on Kate's bed while she tried on her wedding dress. Again.

"What do you mean?" She motioned for me to come over and help her with the zipper.

"I mean I'm forty-five and I still feel like I haven't quite hit adulthood; like I haven't figured it all out yet." I glided the zipper up and slipped the four pearl buttons into their loops at the top. "You look stunning." I smiled, looking at us both in the mirror.

Kate smoothed her hands over the corseted bodice and crinoline skirt and grinned. "I do, don't I?" She turned around so she could see the back. "This dress is gorgeous."

I squeezed her shoulders. "*You* are gorgeous."

"Now I know what you feel like every day." She winked in the mirror and turned as my smile faded. "What?"

"I really wish you wouldn't say stuff like that," I said quietly.

"You wish I wouldn't say you're beautiful?" Her eyebrows furrowed in confusion.

I sighed. Corie had told me I needed to start setting boundaries. What she didn't tell me, however, was how hard it would be. "I know you mean well, and I know you're sincere, but the way you see me is not really how I see myself. And it makes me uncomfortable." I lowered my head. "I just wish you saw me for more than how I look. I don't want to be seen like that anymore."

"Oh, Julie." She rushed over and gave me a hug. "I'm sorry. Of course I see you for more than that. If I had known you felt that way, I would have shut my mouth a long time ago." She stepped back. "It's probably just my own insecurities coming out. I always felt like your less-attractive friend and I guess I mainly focused on how that affected me. I never thought about how saying that stuff affected you." She smiled tentatively, her eyes asking for forgiveness.

"Thanks." I took a deep breath, relieved that the hard part was over. "It's just such a hard standard to live up to. And I'm tired of feeling like I'm failing. I don't want to do that to myself anymore."

"And I don't want to do that to you either," she said. "Thank you for telling me."

I blew out a breath and lay back on the bed. "Do you think our parents had things figured out when they were our age? When I was a kid, they seemed so much older than I feel now. They seemed way more grown up. I mean, I know I was a bit of an extreme case before I stopped drinking, but most people I know who are in their forties still drink and go out and have fun. When I was in my twenties I thought, at some point, people just grew up and became dull."

"Based on what?" Kate lay down beside me, our heads almost touching, just like when we were kids.

I thought for a minute. "Based on our parents, I guess. I never saw my parents party. Back then, being in your forties was old. And old people were responsible. And boring."

Kate laughed. "Little did we know."

"Looking back on it now, I bet my parents did go out and have fun, I just didn't see it. They certainly went to parties and hung out with friends, and there was always alcohol around our house. I was just too young to know what was going on." I rolled onto my side. "I always thought I'd have things figured out by now; that I'd know what to do and make the best decisions."

Kate turned her head. "You made a great decision to stop drinking."

"I know. That's not what I mean."

"What *do* you mean?" Kate sat up and looked down at me.

"Never mind, it's nothing," I said, ignoring her look.

"No!" She nudged me with her knee. "I'm not never-minding. We tell each other everything."

I sat up and leaned back against the headboard, making myself comfortable amongst a dozen frilly throw pillows. "Luke and I almost kissed."

Kate gasped dramatically and leaned in. "What? Really? Tell me more! Do you like him? Does he like you? Do—"

"If you want me to tell you more, you have to refrain from the rapid-fire questioning."

"Right. Sorry," she said, making a motion as if she were zipping up her lips, the way she used to when we were in high school. I laughed.

"The answer to all of your questions is that I honestly don't know."

Kate looked disappointed. "Well, that wasn't worth shutting my mouth for."

"I know, sorry."

"Did you want to kiss him?" She tipped her head to the side.

"I think I did."

"Why didn't you then?" she pressed.

"I don't know. I got scared, I guess."

Kate put her hand on my knee. "You're a great person, Julie. You deserve great things. I hope eventually you start to see that."

"Thanks," I said, eyes down. "I think I'm getting there."

Chapter Twenty-Five

By the end of March, the wedding was almost fully planned. Luke and I were meeting, texting or talking on the phone almost every day. It was exhausting but also filled my cup in a way that I'd never experienced before. Not only was I occupied enough that I had stopped thinking about drinking all the time, but I was also genuinely enjoying myself.

Most of our meetings now happened at his house so he could give Janet a break from taking care of Hannah, and after we'd made it clear to Hannah that we were only friends, I didn't worry so much about always being around.

I would never have said this to Luke, I wouldn't want to put any pressure on him, but I loved meeting at his place. It was homey and comforting, welcoming and warm. I always felt safe and happy when I was there, like their little family had opened their arms and accepted me. Like I was a part of something bigger, even if it was just for an evening.

Hannah was a great kid and we got along so well. If she wasn't in bed already, she would greet me at the door with a hug, her flannel pajamas soft against my skin. If I arrived past her bedtime, a drawing or craft was often waiting for me, my name written on it in block letters. I took everything she made home and put it up on my fridge, always touched and a bit surprised that she had thought of me.

Tonight, she met me at the door, spinning in a princess dress, a whirl of curly red hair, cheeks flushed with excitement.

"Someone is having a hard time paying attention to her father and getting ready for bed." Luke took my light coat and hung it up in the closet, his own face red with what appeared to be exasperation. "Where's Marty?"

I tipped my chin towards my car sitting in the driveway and then back at Hannah, questioning whether or not he had told her I would be bringing my new roommate. I hadn't wanted to burst in with a dog, not knowing what Hannah's reaction would be. I got my answer pretty quickly though.

"Julie's here! Julie's here!" Hannah sang and twirled right into my arms. "Where's your dog?" She looked behind me and then, hilariously, into my purse.

"Hi kiddo," I said. "What's got you so excited?"

"Nothing." She hugged me tight. "I just love my life."

I shrugged. "Can't argue with that." I glanced up at Luke, who looked like he could definitely argue with it. I'd never seen him looking so frazzled. And if Luke looked frazzled, he must have been having a tough night.

"You know what would be fun?" I smoothed Hannah's hair down, trying to hold her still.

"What?"

"Why don't I go get Marty out of my car and then,

after we play with him for a bit in your room, I can read you a story before bed tonight instead of your dad. What do you think?"

"Yes!" she squealed and then turned to Luke. "Is that okay?"

"That is more than okay." Luke ran his hands through his hair, not for the first time it looked like.

"All right," I said, gently guiding Hannah towards the hallway. "But you have to put your PJs on and brush your teeth first, okay?"

Hannah nodded and scampered off to her bedroom.

"Thank you." Luke collapsed onto the couch. "Hannah's normally very well behaved, but sometimes she gets a bit hyper and I completely lose control of the situation. This is clearly one of those times."

"Clearly." I sat down beside him. "You look like you need a break and I would be happy to read her a book."

"Read her two." He yawned. "I really need to clean the kitchen."

"Actually." I stood and cleared my throat. "Before I go get Marty, I have a favour to ask."

"What's up?" His eyes followed my hand as I dug into my purse and held up a key. "I mean, sure, I didn't realize key parties were still a thing, but if that's what you want to do, I'm game," he said, lips twitching.

I rolled my eyes. "Thanks for that, but no. I was wondering if you'd keep a key to my apartment in case I can't get home and I need someone to check on Marty. I highly doubt you'll need to use it, but you know; it would make me feel better if you had one." I looked down.

"Of course I will," he said, taking the key from my hand. "Julie." He stared at me until I looked up. "I know how hard it is for you to ask for help, and I'm really touched you asked me. I'm glad you feel you can trust me with this."

"Well," I said, suddenly shy, "I'm glad I feel I can too." I turned towards the door. "I should probably get Marty out of the car; it's cold out there tonight."

After I had gotten Marty, watched him and Hannah play, and then read not two but three books, Hannah finally calmed down enough to close her eyes and drift off to sleep. I sat with her for a bit longer, knowing Luke could use some quiet time.

"Thanks again," Luke said as I walked into the sparkling clean kitchen, Marty close behind. "Being Hannah's dad is my greatest joy, but it's a lot of work by myself. Having some help is a nice treat."

"It must be hard being a single parent," I said without thinking, instantly regretting it. We hadn't talked about Theresa since he'd told me about her death and I didn't want to bring up anything that would cause him pain. "Sorry, I hope that didn't sound callous."

"Not at all," he said, flipping a dishtowel over his shoulder. "It is hard." He tipped his head to the side. "I don't mind talking about her. Theresa was Hannah's mom. I don't want her to be forgotten."

"Do you still miss her?" I asked as I sat down at the table.

"I do." He pulled out a chair and joined me. "I think about her every day. I think about her whenever I look at Hannah." He sighed. "But it's not as hard as it once was. I was so lucky to have my time with her. To have been able to love her. I think about that now more than the loss."

Only Luke could take grief and turn it into something so perfect. "I'm sorry you had to go through that." I looked down at my lap, touched by the sentiment; embarrassed at the sadness I felt for someone I didn't even know.

"You know what though?" he said, his voice low.

I looked up and was startled to find him staring at me, his eyes deep pools of emerald green. "What?" I whispered.

"I've been noticing things have gotten a lot easier since I met you."

My mouth opened, but nothing came out. Warmth flushed my face from the fire that his words had ignited. I knew what I wanted to express, but I couldn't speak. I couldn't find the right thing to say.

So, instead, I kissed him.

I did it on impulse. Without thinking. Without caring what I should or shouldn't do or what would happen next. I was so touched by his words; I couldn't help myself. And now that I was in it, I didn't know if I could stop. I didn't know if I wanted to.

The softness of his lips against mine was as unexpected as the spark that shot through my body when they touched. He paused for just a second, likely unsure if he should proceed, but my sigh told him he should and he slid his hand behind my neck, deepening the kiss.

Heat pulsed through my body in waves and everything I was thinking dissipated like vapour. All I could do was experience. For once I didn't use my thoughts to push my feelings away.

His one hand lingered under my hair while the other rested on the small of my back, pulling me closer, but not close enough. Never close enough.

I couldn't remember the last time I had felt like this. A feeling so powerful and clear, unclouded by booze and poor decisions. My frozen heart began to thaw; the towering wall started to crumble. He did want me. I hadn't been imagining things. I had been right.

Wait.

Was I taking advantage of the moment? If I was the man in this situation and my friend was telling me about her spouse who tragically passed away, would it be okay for me to give in to what I wanted just because she happened to be vulnerable?

I pushed away, my chair scraping backwards, trying to catch my breath. "I'm sorry, I shouldn't have done that." I looked down at the floor, pretending to be concerned about Marty who had jumped up at the sound. What had I been thinking?

"Why?" Luke breathed heavily. "Why shouldn't you have done that? I was really enjoying myself." He grinned.

"I'm sorry," I said again. "I can't do this. I can't. We're friends. I value your friendship too much. I don't want to ruin it."

His grin disappeared. "Why would you ruin it?"

"Because I would," I said, a bit harsher than I intended. "I have a drinking problem."

"But you've been doing really well," he said unhelpfully.

"Thank you," I said. "I appreciate you saying that. But I still have a long road ahead of me, and I need to focus on me right now, on my recovery. I don't have the effort for anything else."

"Sure." He straightened up in his chair, his face unreadable. "Of course. I understand."

I nodded and we both sat in silence. Eventually he opened his laptop and started scrolling.

"I'm tired actually." I stood and moved my chair back to its place. "Is it okay if we don't do any work tonight?"

"Sure thing." He nodded, closing his laptop. "Whatever you need."

I walked to the front door in a fog and watched silently as he handed me my jacket from the closet.

"Feels like spring might be coming soon," I said as I picked up Marty and opened the door. I couldn't think of anything else to say.

He nodded. "It does."

I walked down the steps and turned. "Text me later?"

"You bet." He tried to smile.

"Bye, Luke." I opened my car door and slid in, tears in my eyes, my heart heavy. I felt awful. Like I'd just lost my best friend. Maybe I had.

I held my hand to wave as I pulled away from his house, but he had already turned to go back inside, head down, shoulders slumped.

And then he was gone.

Present Day

From: Julie
Sent: July 27th 6:50 PM
To: Luke
Subject: I miss you

Hi Luke,

Okay, this honestly isn't fair. I'm hurting too, you know. I miss you more than I've ever missed anyone. Is that what you want me to say? Will that make you come back? I miss your friendship. I miss talking to you. I miss hearing your voice. I miss just being in your presence. Where did you go? Why won't you answer me?

I miss you so much. And I'm sorry, Luke. I'm so sorry.

Please forgive me.

P.S. What if you knew everything? What would you think of me then? Would you understand why I did what I did?

Love, Julie

Chapter Twenty-Six

Three Months Ago

It was a month and a half until the big day and Luke and I had dropped our in-person meetings down to once a week. Most of the planning had been completed and the odds and ends could be discussed via email or text.

Since the kiss, however, the once-fun meetings—the only part of the week I looked forward to—had become very business-like. Luke had suggested we work at his place a couple of times, but I always had a reason why we should meet at a coffee shop instead, not wanting to give mixed signals. He eventually stopped asking.

I missed that house. I missed seeing Hannah and reading to her until she fell asleep.

Luke seemed fine with the new arrangements, and I pretended I was fine with meeting at Starbucks in the evenings, but every time I saw him and was greeted, not with a hug but with a polite smile, my heart sank. It was for the best, though. We weren't meant to be together.

Of course, I said nothing. I just kept pretending I was fine. He didn't seem bothered, so why should I be? He appeared to have gotten over whatever was between us very quickly, so there was no reason to say that I hadn't. To say that I missed him. To say that I was suffering.

One thing I was very good at was pushing feelings away. If I was determined enough, I could shove every good feeling I had about Luke so deep inside that they would never again see the light of day. So, that's what I focused on. It was easier than actually feeling things. It was easier than wanting him. It was much easier than feeling sad.

Luke arrived at Starbucks late, which was unusual for him. "It's disrespectful to be late," he always said.

"Is everything all right?" I asked as he pulled his phone from his cargo pants pocket, set it on the table, and sat down.

"Sorry," he said. "Hannah—"

"Is everything okay with Hannah?" I leaned forward, my chest tightening.

He nodded. "It is now. She fell at school and they called me in from work. She's fine, though, just a couple of scrapes. One was pretty deep and they thought she might need stitches, but she didn't. That's where I was. At the hospital."

"Oh my God, you totally didn't have to come tonight," I said. "If she needs you, you need to be with her. We can do this another time."

He looked up, his eyes softening as they met mine, a proper grin poking at the sides of his mouth. "She's with her grandma and some ice cream, tucked deeply into her happy place. She would kill me if I interrupted that." His eyes shone and I relaxed. I hadn't seen that look in a while. Maybe things were finally getting back to normal. Maybe it wasn't too late to still be friends.

"As long as you're sure." I pulled at my hair and then tucked a piece behind my ear. "Are you doing okay?" I asked as I unconsciously put my hand over his.

His eyes darkened and he slipped his hand out from under mine.

"I'm fine, thanks for asking." He pulled out his laptop and set it between us. "Let's get to work."

As we checked items off our list, knowing all of our hard work would soon be coming to a satisfactory end, I rolled our story around in my head, trying to rearrange the outcome into something I was happier with.

Maybe I'd never had feelings for Luke. Maybe I'd merely gotten caught up in the wedding planning festivities. Of course someone could develop romantic feelings for someone else when everything that surrounded them was about love and commitment and being together forever. It wasn't so much that we had a great connection; it was more the situation. Obviously, it could have happened with anyone.

As soon as this was over, as soon as our part in the wedding was done, we would go our separate ways and rarely think of each other again. Maybe on Kate and Ben's wedding anniversary I would remember our time together fondly, how we had bonded over planning, how we had achieved our goal. That's all it would be.

Soon, I wouldn't have to delete his texts because it made me sad to see his name at the top of my contacts list.

Soon, the texts would just stop coming. Soon, I wouldn't have to try so hard not to think about him, ignoring the tingly buzz of excitement. Soon it would be easy. Because it was never meant to be.

Our friendship was one of necessity. It had developed in a bubble. And that bubble had popped.

Soon, we would never have to see each other again.

And then I would be able to breathe.

If you ever want to get your mind off something, plan a staff party where the only colleague who helps you plan things is unable to because, you know, the party is for her.

All week I had been getting 'helpful' suggestions from the men at work like "we should get a cake" or "we should get balloons from Balloon Bar," when everyone knew that "we" meant "me." Not one of them offered to help.

All of them somehow thought that the party of their dreams just magically appeared without any work. Unsurprisingly, the few other women in the office had asked what they could do to help and what they could bring. The men just asked what time they should show up and "You'll have good beer, right?"

By the time Friday rolled around, I hadn't had time to think about anything else. My days were filled with party balloons and colour schemes and paper plates and drinking games and actually cleaning my apartment, trying to make it look like it was inhabited by an adult. I had even taken the time (and money) to buy a few nice throw pillows and a cozy blanket to cover my threadbare furniture to try to cheer the place up. This was the first party I'd had since the

New Year's I'd stopped drinking the first time—the New Year's Ben and Kate had gotten together—and, if I was having people over, I should probably do my best to make the place look nice.

I left the office early Friday afternoon, grabbed some extra bags of chips on the way, and ran up my apartment steps so I could get myself ready and put the food out in the thirty minutes I had to spare. Much to the displeasure of Kate's cat Mittens, I had left Marty with Kate and Ben for a sleepover. My apartment was going to be full of people and I didn't want to make the little guy uncomfortable.

Not really caring what I looked like—the party wasn't for me after all—I changed out of my work clothes, threw on a pair of skinny jeans and shrugged into a pale pink button-up tunic top. A couple squirts of hair shine to liven up my locks, and a bit of powder to subdue my shiny face, and I was ready to go. Thank goodness I had prepared most of the food the night before or I wouldn't have been close to ready when the first guest arrived.

And, of course, that guest was Ethan.

I had just finished dumping the last bag of chips into a bowl and was walking around the room making sure everything was in place when I looked out the window and saw him walking back and forth in front of my apartment building, looking confused. I opened the window and called out his name, watching him spin around until he saw me like a dog chasing his tail.

First of all, who comes early to a party and, secondly, what on earth were we going to talk about until someone else arrived? At least talking to him, about anything, would take my mind off—

No. I refused to think about Luke tonight. For the next several hours, it would be like Luke had never existed. I had to get over him somehow, and pushing every thought of him out of my mind was the only strategy I could think of.

I buzzed Ethan in and heard him running up the stairs, likely taking them two at a time, trying to get as much benefit out of the physical activity as possible. The stamina on this guy was incredible. My face flushed and I had to shake my head to dislodge the thoughts that were creeping in.

Although, I reminded myself, it wasn't like I was dating anyone. There was nothing wrong with thinking this way. I was single; Ethan was single. What was wrong with a bit of fun? It wasn't like we would get together or anything. No one at work would have to know. What was that saying? Get over someone by getting under someone else?

I can't believe I just thought that.

"Hey Jules," he said, not even close to being out of breath when I opened the door. He handed me six cans of Perrier encased in plastic. "For the hostess with the mostest."

"You sound like my dad." I laughed. "Are you sure you're in your thirties?"

He winked. "Wouldn't you like to know?"

That didn't make sense, but okay. He went to hand me a second six-pack, this one of Nokomis Honey Brown beer, but changed his mind and pulled one out of the plastic cover. "Do you mind if I have one? That run up the stairs made me thirsty." He popped a can open and swallowed deeply before I had a chance to answer.

"Of course not." I grabbed the remaining cans and put them in the fridge. "If I'd made this a dry party, no one would have come."

"I would have," he said, so quietly I wasn't sure I'd heard it. He took another swig of beer, put it down on the kitchen table and unzipped his jacket. I could smell his distinct scent clinging to it as he gave it to me to hang up. He was wearing a tight long-sleeved T-shirt that showed off the results of all the workouts he had "crushed" lately. His triceps tightened the fabric as he slid his hand through his perfectly messy mop of hair.

"So…." I started, not having a clue what to say. All I could think about was running my hands over a different kind of six-pack that was surely hiding underneath his shirt. Thank God the buzzer went before I told him that shirts were optional at my parties.

I buzzed whoever it was in and was relieved to see Quinn burst through the door, overloaded with shopping bags, ready to save me from my impure thoughts.

"Happy birthday!" I cheered and gave her a hug as Ethan took the bags from her hands and set them on the counter.

"Thanks, friend!" she said to Ethan and then looked back at me, raising her eyebrows.

I shrugged. She knew about as much as me at this point.

"Hey, Millennial," she called as Ethan put her bottle of chardonnay in the fridge. "I'll actually have a glass of that."

A flicker of irritation crossed his face before he turned

and pulled the wine back out. "You know you're also a Millennial, right?"

She shrugged. "I'm a Gen-X at heart."

He looked at me, his eyes begging me to come to his rescue.

"Sorry, she's right. I've officially accepted her into our fold." I laughed and playfully punched him in the arm. My goodness, those biceps though.

Quinn opened her bottle of wine and poured herself a generous glass while Ethan looked around my small apartment. "This is a great space," he said, admiring my cheap, random decor. With the exception of what I had just purchased, I had never bothered to decorate, seeing as most of my money used to go to bottles (boxes) of wine. Now that I had a full-time job, maybe I could save up and finally buy myself some adult furniture. Maybe a bigger TV. I was finally starting to realize that I deserved to live somewhere nice. I might as well do my best to make my place more comfortable if I wasn't going to be hanging out at Luke's anymore. A dart of grief hit me in the chest and I forced down a glug of soda water, trying to ignore the sweet aroma wafting from Quinn's glass of wine.

"Why isn't there any music playing?" Ethan said. "Can I plug my iPhone in somewhere? I have a sweet party playlist."

I pointed to the wireless speaker on my bookshelf. "Be my guest."

"What's this?" Ethan picked up a circular piece of plastic I had propped up inside a frame holding a picture of me, Kate and Ben.

"That's my six-month sobriety chip." I walked over and picked it up, smiling at the memory. "From the first time I quit drinking." I hadn't actually attended AA before my meltdown almost a year ago, so what I was holding was actually a poker chip that Kate had written the number six on in black sharpie. I had almost cried when she'd given it to me.

Ethan's eyebrows furrowed. "I thought you said you didn't drink because of health reasons."

"Yeah, I lied," I said, not caring about pretence anymore. "I'm an alcoholic. And I keep this out to remind myself what I can do. I have just over a month to go before I've made it one year." I smiled, proud of myself.

"Nice," Ethan said. "Good for you."

I picked up the picture and pointed to the faces, rubbing off a smudge in the process. "This is my best friend Kate and my brother Ben. The chip lives with them because they're who I'm doing it for. They mean everything to me."

"And yourself, right?" Quinn said, digging into the pretzels. "You're also doing it for yourself?"

"Of course." I smiled. "And myself." I put the frame down and stood the chip back up inside. It seemed like so long ago that I'd gotten it. So much had happened since then. I'd gotten a new job, met some great friends. Met Luke.

An unwanted lump formed in my throat and I swallowed it down. *Focus, Julie.* This night was about Quinn, not about me. She deserved a fabulous, fun party. I refused to think about anything else. I needed to keep my head planted firmly in the present.

"Another beer?" I grabbed Ethan's can from his hand and shook it side to side. I knew it; empty.

"Might as well." He grinned.

Might as well indeed.

If the success of a party could be measured by how many bottles and cans were littered around an apartment after it was over, then mine was definitely successful. Ethan walked around the room with a garbage bag and threw the empty cans in and I dumped the not so empty ones in the sink while Quinn snored on the couch. I'm pretty sure at least two of the empty wine bottles were courtesy of her. No judgment from me though; she looked like she'd had an amazing time.

"Quinn seemed to have fun," Ethan said as I draped one of my new red-and-yellow tartan blankets over her.

"She deserved it," I said, smiling at her tiny snores. "She's been working really hard. And it *is* her birthday. It's about time she was celebrated."

Ethan put down the garbage bag and walked over to the sink, close enough that I could smell the tangy scent of beer on his breath. I wondered when the smell of alcohol would stop being a trigger. When I would stop wanting a drink. Maybe it never really went away.

"You're a great friend," Ethan said. He leaned over so his shoulder tapped mine and I shivered.

"I'm going to close the window." I moved away. "It's getting a bit chilly."

Take it easy, Julie, I thought. Yes, I admittedly was attracted to him, and yes, sleeping with Ethan could potentially help me get over Luke, but I still had a month left before I hit my year of sobriety. Did I want to waste it on someone who probably checked his fitness tracker during sex to see how many calories he was burning?

I struggled to pull down the ancient wooden window frame and Ethan came over to help. Our hands touched once, twice and then his baby finger hooked around mine, pulling my hand down and stroking the top with his thumb.

Just breathe. I tried to swallow, wondering if he could hear the pounding of my heart. This was the moment. This was where I had to make a decision. Either I pulled away and pretended nothing had happened or I turned to face him, knowing that something would.

Should I give in and break my promise to myself? Did it count if it was just sex? If it meant nothing more than giving in to attraction? It was better than finishing off the rest of the wine people had left behind, and I wasn't going to lie, the thought had crossed my mind.

I turned and tilted my head up, gazing into Ethan's clear blue eyes. Eyes that were staring at my lips. "We can't let this affect our work relationship," I whispered, trying to block out the sound of my nagging conscience. A voice that sounded suspiciously like Kate.

I'll be fine, I said to her in my head. *This is fine.*

"It won't. I promise," he breathed in my ear.

His lips nestled in the crook of my neck and slowly slid up to my cheek. A shiver started deep in my toes and came out of my mouth as a gasp. It had been so long.

He pulled me into my bedroom and I closed the door behind us, pushing him gently down on my bed. He reached behind and pulled his shirt over his head in one smooth, practised motion, and I almost lost consciousness. I had never seen a body so perfect; his abs actually rippled when he lay back on his elbows.

Suddenly, I was nervous. What if he expected a body that was younger and fitter? What if he was disappointed? It suddenly occurred to me that I couldn't remember the last time I'd had sex sober. I had never cared what the men I slept with thought. I was always too busy drunkenly acting out their fantasies.

I needn't have worried though. It was pretty clear he was ready before I even took off my shirt. "You are so beautiful," he said as I unbuttoned my blouse. "I dream of that hair, hanging down, brushing my face. Do you know what you do to me?"

"Tell me." I stepped out of my jeans and straddled him on the bed, once again ignoring the voice telling me to stop. I was just nervous because it had been so long. I needed to keep going. It would be worth it when it was done. I would finally be able to move on.

"I think about you constantly." He lifted his hands and pushed my hair off my face, leaning in to kiss my neck. "I feel so good around you. You're the only one who really gets me." He pulled back and looked into my eyes. "I feel like we've known each other forever. I really, really like you."

Using every bit of power I had, I made my hands stop exploring. I could barely think straight. But I did know one thing from experience: I had to make sure we were on the same page. Not only did I not want this to affect our work relationship, I also didn't want him to get hurt. I wanted him to know this would just be for tonight.

I put my hands on the sides of his face. "This is just fun, right? Just sex? I'm not in this for a relationship. You need to know that before we go any further."

He pulled back and tilted his head to the side. "Of course." He laughed. "I'm already in a relationship. What would I want with another one?"

Chapter Twenty-Seven

"You've got to be fucking kidding me." I jumped off the bed, quickly tugged on my jeans and pulled on a faded sweatshirt that had been hanging on the doorknob.

"What?" He was genuinely confused. So confused that everything he said came out like a question. "I thought we were on the same page? You knew I had a girlfriend? We've been going out for almost six years? Everyone knows that?"

"I knew you *had* a girlfriend." I was trying to keep my voice down so we wouldn't wake Quinn and it came out sounding like a growl.

"No." He still looked confused. "I *have* a girlfriend."

"What are you doing with me then?"

"What do you mean?"

Jesus Christ, he was dumb. "Why are you here? With me. Without your shirt on. Kissing me. Flirting with me. Why are you doing all of this if you still have a girlfriend?"

He shrugged. "I don't know, I thought you were into it."

"And what made you think that?" I hissed.

His confusion was slowly turning into anger. "You flirted back." He gestured towards me. "You took off *your* shirt. You kissed me too. I wasn't alone in all of this, you know."

I shook my head with frustration. "Yes, I did take my shirt off because I thought you were single. You never talk about your girlfriend. You never mention her when you talk about your weekend plans. I had assumed—and I wasn't the only one, by the way—that you had broken up with her. I assumed—because you never, ever, *ever* talk about her, and because you are constantly talking to *me*, and because we went on that date or whatever it was, and because you're currently sitting *shirtless* on my *bed*—that she no longer existed. But clearly that was my bad." I held up my hands in mock defence. I could barely contain my fury.

"I never said that was a date." He didn't even have the gall to look ashamed. To look guilty. Was this just what he did? Cheated on his girlfriend as if it were no big deal? Something he didn't think twice about? Thinking only of himself. Not even considering who else was involved. Not thinking that if I had slept with him, I would have unwillingly been a part of whatever bullshit dumpster fire his relationship appeared to be.

"And besides," he continued, "you didn't seem too fussed about it the first time."

My head snapped up. "What?"

He chuckled. "I knew you didn't remember."

"Remember what?"

He shook his head as if to say it wasn't worth talking about. "Never mind, it doesn't matter."

"It does matter." My breath came out fast and shallow.

Prickly beads of sweat poked through the skin on my chest. "Remember what?"

He pulled his shirt back over his head and ran a hand through his messed-up hair. "A few years ago. We met at a bar. You were super drunk or high or something, I don't know. You could barely walk. You took me home to your apartment and I had to help you up the stairs. We had some wine. One thing led to another and then, you know. You didn't care that I had a girlfriend then. You didn't even ask my name."

That fucking wink when we'd first met at the office. That's where it had come from. I felt sick.

"Why didn't you say you knew me on my first day at work?" I whispered. I couldn't believe this was happening. I mean, it would have only been a matter of time before I came across someone I had slept with and didn't remember, but I couldn't believe it was happening now. It felt surreal, and awful and disconnected. I almost felt like I was floating outside of my body.

"I dunno." He shrugged again. "I just thought we were pretending it didn't happen, like it was just one night of fun. Isn't that what women like you do?"

Women like me. I swallowed down the bile that had crept up my throat.

"I stopped drinking. I'm getting better." *Don't cry, don't cry, don't cry.*

"How was I supposed to know?" He looked me right in the eyes. "You seem the same to me. This is not my fault. You were into it as much as I was." He smirked. "Until you weren't."

Fuck you, I thought, seething. "I guess the only difference this time was that you weren't having sex with someone who was too drunk to make proper choices. Someone so drunk that you needed to help her up the stairs. But you fucked her anyways. Because that's what you wanted. You didn't even consider that she might not know what she was doing."

"But you did know," he said, his eyes narrowed. "Women like you always know."

"Get the fuck out of my house," I said, my voice low and even. I pointed my finger at the door like I was banishing a misbehaving dog.

He sighed and opened the bedroom door, pretending to cough into his hand. "Cocktease."

"Get out!" I screamed. Not caring if I woke up Quinn. Not caring if I woke up the whole world.

"Okay, okay." He held his hands up in front of him, grabbed his jacket and shoes from the floor and opened the door. "Is work going to be weird on Monday?"

I shoved him out and slammed the door, sneaking one final look at Quinn who was still snoring away.

I went into my bedroom and closed the door, sliding onto the floor. It had finally happened. My sordid past had caught up with me. In the worst way possible. Now what did I do? How did I go to work on Monday? How did I ever face Ethan again? How did I face myself? What was this whole year for if I couldn't escape all the shitty things I'd done? I had worked so hard to put my life back together and now it was, in every way, falling back apart around me.

I felt gutted. Empty. Embarrassed and ashamed. Nothing

had changed. All the things I had done, the person I was. The feeling of being out of control. It was all back. Like it had never left. Like I had never tried. How was I going to deal with this?

I pulled out my phone and clicked on Luke's number: *I think I made a big mistake,* I typed. *Can you talk?*

But I couldn't hit send. We weren't close friends anymore. We weren't anything.

I was on my own.

Chapter Twenty-Eight

Now that I'd been attending Group for almost a year, I truly believed I wouldn't have survived if I hadn't taken the first step on that hot, sticky day last summer. The openness and non-judgmental support I had received from everyone I'd met had been life-changing.

I no longer felt uncomfortable sharing my deepest secrets and darkest thoughts. I knew nothing I said would go further than this room. I knew everyone here had secrets that were just as bad, and even worse. I knew I could always count on everyone to listen when I was having a tough time. And the best part was, sometimes, the only thing they did was listen. They all knew that there were times to share, but there were also times to just observe. To hear what someone needed to say without commenting.

This, however, wasn't one of those times.

"Why are men such selfish jerks?" I glanced around at the five or six guys in the room. "No offence."

"Not all men are like Ethan," Corie said patiently. I had just finished telling everyone what had happened at Quinn's birthday, ending on my triumphant decision to pour the rest of the leftover wine down the sink.

I puffed out an exasperated breath. "I know." I immediately thought of Luke and then wished I hadn't. I hadn't talked to him in person for weeks and the only time we'd texted had been about the Stag and Doe.

"Okay." I changed tack. "Why are selfish jerks always attracted to me? Do I exude some sort of scent that says I'm game for being an accomplice if a man is in the mood to cheat?"

Some dude snorted and covered up his mouth.

"Maybe you attract those kinds of guys because that's all you think you deserve," Jenn said quietly and then lowered her eyes when everyone else looked her way.

"What do you mean?" I asked, my voice soft.

She looked up hesitantly. Jenn had been back at Group for about a month but still hadn't worked up the courage to talk about her relapse. In fact, I'm pretty sure these were the first words she'd uttered since she'd returned.

"Go ahead, Jenn." Corie gave her an encouraging smile.

Jenn's eyes flickered to mine and then back at her hands, tightly clasped in her lap. "Well," she started. "For me, as long as I can remember, all I ever wanted was for a guy to like me. I was so desperate to be wanted that I didn't care what kind of man I attracted. And after a few bad experiences, and several alcohol-fuelled poor choices, I started thinking that maybe the bad men were the only ones I deserved. The ones who wanted to cheat. The ones who just wanted sex. Who treated you like useless garbage." She lifted her chin and met my eyes. "Maybe when nice guys show you they like you, you don't believe them. So you either ignore them or you push them away. Maybe you're like me."

"That's actually pretty common for women who struggle with alcoholism," Corie said. "Men who are 'selfish jerks', as you put it, often have strong personalities and seem like they're in control of their lives. When you feel your life is out of control, sometimes that's what you crave."

"That kind of makes sense," I said and Jenn nodded.

"But once you've figured that out," Corie continued, "you can be more aware of it and learn to see the toxic traits earlier, eventually avoiding those traits from the beginning. It's a big step. And it's something to always pay attention to." She looked at both of us, her expression stern but kind. "And no one deserves to be treated like that. No matter what you've done, no matter what you've been through. Above all else, I hope you're both learning that from this group."

I smiled at Jenn who smiled back, and this time the smile lit her eyes.

As the rest of the group shared, I gave this some thought. What both women had said made sense. I hadn't slept with a guy since I'd stopped drinking, and when Ethan had flirted and grabbed my hand after the party, I hadn't told him to stop. I hadn't told him that what he was doing was inappropriate. I had thought he was just leading me in the direction I'd wanted to go. The direction I'd been taking my whole adult life. One that was initially satisfying but ultimately led nowhere.

But in the end, I did take control. I stopped it. As soon as I learned he was with someone else, I shut it down. And that *was* a big step. A big step for me anyways. I stopped it because not only did I have a clear head and know it was wrong, I also knew I didn't want to be with someone who could so easily be unfaithful.

I finally believed I deserved better than being a man's fantasy. And I knew exactly what I was going to do about it.

Chapter Twenty-Nine

"Holy crap, Julie, what did you do?" Kate met me at her door, eyes wide, hand clasping her chest like she was about to have a heart attack.

"Thanks, I'm glad you like it," I said dryly as I slipped past her, set Marty gently on the floor, and shrugged off my spring jacket. I had come to accept the fact that I was now one of those women who carried their small dogs with them everywhere they went.

"What happened?" Ben walked into the living room. "Oh my God." He stopped in his tracks when he saw me. "Are you…are you okay? What happened? Are you…did you…?"

"I am not now nor was I drunk when I made this decision." I hung up my coat. "And while I can understand why you would think that, I'm still almost twelve months sober. And honestly, I wouldn't mind a bit of support here."

I stared at them both, trying to put on a brave face. At the time, the decision had seemed, while maybe slightly rash, a perfect step forward to celebrate my personal growth.

Kate, instead, started crying.

"Why are *you* crying?" I asked, walking over to give her a hug. "I'm the one who cut off all my hair."

"I'm sorry I haven't been there for you." She sobbed onto my shoulder. "I know I've been busy and now obviously something horrible has happened and I wasn't there to give you any support."

I gave her a squeeze and then held her at arm's length. "Kate, I'm fine. And honestly, a reaction like yours is one of the reasons why I cut it. Why is it so shocking when a woman cuts her hair, or stops dying her hair, or changes her look in any way? Men don't get shit for shaving their beards, or going grey, or gaining a few pounds."

"But it was so pretty." Kate sniffed, reaching down to pet Marty, who appeared to be very concerned about her tears.

"Exactly. I'm tired of hiding behind my hair. There's more to me than long blonde hair. I don't want to be judged purely on what I look like anymore. I have other things to offer."

"I think it looks great." Ben walked over in two strides and pulled me in for a tight hug. "And I'm so happy to hear you say that. It's something I've always wished you could see about yourself. You *are* beautiful, good genes run in this family." He laughed. "But you're also funny and smart and kind and caring. I'm glad you're starting to see that too." He stepped back and examined my newly shorn pixie cut. "I like it. It actually suits your personality more than the long hair did."

"Sharp and shocking?" I joked.

"No," Kate said. "Fun and flirty. Bold and bright. Ben's

right, it does suit you." She reached out and touched the top, still a bit unsure. "I'm sorry I lost my shit a bit."

"A bit?" I laughed.

"I just thought something had happened, you know, like you pulled a Felicity. I do like it now that I'm getting over the shock." She grinned. "Are you sure nothing happened?"

"Well." I sat on the couch. "Something did happen, but it wasn't that terrible. It was more of a wakeup call than anything."

Kate perched on the couch beside me and Ben curled up in the overstuffed armchair. I told them about Ethan and the flirting. I told them about the night of the party, and then I told them about my decision to cut my hair after I went to Group.

"I slept on it," I said. "And after I woke up, it was still what I wanted to do."

"The mistake with Ethan wasn't your fault." Kate frowned. "It sounds like he knew exactly what he was doing."

Ben nodded, arms crossed. "What a jackass," he said under his breath.

"I know," I said. "I know it wasn't my fault this time. And I know I didn't deserve to be treated like I was just around to entertain some clueless man who was bored with his girlfriend. I honestly think Ethan was placed in my path to help me finally see that."

Kate's eyes filled with tears again. "You've come so far this last year, Julie. I'm glad you're finally seeing what everyone else sees. You are so much more to me than my 'pretty best friend.' Now you know why we love you so much."

I dabbed my eyes with the corner of my sleeve. I knew how lucky I was to have such great people love me.

It was time I started to love myself just as much.

I will admit, after Kate's reaction, I was a bit nervous about going into work on Monday morning with my new hair and subsequent "fuck it" attitude. What would people say? Would they say anything? Would someone tell me I looked much younger with my hair longer and "why would I do something like that to myself" like the barista at Starbucks?

At 7:30 a.m. I decided I might as well get it over with. I grabbed my denim jacket from the closet, checked the mirror by the door, smoothed some stray hairs behind my ears and stepped out into the cool morning, Marty trotting happily behind me. "You don't care what I look like, do you?" I said as he bounded into the car, ready for a day of eating scraps off the office kitchen floor. "I wish more humans were like dogs." Marty licked my nose in agreement, jumped into the back seat, turned around three times and snuggled into his blanket.

I breathed in the crisp, dewy air and smiled. I loved spring. And while it wasn't quite warm enough for the trees to start budding or for the flowers to wake up, the snow was gone and everything smelled fresh and clean. Winter had washed away all the crap from the year before and everything was new again, ready to be reborn.

Just like me, I thought.

I climbed the two flights of stairs at the office with a bit of a skip in my step, ready to face whatever shocked looks and sentiments my short, "unfeminine" hair elicited. I pulled open the heavy oak door, set down Marty who took off like a shot, and walked into the empty lobby, head up, confident, ready to take on the shit-talkers.

No one was there.

Fine. This was just fine actually. I hadn't admitted it to myself, but I was also nervous about seeing Ethan for the first time since I'd told him to get the fuck out of my house. I had a plan for that too though; I would just need to stick to my guns. I had firmly decided that I would be in control of our 'relationship' moving forward. No longer would I be waiting to see what a man did first and follow along. Today was the day I started taking my power back.

I didn't have to wait long.

Ethan walked in just seconds after I sat down, dazzling smile at the ready. It was almost comical how quickly it disappeared after he registered that it was, in fact, me sitting behind the desk.

"Jesus Christ, Julie, what did you do to your hair?" Apparently, he was so shocked he couldn't even pretend he liked it.

I smiled sweetly and ran my fingers through it. "Oh this? It was time for a change."

"It looks…."

I laughed at what appeared to be him struggling to choke out a positive word. "Different." He finally landed on.

"Thanks. That was the intent."

He nodded. "Right." He touched his hair and walked

slowly up to my desk, perhaps scared that I would leap over it with some scissors and cut off his own cherished locks.

"So." He leaned on the desk and shot me a wide, toothy grin, seemingly recovered from the hair trauma. "About Friday night. No hard feelings, right? I mean, it was just a misunderstanding. I'm game to pretend it never happened if you are. Still friends?" He tipped his head and looked at me with his soft blue eyes.

I held his gaze without blinking. "No."

His grin momentarily faltered and his head jerked back. "What do you mean no?"

"I mean no," I said, firm and unsmiling. "No, we cannot just pretend it didn't happen and, no, we're not still friends."

His eyes narrowed in confusion.

"What you did was not cool," I continued. "I don't care if you're in an unhappy relationship; cheating on your girlfriend is not cool. Deciding that you're attracted to me and then acting on it without regard for anyone else involved is not cool. Bringing me into whatever bullshit mess your life is without my consent is not cool. And, most importantly, thinking that I would just go along with it, thinking that I would jump at the chance to sleep with you without caring about the consequences because that's just the kind of person I am is not cool at all."

He opened his mouth to speak, but I held up my hand, not finished.

"I will, however," I continued, my voice steady and calm, "grant you the undeserved courtesy of keeping this to myself because we work together and because I'm an adult. But moving forward, we will maintain a professional relationship only. I will be friendly and cordial to you at work so we don't cause any drama, but no matter how friendly I am, don't ever make the mistake of thinking we are friends. I don't like you. I don't respect you. You have lost all of my trust and it would be a grave error to think that you will ever win it back." I paused and settled into my chair. "Understood?"

"But—" he started.

"No, Ethan. This is how it's going to be. Nothing you say will change that. Understood?" I said again.

He stood up, shoulders sagging, a scowl forming on his handsome face. "Fine. Understood." He sighed. "Would it help to say I was sorry?"

"Nope."

He nodded and walked away.

"Oh my gosh, I'm so proud of you." A whisper behind me made me jump.

"Oh shit, you heard that?" I said as Quinn walked up and gave me a hug.

"Don't worry; I won't tell anyone. I am so, so proud of you." She squeezed even tighter. "And I'm so sorry." She released me from her bear-like grip. "Are you okay? Ethan is such an ass."

I smiled. "Yes, he is. And I'm fine actually. More than fine. This is the first time I've ever stood up for myself like that. The first time I've felt like I deserved more than sleeping with someone and pretending it didn't happen. I honestly feel pretty good about it."

"I'm glad you finally see that," she said. "You deserve so

much more; you always have. And, holy crap, I absolutely *love* your hair. It looks great on you. You look like you just walked off the cover of *Vogue*. Absolutely gorgeous!"

"Thanks." I smiled and touched the side, still getting used to the feel of the rough edges beneath my fingers. It was funny, I had finally gotten the reaction to my hair that I'd been hoping for, but I felt the same. *I* liked my hair. *I* thought it looked good. And, right now, that was all that really mattered.

Present Day

From: Julie
Sent: July 28th 4:50 AM
To: Luke
Subject: Thank you

Dear Luke,

I think it's time I told you the truth. This is going to be a long one, so if you're actually reading this, I would recommend getting a snack.

Okay, here goes:

When I told you why I started drinking so much, I didn't tell you everything. Mostly because I've never admitted this to anyone, not even myself until recently. When I said I drank a lot because of what happened in my past, to keep it buried so I wouldn't have to process it, I was telling you something that I think I've always known. No matter how much I tried to deny it.

But, when I did finally process it, I realized there was more to my drinking, to my alcoholism, than what had happened to me. And I didn't like what I found.

I think I also drank so much because I liked being out of control. I liked that it gave me an excuse to do things I would never do when I was sober.

But I've recently also realized something else: when I drank too much—when I allowed taken men to flirt with me and make suggestive comments; when I would flirt back and feel flattered; when I would sleep with someone and pretend it never happened—each time I did this I was giving up my self-worth.

I was continuously perpetuating the idea that I'd always had about myself: I was only worthy of being intimate with someone who didn't want to commit.

When I was drunk, I told myself I was being brave. I was doing what I wanted to. I was doing what I was inhibited from doing when I was sober. I thought I was being free and having fun and living life to its fullest and not caring about society's expectations.

But I was really being a coward. I was admitting defeat. I was letting men take advantage of my low self-esteem; of my need to be liked; of my desire to be wanted.

But since I stopped drinking, since I met you, Luke, I've become stronger. Through your eyes I could see that I was worth more than one-night stands and settling for men who didn't know what they wanted.

I now know that I deserve better. I deserve someone who loves me for all that I am—even the faulty parts. Someone who isn't keeping me as their weekend escape or backup plan. I deserve romance and commitment and love. I know that now. I know that I'm worth something. I finally feel worth something. And I have you to thank for it.

I will never forget this gift you have given me.

Love, Julie.

Chapter Thirty

Two months ago

It was the day before the Stag and Doe, it was midnight, and I was still awake. As I waited at my kitchen table for Luke to email me the final wedding seating chart so I could proof it before it went to the venue, I laid my head down, cradled in the crook of my arms. I was tired. And sad. I wished we were meeting in person. It was much more fun staying up until midnight when you had someone to share your exhaustion with. Now it was just lonely.

I watched the minutes flip by on the bottom corner of my laptop and marvelled at how things had changed so dramatically over the past couple of years. Staying up until midnight, or much later, never used to faze me in the slightest. Two years ago, on a weeknight, it wouldn't have been unthought-of to be finishing off my first bottle of wine, waiting for my Tinder selection of the night to show up.

Since I'd sobered up, since I'd gained a better understanding of why I'd drunk so much, I'd started wondering if meaningless sex was part of the toxic pattern.

Was it just something else I had been using for comfort? Something else I'd been using to cover up the pain? I'd always felt so powerful when men had wanted me. Had I actually been giving up my power in exchange?

Until I'd told Luke about the rape, I hadn't considered that I might not have properly processed such a defining moment in my past. I'd always thought it was something I'd asked for. If I hadn't been flirting. If I hadn't been drunk. If I had just left earlier. If. If. If.

I hadn't realized how one terrible night could affect the rest of my life.

My phone dinged with a new email and my heart fluttered in my chest. I smiled as I woke up my computer screen and Luke's name popped up. What a difference a sober year and a clear mind can make.

I couldn't put my finger on what I was feeling the night of the Stag and Doe. Nervous? Excited? Both? Luke had been so busy that I hadn't seen him in weeks. I hadn't seen him since I'd almost had sex with Ethan.

I had really missed him though. Had he been missing me? Would we just start seeing each other less and less now? My stomach churned at the thought. And there was also the issue of my hair. As much as I loved it, and as much as I didn't want to care about what other people thought, it was hard not to be nervous when most people's reactions had been either shock or disappointment. Marc had come right out and asked why I'd done it. "It makes you look way older," he'd said as if he was doing me a favour.

I was happy that Quinn loved it. And not fake loved it

like a lot of people attempted. Every time she saw me her eyes lit up. "I love your hair so much!" she would exclaim. "It's so perfect for your face."

What would Luke think? I ran my hand over my scalp, smoothing it down, brushing the bangs across my forehead. I wasn't used to being this nervous before seeing someone. I didn't like it.

I'd had a hard time choosing my outfit for the night. What did a forty-five-year-old woman wear to a night of karaoke? Especially if that woman didn't like karaoke. The only thing worse than watching a room full of drunken people sing-yelling '90s pop songs all night was watching it when you were sober.

I looked at myself in the mirror, pulling the waist up on my boot-cut jeans and smoothing a short-sleeved cream-coloured sweater over my hips. My jeans had gotten a bit tighter over the past year, but, surprisingly, I didn't care anymore. Having an excuse to buy new clothes certainly wasn't a bad thing, especially now that I was making a steady income.

I smiled at my reflection, and enlightened eyes stared back at me. A year ago, if my jeans were getting too tight, I would have starved myself, never eating, getting all my calories from wine. But now? Now it didn't bother me. If someone didn't like me because I'd gained a bit of weight or cut my hair that was their loss. The people I surrounded myself with provided me with all the unconditional love and support I would ever need. That was what was important to me now.

The karaoke extravaganza was in full swing at Sparky's when I got there; the lights were low and everyone was shouting out the words to "Paradise by the Dashboard Light," much to the displeasure of the two singers who had clearly wanted to put on their Meatloaf show without the assistance of the audience. Thank God I'd come in close to the end of the song. Every time I'd been forced to go to karaoke, there was always someone who wanted to sing the longest song in all of human history, and every time it was my least favourite part of the night.

I looked around the room—the lights from the neon "Molson Canadian Rocks" signs reflected off golden banisters and illuminated Saskatchewan Roughrider and Pilsner Beer pennants adorning the wood paneling. I quickly spotted our table as it was the biggest and rowdiest in the pub. The only one full of middle-aged men and women away from their kids and out past bedtime. Ben waved me over, a huge grin lighting up his face. The mere fact that he looked like he was having a blast made me smile. This was why I had come. Despite being one of the shyest people I knew, Ben killed at his newfound karaoke passion. It had only taken him forty-seven years to find his jam.

"You made it!" he said and gave me a sweaty hug. "You just missed my excellent rendition of 'Funky Cold Medina.'"

"Aw, that's unfortunate," I said in a way that made it clear that I didn't think it was unfortunate at all.

"Come sit." He pulled out an empty chair beside someone in a familiar plaid shirt.

Luke was deep in conversation with a petite woman who was leaning so far forward I could only see her cleavage. Had Luke brought a date?

"Kate's in the washroom." Ben pointed as he sat down.

I had just turned in the direction he had pointed to see if Kate was on her way back when I heard a familiar voice squeal my name. Or, at least, the version of my name I disliked the most.

"Julsie! Is that you? Holy shit, what did you do to your hair?"

Ugh. Now I knew who Luke was talking to.

I turned around, trying unsuccessfully to hide an already formed scowl. "Hi Marnie."

She stared at me, stunned. So stunned, in fact, that she had stopped scrolling through her phone and was giving me her full attention. "Seriously, what happened to your hair? Like, did you lose a bet or something?"

"No, Marnie, I cut it on purpose." I tucked a short piece behind my ears, trying not to look at Luke's expression, trying to pretend this experience wasn't completely horrifying.

"I like it," Luke finally said, nudging her arm, probably trying to get her to close her mouth, which had dropped and stayed open.

"Oh, sorry," she said, misinterpreting the nudge. "Have you met Luke?" She placed her hand on his knee.

"No, I haven't had the pleasure. Luke, is it?" I joked, holding out my hand, ignoring where Marnie's hand was placed, ignoring the fact that she looked young and fresh and comfortably perfect sitting next to Luke.

He smiled and stood. "Hi Julie."

"Oh my God, *duh*." Marnie crossed her slim legs and her tight dress slid up her thighs. "I totally forgot about Christmas Eve. And aren't you guys planning the wedding together or something? How is that going anyways?"

"It's going well, thanks," I said as she stood up and walked away, my voice trailing after her. "How are you?" I said to Luke. "I haven't seen you in a while."

Luke tugged on his left ear, something I'd learned he did when he was nervous. I was glad I wasn't the only one. "I'm good." He turned his head, looking for Marnie, and then turned back to me. "And you?" he said as if it was an afterthought.

Cool. I'm *so* glad this wasn't awkward.

"I'm good. Staying out of trouble." I smiled. "I see you're hanging out with my best friend, Marnie." I pointed towards one of the large speakers, upon which Marnie was now dancing to Katy Perry's "I Kissed a Girl" while the karaoke host gestured wildly for her to descend.

"She's actually not that bad," he said. "We've been having a great conversation."

"You've been having a great conversation with Marnie?"

Luke turned at the sound of his name. "Come help me down!" Marnie shouted.

"Please tell me you're not going to help her," I said. "There are three men right there who seem to be willing to help her with anything she needs." It wasn't lost on me that my sour attitude might have been coming from just a *wee* bit of resentment. It wasn't that long ago that it would have been me up there, youthful and vibrant, eating up all the attention. Had I been that annoying though? It suddenly hit me that I probably had been.

"Of course I'm going to help her," Luke said. "I'm not going to leave her in the company of strange men after she's had too much to drink."

I watched him as he strode over purposefully, wrapped his strong hands around her waist, and gently lifted her down. I couldn't help but wonder where I would be now if I'd had someone like that to take care of me when I was her age.

I sighed, trying to ignore the envy that had settled in my stomach. As I glanced around, silently begging someone to come save me from standing there like a jilted lover, I spied Kate walking back to the table out of the corner of my eye.

"Julie! I'm so glad you're here." She pulled me in for a hug. "I've signed us both up to do Shania. 'Any Man of Mine.' And you have to do it. Because it's my party."

Perfect.

The rest of the night wasn't terrible. But I wouldn't go as far as to say it was fun. Our table dominated the karaoke floor, with Ben and Kate singing two songs each and a combo. Luke did a couple of songs, including a not bad version of "Sweet Caroline." Marnie, while not a bad singer, failed miserably while trying to make Kesha's "C'mon" into a sultry rap, which she directed at Luke.

The whole Marnie and Luke thing wouldn't have bothered me so much if Luke and I were still as close as we used to be. I mean, to each their own, right? If Luke liked Marnie, so be it. She was pretty and bubbly. And probably fun to hang out with, who knows? She wasn't the smartest person in the world, but being able to carry on a conversation about anything other than celebrities wasn't everything. It wasn't like I had any girlfriend-type claim on him. What I really missed was selfishly having Luke to myself.

"Are you okay with this?" Kate asked as the night started winding down. She gestured in the direction of Luke and Marnie, whose heads were almost touching in conversation.

"Why wouldn't I be?" I tried to arrange my face into a convincing look of apathy.

"I don't know." Kate shrugged. "I kind of thought you and Luke might have had something going on. You seemed to have a great connection, but you barely even talked tonight."

"Nope." I shoved my hands in my back pockets. "It probably seemed that way because we were thrown together to plan your wedding and we had that in common. Now that it's almost here, we don't really have anything to talk about."

"You just seemed so good together." Kate's eyes were searching mine.

I shrugged. "Luke and I are friends. And even if I did have feelings for Luke, which I don't"—I raised my eyebrow as Kate looked at me sceptically—"he has a daughter. Whoever he ends up with has to be someone who would be a good mother to her."

"Someone like Marnie?" Kate laughed.

"Hopefully not," I smiled. "But if that's what Luke wants…."

"I'm pretty sure that's not what Luke wants." Kate zipped up her coat. "He was looking at you all night. If you had been paying more attention to him instead of trying to kill Marnie with your facial expression, you might have noticed."

"I'm sure you're mistaken," I said as I shrugged my denim jacket on. "They looked pretty inseparable to me." I walked towards the door. "And that's totally fine."

"Julie." Kate pulled on my arm and I turned around.

"What?"

"Why are you fighting this so hard?" she asked.

"Fighting what?" I tried to look innocent but immediately gave up, knowing Kate could read me like a book. "I'm not fighting. I'm just accepting. It's too late for anything else."

As we'd been talking, the lights had flickered on in the pub and people had started leaving. Our table was the only one left and the karaoke host was looking at us like we could go any time now, please.

Kate looped her arm through mine as she pushed open the door and we walked outside. "I don't think it's too late," she said. "I think you should talk to him."

She gestured towards the door as it opened one last time and Marnie bounced out, followed by Luke carrying her purse.

"Luke, can I talk to you for a second?" I blurted without thinking.

He opened his mouth to speak and was interrupted by

Marnie yelling from her car, wondering where her keys were.

"She's not driving, is she?" I asked. "She's probably over the limit."

"No." Luke pulled her keys out of her purse and pushed the button on the key fob so she could get inside. "Can we talk another time? Marnie's waiting for me."

"Oh. Okay, sure." I stepped back out of his way. "Are you…are you guys…?"

"See you Saturday," he said over his shoulder as he quickly walked towards Marnie's car.

Kate waved at Luke and turned back to me. "His loss," she said as I tried to arrange the hurt on my face back to what I hoped was something more neutral.

"Exactly." I slipped my hands into my jacket pockets, the cool of the spring evening biting at my fingertips. "Like I said, it's too late."

My shoulders slumped slightly as what I had just said started to resonate. If this was the case, and especially if he was with someone else, maybe I should just cut the cord. Sure, I would miss Luke's friendship, but I had other friends. I had Quinn. I had Ben and Kate. I had Group. If I really wanted to prove I had my life together, maybe choosing my own well-being over something that was never meant to be was the healthiest path to take.

"See you on Saturday?" Kate called as I made my way to my car.

I stopped and turned back, forcing a smile, willing my voice to produce even a modicum of joy. "Of course. My two favourite people in the world are getting married. I can't wait."

Kate bounced on her toes and then turned to join Ben who was waiting in the car.

I unlocked my car door and slid in, throat tight with the unshed tears of a difficult decision made. All I needed to do was get through Saturday I told myself as I pulled out of the parking lot.

And then I could start the process of removing Luke from my life for good.

Chapter Thirty-One

I was awake early the morning of the wedding. The sun had barely peeked above the horizon and Marty was still snoring, curled up at my feet, when I determined I would no longer be able to fall back asleep. The day was finally here. The day Luke and I had worked so hard to make perfect. The work was almost over and now the fun could begin.

I should have been excited. I should have been relieved. Not only were my brother and best friend getting married, but today I would finally prove I could not only take care of myself but show up successfully for the ones I loved. So, why couldn't I get out of bed?

I lay perfectly still, eyes barely open; the nagging voice inside my head telling me I needed to jump right up and start the day. As maid of honour, and, more importantly, co-wedding planner, I still had a lot to do. I knew that if I checked my phone there would be at least one text from Kate waiting, asking me to pick something up on my way to her place. But still, I lay on my back, watching the sun hit the tree outside my window and flicker across the ceiling. I couldn't even be bothered to pick up my phone.

I knew that part of being a recovering alcoholic was learning to roll with the low days. Days where I felt so shitty that all I wanted to do was stay in bed. Days where my body was so heavy I could barely move. I hadn't had one in so long I'd almost forgotten they existed. Why did my brain have to choose this day to remind me?

Normally when this happened, I would just stay away from people. I'd snuggle up with a good book or TV show, maybe call in sick to work. I knew when I had down days I needed to focus on self-care.

But I couldn't do that today. Today, I couldn't think about myself. I needed to be there for Kate and Ben. It was their wedding day, the happiest day of their lives. I needed to get my shit together so I could give them the wedding they both deserved.

I groaned and rolled onto my side, hiding my face under my comforter. I'd called Luke after the Stag and Doe to see if he'd wanted to run over the plan once more, destructively wanting to savour our time together before I would sever our ties for good.

Of course, I hadn't said that I'd also called to see if I could hear Marnie in the background. And he didn't offer any insights into what had happened with them after karaoke. Was that why I felt so bummed?

After dragging myself out of bed and showering off the self-pity I'd been feeling since Thursday night, I pulled on a pair of faded leggings and one of Ben's old, discarded University of Toronto sweatshirts. I then sat down at my kitchen table with my laptop and a cup of strong coffee, ready to go over my list one final time.

Kate and Ben had decided to do a short late-afternoon ceremony in the room at the Hotel Saskatchewan where they were having the dinner and dance. Neither of them was religious and neither wanted a church wedding. Ben was going to ask one of his buddies to get his certification online and officiate, but then Kate reminded him that his buddy had never been on time for anything in his life, so they decided to go with a justice of the peace.

The plan was for the bridesmaids to meet at their new house, which Kate had claimed as her home base, and the groomsmen were to meet at our parents' house so our dad could take part. Hannah had, unfortunately, come down with a cold and was staying with Janet so, after dropping Marty off in an effort to lift her spirits, I called Ben from my car on my way to meet up with the rest of the lady crew.

"Hey." He picked up on the first ring.

"How're you doing?"

"Good. Fine. Good." He sounded manic.

"You sound manic."

He took a deep breath. "I'm good. Seriously. I'm just nervous."

"And happy?" I knew he was.

"So happy." I could hear him smile over the phone.

"You took your meds this morning?"

"Yes, Mom, I took my meds this morning." He chuckled.

"How's Dad?" I asked, knowing he was very likely nervous as well. Despite our parents' limited involvement in our lives, they were far and away the superior pair if you were to compare them to Kate's. Kate hadn't seen her absent dad in years and her mom had selfishly declined the wedding invitation due to a river cruise she "just couldn't get out of." Kate was initially upset, but she knew it was for the best. She had cried tears of joy when our dad had offered to walk her down the aisle.

"He's not bad actually," Ben said. "He walked me down the hallway five times to practise, so I think he's feeling pretty good about it."

I laughed. "Aw, that's so cute."

"Are you on your way to our place?"

"I'm sitting in the car outside."

"Why aren't you—" he started.

"Marnie's already here."

"Right. Well, you'll have to get it over with at some point."

I sighed. "Yes, I will," I said. Then, so his wedding day wasn't all about me, I added, "Everything is going to be great. You and Kate are so perfect for each other it honestly almost makes me puke."

He laughed. "Thanks?"

"And that's all that matters," I continued. "No one else matters today. Just the two of you. Just the two of you together."

"Love you, Jules."

"Love you too."

Fifteen minutes later, I walked in the door of Ben and Kate's and was met by absolute chaos. And by chaos, I mean Marnie.

"Julie!" she squealed as she grabbed my hands and

squeezed. "Isn't it so exciting?" She held her phone up to my face. "I'm documenting the whole day on my Insta stories. Smile!"

At the sound of Marnie's screech, an older lady with platinum blonde hair and Marnie's startling blue eyes spun into the room, a wave of flowery-smelling perfume following in an oppressive cloud behind her. "You must be Julie!" she shouted like I was ten feet away and then aggressively pulled me in for a hug. "Isn't this exciting?"

Good Lord, there are two of them, I thought, my eyes watering from the sting of whatever sweet hell this woman had sprayed all over herself.

"This is Lydia, my mom." Marnie strutted towards the kitchen like she owned the place, stepping over boxes that, after four months, were still waiting to be unpacked. "Coffee and Baileys?" She held up the bottle, took a picture of it, and then shook it side to side with her eyebrows raised.

"I don't drink, Marnie."

She rolled her eyes. "It's only Baileys."

"Just coffee, please."

"You're no fun." She pouted.

I was just about to show her how much fun I wasn't when Kate quietly floated into the room. My mom walked behind, holding Kate's bouquet, face flushed, eyes glistening. I gave Mom a hug and then stood in front of Kate, taking everything in. She looked absolutely stunning.

The jewelled bodice of the ivory dress hugged her figure perfectly, pouring out into thick waves of rippling silk that lightly brushed her rose-gold sparkling heels. Her hair was pulled away from her face in a sweeping French twist, loose chestnut curls framing her face.

"You look beautiful," I breathed.

She turned towards the oval mirror hanging in the hall and then back to me. "Do you think Ben will like it?"

"Ben will love it." I smiled and squeezed her hand.

"He'll love ripping it off tonight!" Marnie yelled and then mimed a mic drop. "Boom!"

And the spell was broken.

Kate stepped forward and gave me a hug, whispering in my ear, "She's driving me bananas."

"Come on," I said, smothering a laugh, "let's go see if my dress still fits."

The parking lot at the hall was almost empty as our ridiculous party bus limo (Marnie and her mom's gift to the bride) pulled in and parked at the front. The door slid open and we all piled out—me, Kate, Marnie and the moms—in a flurry of sparkles and satin. Marnie and her mom had managed to polish off an entire bottle of champagne on the twenty-minute drive over and they were a bit unsteady on their feet, giggling into their hands on their way to the door, trying to follow Kate, who jogged in so Ben wouldn't see her.

Kate had held firm on giving me a plus one, just in case I "met someone," so Quinn, thankfully, had agreed to be my last-minute date. She'd planned to meet me at the venue early to help out if needed, but we were almost a half an hour late due to Kate's cat Mittens not wanting to enter his cat carrier and, unsurprisingly, even more not wanting to wear a tiny top hat Kate had been trying to gently fasten onto his head.

"Why are you doing this to your poor cat again?" I'd asked.

"He's the ring bearer, Julie," she'd said, as if the answer was obvious.

"Well, couldn't he be the ring bearer without a hat? Why don't you just weave the ribbon around his collar?"

She stared at me with barely contained exasperation.

"I'll take care of it." I gently took the hat and ribbon from her clenched fingers. "Don't worry; everything will be perfect."

By the time I'd gotten Mittens into his carrier, I realized I hadn't had a chance to text Quinn to tell her we'd be late.

You here? I texted her from the parking lot, picking up one of the many feathers that had moulted off the boa Marnie had insisted on wearing.

I'm inside, I read as I walked through the door of the hotel, holding the cat carrier like a purse.

And there she was, quietly shimmering in her own unique brand of colourful radiance. She looked amazing in a gorgeous chocolate-brown retro smock dress, sprinkled with bright teal and yellow polka dots, flared at the arms and hanging just below her knees. Her hair was pulled back in a purple scarf she had fashioned into a headband, and a perfectly curled, perfectly teal ringlet brushed her cheek.

"You look amazing," I exclaimed. "Your sense of fashion just blows me away."

"So do you." She stepped back. "Your dress fits perfectly."

We walked up the stairs and were met by an anxious Luke, his wide-eyed expression indicating that he wasn't super pleased with my tardiness.

"You're late." I could tell he was making an effort to keep his voice calm.

"Sorry, didn't Marnie text you we were running behind?" I said as I put the cat carrier down. I knew I was being childish, but I didn't care.

"No, why would….Never mind, we need to do a walk-through to make sure everything is ready to go."

"Really?" My eyebrows rose. "Shouldn't the hotel staff be doing that? Also, this is Quinn." I gestured to Quinn and she waved.

"Nice to meet you, Quinn." He smiled, but I could tell he was flustered. He turned back to me. "I'd still really like to do one final check. Just so we can make sure for ourselves."

"Of course." I nodded and then turned to Quinn. "Would you mind taking Mittens to Kate's room? I'll meet you there in a bit."

I turned back to Luke and placed my hand on his shoulder. "Everything is going to be fi—"

"Um, Julie?" Quinn's normally confident voice was unusually hesitant.

I glanced back and followed her gaze.

To the wide-open door of the cat carrier.

Chapter Thirty-Two

"*No!*" I whisper-shouted and fell to my knees, poking my arm into the cat carrier just in case Mittens was somehow hidden in the back. "Where is he?" I asked no one.

"Oh God, oh God, oh God," I rambled, crawling on the floor in my dress, head snapping back and forth, trying to view every corner of the lobby at once. "If Kate finds out I lost Mittens, she'll never forgive me."

Luke kneeled down and gently placed his hands on my shoulders, which were now rising and falling in rapid succession as I tried to catch my breath. My heart was racing and my mouth was dry. Was this what a panic attack felt like? Was I going to die? I almost hoped that was the case.

"Julie." Luke's voice floated into my consciousness. "Look at me."

I did.

"It's going to be okay, we'll find Mittens. He couldn't have gone too far. He probably just wanted to get out of the carrier and find Kate; you know how he hates that thing." He pulled me back to standing and guided me into the coatroom, peeking into a cardboard box that was sitting in the corner.

"But what if we don't?" I said as I looked behind a coatrack, trying not to cry. "What if the wedding is ruined? This was my last chance." I knew I sounded hysterical.

"Last chance to what?" He stopped searching and faced me, tipping up my chin when I lowered my head. "Last chance to what, Julie?" he asked again.

"Last chance to prove that I have my life together," I said as a rogue tear slid down my cheek. "To prove that I'm not a mess anymore."

"Julie," he said, his eyes flashing with emotion, "no one thinks that about you. No one thinks you're a mess. Where is this coming from?"

I looked into his eyes and melted into their warmth. His hands on my arms, soft yet firm, held me up like a life raft. It was then that I knew. I couldn't remove him from my life. Not when he was the best part of it. I opened my mouth to speak. Ready to tell him everything.

"Found him!" Quinn burst through the door, holding a squirmy Mittens in her arms. "He was snooping around in the kitchen. Much to the displeasure of the staff, I might add." She stopped, eyes moving back and forth between us. "Should I…? Did I interrupt something?" She shot me an apologetic look.

"No, this is great!" I stepped forward, taking Mittens from her and burrowing my face into his fur, pretending nothing more had been happening than a furtive search. "I am so happy to see you," I murmured into his neck, tears of relief now forming in my eyes. "You scared me, you silly cat." I walked back into the lobby and put Mittens into his cat carrier, wiggling the door to make sure it was closed.

"Thank you so much," I said as I gave Quinn a frantic hug. "You saved the wedding. You saved me. I don't know what we would have done if we had lost him."

"Happy to help." She gently pulled away from my tight embrace and picked up the cat carrier. "I'll take him to Kate's room and see you later, okay?"

I watched her leave and my breath came out in a whoosh of relief. "That was close," I said to Luke. "Thanks for calming me down."

He nodded. "I'm glad Quinn found him."

"You look nice," I said, just now noticing what he was wearing. He cleaned up well in his dark grey suit, complete with a rose-coloured tie and pocket square. He looked handsome. His red hair was a bit longer now than when we'd first met, and wisps of it curled below his ears. His beard was neatly trimmed. I almost reached up to touch it.

Instead, I tugged playfully on his tie. "You remembered."

He brushed my hand away and smoothed it out. "Of course I did. When the bride asks you to match her bridesmaids, you match her bridesmaids."

We walked to the kitchen and checked on the hors d'oeuvres, some of which were laid across the counter on silver trays, some ready to be put in the oven. I could smell the coffee brewing and spied two large urns waiting to hold it and keep it warm. The wedding cake stood tall and proud in the corner, red velvet covered in smooth pink icing with a little plastic bride and groom on top, holding hands and looking lovingly into each other's eyes.

"This turned out well." I walked over to admire it. I

hadn't noticed from far away, but tiny candy beads dotted the top of the second layer.

Luke nodded his approval and made a checkmark on his clipboard.

"It looks like snow," I whispered, remembering the night Luke and I had stood by the snow-covered field. The night we had almost kissed. I looked up and was startled to see him staring, the look on his face telling me he was thinking the same thing.

"You look amazing," he said quietly.

"Oh. Thanks." I smiled, trying to will the blush from my face. "The seamstress did a great job. I think it fits pretty good." I smoothed my hands over my hips.

"It does," he said. "Fit. Pretty good." He shook his head as if trying to clear it. "Okay, let's go check the tables."

I turned again to leave and then turned back. "Luke?"
"Yeah?"

"We did good, you and me."

He nodded. "We did."

"We make a good team."

Another nod was his only response as we silently left the kitchen.

The ceremony, of course, went flawlessly. Even Mittens cooperated, silently following Kate's friend's daughter Abigail with only a couple of encouraging tugs on his leash, rings hanging from a satin ribbon tied around his tiny collar.

Kate was radiating happiness and Ben only had eyes for her. The room could have fallen down around them and they wouldn't have cared. They were so in love; the vibration from their beating hearts was palpable.

After their vows and the "You may kiss the bride," they both turned in unison and walked back down the aisle hand in hand to cheers and confetti and Taylor Swift's "Love Story" because Kate, in no uncertain terms, had vetoed Ben's selection of any song by Bryan Adams.

I watched it all with misty eyes, my hatred of all things wedding-related replaced by a mushy faith in love. I knew I had Luke to thank for that.

I finally made it to the table where Quinn was sitting, sneaking away after most of the guests had made it through the receiving line. "I'm so sorry," I said. "I hadn't realized it would take this long. Honestly, I used to be so drunk at weddings by this point that I never considered there were other things going on."

Quinn laughed, cheerful and understanding as always. "Totally fine, I expected it. I've been having a great time here at the cousin table." She gestured around to all the cousins, who waved politely.

"Of course you have." I smiled. "But I'm going to have to steal you away. Kate made room for you at the main table so you wouldn't have to sit by yourself, although I should have expected you would immediately make friends."

She stood up and leaned in to whisper in my ear, "I scouted out the table for potential dating options if you're interested."

"Oh, I'm so sorry," I said, feigning sincerity. "I should have mentioned at the outset that I don't want to date anyone who is related to me. I'm pretty sure that's illegal."

She laughed. "They're not *all* related to you. Some of them are Kate's cousins."

I rolled my eyes. "Thank you for thinking of me, but I think I'll pass on the cousin hook-ups tonight. I've got too much going on."

"Do you?" She winked. "Or do you have someone else in mind?" She shook her head at my confused expression. "Don't play dumb. I've seen the way you look at Luke."

"I'm pretty sure he's taken." I gestured with my chin to Luke and Marnie sitting beside each other at the head table, heads close in what looked to be an intimate conversation.

"Oh, I don't know." She looked at them suspiciously. "Something tells me, no matter how much she wants that to be true, his desires lie elsewhere."

I opened my mouth to give a smart retort and then realized I didn't have one handy. Luckily, I didn't have to follow through as we'd reached our destination. We walked up to the main table just as Ben and Kate were sitting down, their names clearly labeled on the adorable place cards that Hannah had made. I reached for my phone to take a picture so I could show her and then realized I didn't know when I would see her again. A wave of grief swelled through my chest and I pushed it back down before it could reach my face.

"Finally!" Kate was halfway seated but bolted up when she saw us. "We finally get to meet the famous Quinn!"

Quinn blushed, uncharacteristically shy, and stuck out her hand, which Kate ignored as she pulled her in for a hug. "I'm so glad to officially meet you. I thought it was you when you dropped off Mittens, but Marnie had just jabbed me in the head with a bobby pin so I was a bit otherwise engaged."

I glanced at Luke to see if he was still talking to Marnie and he met my eyes and smiled.

"Isn't Quinn a man's name?" I heard Marnie loudly whisper. "I thought Julie had finally found herself a man. Guess not." She giggled.

I pulled Kate's arms loose from Quinn, ignoring Marnie. "Jesus, Kate, you're like a boa constrictor."

Kate reluctantly pulled away and Ben stuck out his hand. "I'm not really a hugger, no offence."

"None taken." Quinn laughed and shook his hand. "And congratulations, the ceremony was beautiful."

"Thanks," Kate and Ben said at the same time and then laughed, staring at each other like there was no one else around.

"Ugh, get a room," I said through a smile. "Let's go sit down." I pulled Quinn towards the end of the table, the opposite end to where Marnie and Luke were sitting. I didn't want any part of what was going on over there.

"Julie, wait." I turned to find Kate and Ben still standing, both of them moving closer as Quinn went and sat down.

"We just want to say thank you," Ben said as Kate grabbed my hand and squeezed. "Now, I admit," he continued, "I had my doubts when you first brought up the idea of planning our wedding, but you proved me wrong, and not only that, you blew all of my expectations out of the water."

Kate nodded as my eyes filled with tears. "It was mostly Luke," I said, once again glancing his way.

"No," Kate said firmly. "I know you think that Luke carried the bulk of the work, and maybe he did do a lot of the organizing, but this"—she swept her arm around the room—"the thought and care you put into the decorations, and the guest gifts, and the seating plan, and the entire day itself; the way you knew exactly what we wanted; the way you knew exactly how we wanted to feel when we walked into this room—that was all you. And I can't even begin to thank you enough."

"Julie," Ben said when I was clearly too speechless to respond, "I know you sometimes think you're a disappointment. I know you think that you need to prove you have your life together. But you don't. You proved yourself to us the second you walked into that meeting a year ago. And you've continued to prove it to us ever since."

"Not that you need to," Kate said. "Prove yourself to us."

"Exactly," Ben said. "We've loved you, and we will continue to love you, exactly as you are."

"Well…." I started, but didn't know what else to say. I'd had no idea they felt that way. I had been proud of what Luke and I had done, and I'd worked hard to make their day special, but I hadn't realized they'd seen it too. "Thank you for saying that," I finally said. "I just really wanted to make up for all I did in the past."

Ben shook his head. "Your perception of yourself is so different to the way others see you. Do you realize that you basically saved my life when we were kids? You cared for me and stuck up for me and made me feel loved and accepted when no one else did. You helped me see that I wasn't my anxiety. You helped me get through the worst parts of my life. That's what families do." He grinned his shy half grin. "I was merely returning the favour."

"I love you both so much," I said, my voice cracking, as I leaned forward to give them each a hug. "I'm so happy for you."

It was funny, I thought as I made my way to the end of the table to join Quinn, dabbing at my eyes with a tissue, all this time I'd thought I was staying sober and planning the wedding to prove I was worthy to the two people who had already believed it, when really I'd needed to prove it to the person who hadn't.

Me. I had needed to prove it to me. And I'd finally done it.

After the main course was served, Quinn nudged my arm. "You're not being that great of a date."

"What do you mean?" I asked as I speared a cabbage roll with my fork.

"I mean you haven't said one word since you sat down. All you've been doing is giving the stink eye to poor Marnie over there."

"Sorry, was I that obvious?"

"Yes, you were that obvious. Why don't you go talk to him?"

I sighed. "I don't know. No, that's a lie. I do know. I don't want to talk to him because I don't know what to do. Do I think he's a great guy? Yes. I am attracted to him? Yes. Do I think about him all the time?"

"Yes!" Quinn cheered.

"Yes. But…."

"But?"

"But I think I might have missed my chance. It looks like he's with Marnie now."

Quinn glanced in the direction I was gazing. "Are you sure about that?"

I picked up my champagne flute of sparkling water and took a sip. "Okay. So, let's suppose he's not with Marnie; the question I keep asking myself is: Am I ready for a relationship? And the answer is: I don't know. And I think Luke's a relationship guy. I don't think Luke's a 'Let's sleep together and see what happens' guy."

"I don't think he's that kind of guy either," Quinn agreed.

"But what if that's the only thing I can do? What if I hurt him? If I did, I could never forgive myself." My eyes filled with tears and I angrily poked at them.

"And what if you don't?" Quinn asked, logical as usual. "What if you give yourself permission to fall in love? What if neither of you get hurt?"

"Excellent questions." I sat back in my chair as if to end the conversation. "I'll think on them and get back to you."

"Julie." She gave me a look that said she wasn't going to put up with my bullshit.

"What?"

"We both know you deserve something great. I think it's time you did something about it."

Chapter Thirty-Three

The clock struck midnight.

It was June 4th.

I had officially been sober for one year.

But the only person I wanted to celebrate with had left the wedding an hour ago with Marnie.

"They're not together," Ben had said, his arm around me for brotherly support after he and Kate had given me congratulatory hugs.

"They sure look like they are."

"They're not," he reaffirmed. "Trust me."

And so here I was. Trusting Ben. Standing on Luke's doorstep at 12:30 a.m. Hoping the door wasn't answered by Marnie in her underwear and one of Luke's plaid shirts.

The door opened and there stood Luke, still dressed in his suit pants, tie loose around his neck. Still looking handsome. Still one of my best friends.

"Hey," he said, face questioning.

"Hi. Sorry, I know it's late. I hope I didn't wake Hannah."

"She's at her grandma's. With your dog, remember?" Luke looked behind him and then back at me. "Are you okay?"

I looked over his shoulder. "Do you have company? Is Marnie…?"

"No. Marnie is not here. Why would you think that?" He sounded irritated. Maybe this had been a mistake.

"You just…you left with her so I was…I thought…."

"Well, you thought wrong." He ran a hand through his hair. "I drove her home. She wanted to call an Uber, but I didn't trust one to get her there. She'd had a lot of champagne."

"Oh." I looked down at my shoes. "That was kind of you."

"Did you want to come in? It's a bit chilly out." He stepped back and I walked through the door. I breathed in the familiar comforting smell of his home—coffee and cinnamon with a touch of lavender air freshener—and a lump formed in my throat. I hadn't realized how much I'd missed it.

"Is that why you drove her home from the Stag and Doe?" I asked as I slipped off my heels.

"Yeah. Same thing." He sat on the couch and gestured for me to do the same. "It's not safe for women who have drunk a lot to be out on their own." He looked at me knowingly, which, to be honest, stung just a bit.

But it was true. I, more than anyone, should have known that. My throat tightened with shame as I realized how judgmental I'd been towards Marnie. Thinking the same things about her that other people used to think about me. All of a sudden, I knew why I didn't like her. It was because she reminded me so much of how I used to be. All the parts I hadn't liked about myself. All of the parts that were once so broken. *That poor girl,* I thought. *I wonder what kinds of things she's been hiding.*

"So, is that why you're here?" He propped his elbow up on the back of the couch and rested his head in his hand. "To talk about why I've been driving Marnie home?"

"No." I smiled. "I just wanted to tell you what a great job you did as co-planner. The wedding was perfect. Kate and Ben are very happy." I nodded and stood up like I'd completed my mission as planned. Now he knew. Now I could go.

He didn't move. "You came all the way over here, at 12:30 in the morning, in your bridesmaid's dress, to tell me that I did a great job of co-planning." It was more of a statement than a question.

I shrugged. "Yeah. I wanted to let you know right away. I thought it was important."

"Okay then." He sat back on the couch, eyes twinkling. "Nice of you to stop by."

I padded over to the door in my bare feet and reached down for one of my impossibly high heels. "Also," I added, "it's my anniversary. I've been sober for one year. I thought you'd like to know."

He jumped up and gave me a hug. "That's so great, Julie. Congratulations. I knew you could do it."

"Thanks." I pulled away and looked down. "I couldn't have done it without your support."

He nodded. I nodded. He nodded again. This was so awkward.

"Fine," I sighed out in a puff of exasperation. "You win. I didn't come over just to tell you that you did a good job and about my sobriety anniversary." This was infinitely harder than I had thought it would be.

"Why did you come then?" he asked softly.

I struggled to raise my eyes to meet his, holding my hands against my thighs so he wouldn't see them shaking. I cleared my throat. "I missed you." I pushed the statement out with the force of a cough. "I missed you," I said again, this time softer.

His eyes softened into a deep emerald. "I missed you too." His voice was like sandpaper, his words catching on the rough edges.

"Now what?" I said after a stretch of silence. "I don't know how to do this."

He stepped towards me and my stomach fluttered. "What do you want, Julie?"

"I don't know." I shook my head. But I did know.

"Well, I know what I want." The way he looked at me. The hope, the longing, it made my legs weak.

"Tell me," I whispered.

He moved in closer and grabbed my hand, swallowing it up like a protective shell. "I think you know."

"Tell me anyways."

He chuckled and shook his head, used to giving in to my indulgences. He stepped forward one more time, closing the gap between us. Our thighs touched and a jolt of electricity shot through my body.

Run. I thought immediately. *Run before you get in too deep.*

But I didn't run. I followed as he pulled me over to the couch to sit down.

"Do you know why I've been keeping my distance for the past few months?" he asked.

"Well, I thought it was because you were with Marnie."

"I'm not with Marnie." He held up his hands in protest.

"I know," I said. "I thought that's what it was. But now I don't know. I guess maybe you were mad because I pulled away a bit after the night we kissed?"

"Jesus, Julie, no," he exclaimed, his expression a mixture of alarm and outrage. "Of course I wasn't mad. I would never expect you to do something you weren't comfortable with. I'm honestly a bit offended that you would think that." He shook his head.

"Sorry. Habit, I guess. What was it then?" I asked. "Is it that you don't want to be with me?"

He leaned in and grabbed my other hand. "Julie, I respected your decision that night. If you didn't want to take our relationship any further, I wasn't going to pressure you. But that didn't mean I didn't want to. So, keeping my distance was more for self-preservation than anything else. I do want to be with you. I can't stop thinking about you. No matter how hard I've tried. You are the first thing I think about when I wake up and the last thing I think about when I go to bed. You dominate my thoughts; you dominate my life, Julie, even when you're not around…especially when you're not around."

As he spoke and his hands held mine, my body relaxed for the first time in what felt like forever, his words wrapping around me like a hug.

But I also felt something else. His words filled my heart, but our proximity—our thighs together and his hands squeezing mine—caused my whole body to hum. I was almost shaking with how much I wanted him. And that scared the crap out of me.

"Why didn't you tell me this before?" I asked, trying to keep my voice steady.

He laughed softly. "You're not the easiest person to read, Julie. At the beginning, I didn't know if you felt the same way. In fact, at the beginning, it was pretty clear that you hated me."

"I didn't hate you." I smiled. "I just thought you were annoying."

"Thanks for clarifying." The corner of his mouth pulled into a wry grin. "But," he continued, his face suddenly serious, "after the night at the field, when I thought you might feel something other than annoyance, I didn't want to push anything because of your past. I didn't want to come on too strong and scare you away. And, if I'm being honest, I didn't know what I wanted to do either. I had to be logical. I had to think of Hannah." His eyes flickered down, touching on my lips. "However, logic aside, you have no idea how much I wanted to kiss you that night."

Heat flushed my cheeks. Could he tell that I couldn't breathe? "I think I do know."

He reached up and cupped my face, the tips of his fingers brushing my hair. I leaned against its warmth and closed my eyes. Feeling safe. Feeling like I could finally let go.

"I thought you might." He smiled. "But when I finally realized I couldn't get you out of my head, I didn't want to pressure you. I wanted to wait until you were ready."

I opened my eyes and met his. "And then when you thought I was ready, when we kissed in your kitchen…."

He nodded, bringing his hand down to his lap. "You ran away. Which is fine, like I said, I didn't want to pressure you. But, after that, I was…."

"Confused," I finished.

He nodded. "Yes. I had thought we had something, a strong connection. But then I thought maybe I'd been wrong."

"You weren't wrong." I leaned forward and our foreheads touched, our lips so close we were breathing as one.

"You are an amazing woman, Julie," he said. "So smart and so strong."

I laughed softly. "I guess now that I cut my hair, I need to get used to no longer being described by how I look. I can live with that."

"Well, that's where you're wrong," he said, his thumb brushing my lower lip, sending shivers down my spine. "To me you've never been more beautiful." His hand slid around to the back of my neck, his fingers sliding across the wisps of hair.

And that was it. I made my decision. I closed my eyes as he tipped up my chin with the crook of his finger. I softened into the safety and the warmth of his touch. I completely gave in.

And then he kissed me.

I didn't know it could be like this.

I didn't know I could feel this way. Letting go so completely, connecting without words, bodies moving as one, not thinking, just doing.

I had done this so many times, slept with so many men, but it had never been like this.

With Luke, I wasn't pretending; I wasn't performing; I wasn't acting out his fantasy, moaning and writhing, playing the part.

With Luke, I was real and I was alive and I was experiencing everything with the newness of just waking up. I was only me, all of me, right at this moment, and it was the freest I'd ever felt.

When his mouth brushed my skin, my senses sizzled, the nerve endings still buzzing well after his lips had moved on. He was so confident and sure, his hands instinctively finding the spots that made me lose all sense of reality.

When he pulled off his shirt and I ran my hands down his arms, I knew that I had never wanted anyone so badly. Was it because I had never cared for anyone so much?

"God, Julie," he whispered as I unzipped my dress and let it slide from my shoulders.

He cupped my face in his hand and slid his lips across my neck, his tongue finding the spot behind my ear that instantly made me shudder. I sighed as his fingers lightly skimmed the bare skin on my thigh and then, with an urgency that matched my own, he pulled me in closer, skin against skin, the combined heat of our bodies almost too much to handle.

I lay back on the couch, quickly pulling him down, gasping for air, needing his mouth on mine so I could breathe again. The passion was intense, the yearning palpable. I thought of nothing but could feel everything.

"Is this okay?" Luke pushed himself up with his hands, his dark eyes searching mine.

I nodded, almost drunk with desire, wanting him to settle and close the gap; missing him in the space that his upper body once filled.

"Are you sure? I don't want you to feel like you have to do anything you're uncomfortable with."

"I'm sure," I whispered, sliding my hand down his chest.

A soft groan escaped his lips and he closed his eyes, pressing against me, sliding his hand down to meet mine.

And then I lost myself completely.

The soft sounds of chirping birds greeted me as I slipped back into reality. I couldn't remember the last time I'd stayed up long enough to welcome the sun. I breathed a sigh of contentment as I snuggled closer into Luke's warmth, my head resting on his chest, the coarse hair tickling my cheek.

As my head cleared and my breath steadied, a soft tinge of unease vibrated in my belly. As much as I had wanted this, as much as I had loved every second of it, had giving in to what I'd craved been the right choice? As someone who had for the better part of her life only lived for pleasure, never caring about the consequences, it was still often difficult to be confident in my own intent. Did I do this just for me? Only wanting to satisfy myself? Now that we'd slept together, what came next?

And then it happened. I got the answer I was looking for.

"I think I'm falling in love with you," Luke whispered and then gently kissed the top of my head.

I froze.

"You don't have to say anything back," he said after it

was clear I wasn't going to. "I just wanted you to know." He chuckled. "Hannah is going to be so thrilled to find you here when she gets home. She won't stop talking about you. We still have a couple of hours before she arrives though," he said as he ran his fingers down the length of my arm. "I bet we could think of something to do to fill the time."

I made a noncommittal noise, my arm now numb to his touch. There was so much going on in my head I couldn't think straight. Luke was falling in love with me. Hannah would want me to stay. This was too much to deal with, too much that I would be responsible for.

What had started as an amazing night between me and Luke, with only the unknown before us, had quickly evolved into so much more. Could I barrel into this headfirst, throw caution to the wind, baggage and all? Could I risk hurting the greatest, kindest, most amazing man I'd ever known? Could I risk hurting an innocent little girl? Just to get what I wanted?

Failing at a relationship and hurting myself was one thing, but when there were more people involved, people I truly cared about, it became much more real. Sticking around just to see what happened didn't seem fair. Old Julie would have thrown caution to the wind. She wouldn't have thought twice about taking what she wanted; she wouldn't have cared about the casualties. She would have only thought about herself.

I knew I wasn't that woman anymore, but I still had a sinking feeling that Luke deserved more than I could offer. Maybe Quinn had been right. No matter what I changed my story to, maybe I would always veer in the direction of self-sabotage.

I couldn't live with myself if Luke followed me down that path. I had to stop this. I had to save him.

"Look, Luke." I turned, forcing my face into an expression of apathy. Ready to give the talk I'd practiced on random men for so many years. "This was great, but you know me, I don't really want to be tied down."

His face fell and my heart broke.

"What…really?" he stuttered, confusion softening his features. "But I thought…."

I cleared my throat and stood up, tugging on my underwear, picking my dress up off the floor and slipping it on. "I'm sorry. I guess I thought you understood me better than this." I couldn't look at him. I couldn't bear to see how much I was hurting him.

"So, you mean…you mean…for you, last night was just…." He couldn't finish. His voice caught in his throat.

"Yes." I swallowed and forced the next words over the lump that had started to form. "It was just sex." I sat back down, wanting desperately for this to be over but unable to actually leave. "I mean, it was great sex, but I don't really think you and I would be a good match for a relationship. I would just prefer to stay friends, if that's okay." I tried to stretch my lips into a smile, but they wouldn't cooperate.

"But why?" he choked out. "Why did you do it when you knew how I felt?"

I finally looked up. Looked into eyes so full of pain that I almost doubled over. *I did this,* I thought. *I made him feel like this.* I wanted to take it all back. I wanted to tell him

I was wrong. I wanted to run into his arms and feel them wrap around me, forgiving me for doubting. I wanted to say I was sorry for hurting him and that I would never do it again. But instead I said, "I'm sorry if I misled you."

I could see the flash in his eyes the second his heart broke and I forced mine closed so he couldn't see the same thing reflected back at him. I knew this was it. I could never go back.

"I think you should leave," he whispered.

I nodded, stood up and stumbled over to the door, the sorrow so heavy in my heart it hurt to move.

I could feel him watching me while I tried to put on my shoes, gave up, and grabbed them, ready to walk to the car in my bare feet, hoping Janet would be awake so I could pick up Marty.

"Say bye to Hannah for me?" I held his eyes until he looked away, his lips pulled into a tight line. Lips that had softly touched mine a lifetime ago.

He didn't respond. He couldn't respond.

So I opened the door and headed straight to my car, wiping the tears from my face as I ran.

Chapter Thirty-Four

Present Day

It had been two months since I'd last seen Luke. Two months since he'd closed the door behind me the day after Ben and Kate's wedding. Two months of holding everything inside.

"I have to tell you something," I said to Quinn, placing my plastic container of fruit and cottage cheese on the park bench beside me, gently brushing Marty's nose away when he poked it inside. We were now eating our lunches in Victoria Park in an effort to get the most out of the warm weather. In typical Saskatchewanian fashion, we didn't want to waste any part of our short but sweet summer.

"Oh, wow, this is a food-down conversation," she said, wrapping her hot dog in a napkin and placing it deliberately on her lap. "Okay, I'm ready."

"You have to promise not to judge me." I looked down.

"Of course, I promise." She dipped her head, trying to meet my eyes.

"Because you couldn't possibly judge me more harshly than I'm judging myself."

"Julie, what's going on?" She nudged me with her elbow. "Are you finally going to tell me you slept with Luke?"

My head snapped up. I was, for once, at a loss for words.

"Of course I knew," she said. "Don't you think I know you well enough by now?"

I opened my mouth to speak but closed it again. I honestly couldn't think of what to say.

"You've been a different person these last two months. Since Luke's been gone," she said. "That's how I knew."

I nodded. I guess I hadn't been as stealthy as I'd thought.

"Do you love him?" she asked, not mincing words, as usual.

"I don't know," I barely whispered.

"What *do* you know?" she asked.

I took a deep, shaky breath, pressing my palms into the wooden bench as if to prop myself up. "I miss him. I know I miss him. Like more than I've ever missed anyone. At the time, I thought I'd messed up. I thought sleeping with him had been a mistake. When I realized he wanted more, when he said he was falling in love with me, I got scared. And I ran. And I broke his heart. I will never forgive myself for that."

I paused, trying desperately not to cry in the centre of downtown Regina. "Honestly, and I'm embarrassed to admit this, I kind of thought we'd eventually get past it, just like we did with the kiss. Sex had never been a big deal to me; it had always been more transactional than anything."

"Did you feel that way with Luke?"

"No," I said, ashamed that it had taken me this long to admit it. "It meant so much more to me. And the worst thing is I knew it meant that much to Luke all along. I knew what I was doing. I just got so scared. I thought I would eventually ruin things."

Quinn shook her head. "Oh, Julie," she said, sadness softening her words. "You are your own worst critic. Have you talked to him about it?"

"I've tried, but he won't answer my texts or my emails. I don't know what else I can say." I hung my head. It was so heavy. I was so tired.

"Julie." Quinn nudged me in the thigh with her knee.

I didn't say anything.

"Julie, look at me."

I did.

"So." Quinn ripped a piece of her hotdog bun, popped it in her mouth, chewed, swallowed and then continued. "I know you don't like feeling things."

"That's not true," I protested. She raised her eyebrow and I smiled. "Fine, it's true, I really don't. Honestly, after this past year of feeling all of my feelings, all I want to do is crawl into bed and never come out." I picked up my lunch, took a bite and fed a piece of melon to Marty.

Every day felt like I was waking up after the benders of my past, a rock of regret in my stomach, my chest tight with grief. For a brief second, I'd feel the bliss of not remembering, but as soon as I woke up fully, I tumbled down into a depression I just couldn't shake.

"If this is what being in love feels like, I don't want it."

I gasped, realizing what I had just said, and almost choked on a piece of pineapple. I looked at Quinn, who was beaming ear to ear.

"I knew it!" Her fists clenched excitedly at her sides. "I knew you loved him."

"How did you know?" I was still stunned at my own admission. "I didn't even know. I still don't know. How do I know? I don't think I've ever truly been in love before." My voice was getting more panicky as I spoke.

Quinn placed her hand on my knee in what I was sure was an effort to prevent me from losing my shit in a park full of corporate employees. "Calm down, take a breath," she soothed. "Let me tell you how I knew first, and then we can figure out you. I knew because your eyes would light up every time you talked about him, and after seeing him, you couldn't stop smiling. You planned an entire wedding with him. Willingly. What do you think that says?"

I nodded, knowing she was right.

"Remember how jealous you got when you thought he was with Marnie?"

"I wasn't jealous," I scoffed. "I just thought he deserved better."

She raised her eyebrows.

"Fine. I was jealous." I crossed my arms.

"What else?" she said.

"What else, what?"

She shook her head. "You are seriously the most stubborn person I know. Don't pretend to be ignorant. Stop pretending for once, Julie. You know exactly what I'm talking about."

I did know. There was more that drew me to Luke than having fun with him planning a wedding. So much more. It was the way he looked at me, making me feel like I was the most important woman in the world. The way my chest tightened and my stomach fluttered and my heart beat faster whenever he was around. The warmth and the kindness and the strength he gave me, even when I didn't deserve it. It was his sparkly green eyes, and how his face lit up when he smiled. It was his humour and, surprisingly, his positive outlook on life. It was the way he parented Hannah. The love he had for her, and the patience he displayed, was more attractive to me than any pair of dancing pecs could ever be. I had even started to think plaid was sexy.

"Hello?" Quinn finally said. "Are you in there, Julie? You drifted away somewhere."

I blinked. "I am in love with him," I said, astonished. "Is this what love is? Wanting to be with someone every second? Wanting to take care of them and make them happy and make sure they're safe? Never wanting them to hurt as much as I hurt right now?"

"How do you feel when you think of never seeing him again?"

"Broken," I said, my eyes again filling up with tears. "I feel broken."

"So?" she said, the expression on her face urging me to come to my own conclusion.

"What if he's found someone else? What if that's why he's been gone for so long? What if that's where he is right now? With her?" My stomach churned at the thought.

"How would you feel about that?"

I knew the answer, but I didn't want to admit it out loud. "I would be gutted. But I want him to be happy more than anything else. If he has found someone, and that person is who he wants to be with, I would be happy for him. The last thing I want is for him to feel like this."

"Yes!" Quinn pumped her fist in the air. "Go get him, girl!"

I jumped off the bench, knocking the empty container that had once held my fruit salad to the ground, paused, and then sat down again. "But what about Hannah?" I said, letting Marty lick the empty box as an apology for scaring the crap out of him.

Quinn sighed. "What *about* Hannah?"

"What if I can't be the role model she deserves?"

"Julie." Quinn turned to face me. "The things you just said in the past twenty minutes were the most selfless things I've heard you say in the past year. I think you're ready. I think you're more than ready."

I sat up, a look of determination on my face. Quinn was right. I *was* ready.

And I finally knew what I had to do to make things right.

The heat was oppressive as I slid out of my air-conditioned car, feet firmly planted on the pavement. I instantly started to sweat and peeled off my sky-blue blazer in the lobby of my apartment building before I went up the stairs, Marty following close behind. Despite the fact that I had closed all the windows and curtains in preparation for another record-setting day of heat, I knew it would be almost unbearable in my apartment. I was glad I had plenty of fans.

I trudged up the carpeted stairs that desperately needed a steam clean and ran my hand along the wall, paint chips falling between my fingers. I needed to find a new place. Now that I was in my apartment more, and wasn't passed out for most of it, I'd been realizing what a dump it was. And seeing as I'd recently found out that my role at the agency was going to become permanent, maybe I could actually start looking for somewhere new to live. Somewhere nice and cozy that felt like home. Somewhere like Luke's.

I sighed as tears welled up in my eyes. I missed him so much. I missed him and Hannah and being with them together in that house. I felt more at home there than I did where I grew up. And now I might have lost them both forever.

I opened the door to my apartment and walked through the heat like I was walking through sand, turning on a fan in the kitchen and then one in the living room, refilling Marty's dish with cool water. The last stop was my bedroom where I stripped off my soaking wet T-shirt and skirt and replaced them with a thin grey tank top and a pair of pink-striped boxer shorts.

I ran a hand through the short, feathered wisps of my hair. Two months after cutting it and I still loved it. It was much easier to get ready in the morning when I didn't have to style something that I would inevitably just hide behind. And I sure didn't miss the oppressive weight on my neck in weather like this. I looked in the mirror and smoothed down some wayward strands. I certainly didn't have plans to grow it out anytime soon, no matter how many people thought I'd made a mistake. Besides, Luke had said he loved it.

Luke.

What was I going to do about Luke? Despite my constant emails, he had yet to respond. I knew this because I checked my phone every thirty minutes. I knew from Ben that he was okay; that he had taken Hannah on an extended summer vacation, but that's all Ben would tell me and I didn't want to put him in the middle of something he had no desire to be a part of.

I had never felt like this. I had always loved being alone. Being alone was easy. I didn't have to compromise. I didn't have to change my ways.

But now? Now that I'd felt something real; now that I knew what it was like to care for someone as much, if not more, than I cared about myself; now that I knew what it was like to ache for someone when they weren't around, I didn't think I could go back.

If this was what love really felt like—not dependence, not fear, not what I'd felt in the past—then maybe it was time to actually feel it. I was so tired of all the pretending. I had been pretending to feel things and not feel things my whole life. Maybe it was finally time to stop.

I went into the kitchen and poured myself some ice water, holding the glass against my forehead to cool down the flush that had reddened my face. What if it was too late? What if I had ruined everything? I sipped the water, trying to wash down the lump that had formed in my throat, and sat down at my kitchen table.

There was only one way to find out. I took a deep breath, opened my laptop and wrote the hardest, most important email I'd ever written.

From: Julie
Sent: August 7th 8:14 PM
To: Luke
Subject: Final email

Dear Luke,

This will be my final email. After I send this, if I don't hear back from you, I will know it's over. I'll know I ruined it. And I will understand. I will truly understand.

I've been writing this email for two hours. Writing, deleting, rewriting. I want to make sure I get this right. I know this is my last chance.

I have never felt safe in my adult life. You know why this is. This email isn't going to be about my traumas and what an unfortunate victim I've been; you've heard enough about that.

The point of this email is this: The first time I ever felt one hundred percent safe, the first time since I was a kid, was the moment I felt your hand reach for mine that night and hold it tight. Of course, you know which night I'm talking about. The night in the snow. The night that changed my life.

I felt it instantly. I felt my body relax. I felt my guard start to slip. All of my fear disappeared into the safety of your protective grip. You held the fear with me. You held it for me. And I could finally breathe.

Over the next few months, the wall I had carefully and purposefully built over decades didn't just start to crumble; it was levelled. And feelings surfaced. Feelings that I hadn't felt for so long flooded the space where the wall once stood. And they came so fast that I didn't know how to handle them.

At first, I was upset. Why couldn't I rein them in? I didn't like it. I no longer liked the feeling of being out of control.

But, thanks to you, and your kindness and patience and strength, I learned the beauty in letting go. I learned that there was power in feeling powerless. That it was worth opening myself up, because that's how the sun got in.

You taught me how to like myself. You taught me that I was enough. And even though I truly believe that now, I still, perhaps selfishly, want more.

Because I love you. I love you so much, Luke. And I'm sorry I couldn't see it. I'm sorry I wouldn't see it. I've loved you for longer than I know. I'll love you for longer than I can ever comprehend.

The night we spent together meant more to me than anything ever has. I am so, so sorry I pretended that it didn't.

You have such greatness about you, a unique way of making those around you feel seen. Of making them feel safe. You have all this love to give and you give it so easily and graciously it's like a superpower. I'm so grateful that I was able to be a part of that for what, unexpectedly, turned out to be the best year of my life.

You make me want to be a better person, Luke. I know I can be that person when I'm with you.

I miss you. I miss Hannah. I miss our time together.

Please come back.

Love, Julie

Chapter Thirty-Five

I hadn't been to Group in months. At first, I'd been too busy with the wedding and then I'd been too sad to leave my house. And now, two days after I'd sent Luke my final email, I'd added the glorious feelings of heightened anxiety and crushing despair as I waited for him to respond. Every time I got an alert on my phone, my heart felt like it was going to beat out of my chest. And every time it wasn't him, I felt it fracture just a tiny bit more. It was official: feeling things was stupid.

All I wanted to do was get rid of the sadness; all I wanted was to be numb. And the only way I knew how to do that was to drink. So, knowing myself better than I ever have in my life, I picked myself up off the couch, threw on a pair of ragged jean shorts, a sports bra and a very old Chip & Pepper tank top, and took my sorry ass on over to a meeting, making a phone call on my way.

Everyone was already seated when we arrived and they all turned when we walked in the door. I was, at first, startled by the looks of confusion—it hadn't been that long—but then I remembered I hadn't been there since I'd cut my hair. It had grown a bit, but it was still shockingly short, and I ran my hand through it nervously.

As a tentative smile curved my lips, looks of confusion turned to recognition and then to delight. "Julie!" Jenn yelled. "Oh my God, I love your hair!" Everyone stood up and walked over to greet me, some with hugs, others with kind words, all with warm smiles. I immediately felt better. These were my people. This was where I belonged. I couldn't believe it had taken me this long to come back.

"So." Corie leaned towards me hesitantly after we had all sat down. "How are you, Julie?"

"I'm okay, thanks." I looked around and as soon as I saw the concerned faces, I understood the hesitation. "Oh!" I held up my hands and smiled. "I'm fine, don't worry. I didn't cut off my hair in a drunken stupor. I haven't fallen off the wagon." Everyone visibly relaxed. "I've just been busy," I finished.

"Oh good." Jess put her hand on my leg. "We were worried about you!"

I shrugged away her concern, not needing it but grateful for it. "In fact," I said, "I made it to my one year of sobriety. Over a year now, I guess." Time flies when you're miserable, apparently.

I jumped as the room erupted. Cheers and whoops and "congratulations" and even a couple fist bumps. Everyone was so happy for me that I couldn't help but be happy along with them. I hadn't celebrated my achievement, with the exception of a quiet dinner with Kate and Ben. It felt good to be acknowledged. To be recognized for something that I'd worked hard for by folks who had gone through the exact same thing as I had. I hadn't known I'd needed it.

"Oh," I said, gesturing to the person sitting beside me

who was gripping her phone like a lifeline. "This is my friend Marnie, she's new." I gave her a warm smile, which she returned hesitantly. She lifted her hand in a small wave and her smile widened as everyone welcomed her into the fold.

"Thank you," she whispered and I squeezed her hand, grateful for all the people who had helped me; grateful for the opportunity to now help someone else. I couldn't go back to my past self and give her the support she needed, but I could do my best in the present with Marnie. She deserved much more than my misplaced resentment.

As I sat back and listened to the shared stories of achievement and challenges, I realized how proud of myself I was. How lucky I was to have joined this group over a year ago. I may not have gotten a "You are all my heroes" cake or a one-year sobriety chip, but I wouldn't have had it any other way.

After Group, for the first time in a very long time, I drove home feeling content. The positive energy of the meeting had filled me with bubbles of hope and, after dropping Marnie off, I sang along to my Spotify playlist as I drove. What a great meeting. I couldn't wait to text Luke and tell him about it.

Fuck.

The thought had popped out of nowhere, and as it floated away to oblivion, so did my good mood. Why did I have to wreck everything by thinking something stupid?

I stood at my apartment building, rummaging in my purse for my keys, wondering why I didn't just hold on to them when I got out of the car like a normal person, and, for the first time, started to feel angry. How dare he wreck my good mood by bursting his way into my thoughts? How dare he wreck the first good day I'd had in a month?

I pushed the heavy metal door open and pulled my key out so hard I almost broke it. How dare he not answer my email? I'd poured my heart out to him, for shit's sake. I'd never done that before. To anyone. And he *knew* that. He knew that, and he couldn't even acknowledge that he'd received it. He couldn't even be bothered to reply to me at all.

I stomped up the stairs like a five-year-old, not caring who I was disturbing. How dare he just leave like that? With no goodbye. With no word at all. I'd said I was sorry. I'd said I loved him. What else could I possibly do?

I made it to my apartment door, out of breath and full of fury. I jammed my key into the deadbolt and rammed the door open with the heel of my hand, ready to throw my purse across the room in an anger-fueled eruption of immaturity.

"Fuck!" I yelled in a cleansing burst of rage, pulling my arm back, gripping my purse like a football.

But that was as far as I got. My hand fell to my side, my purse tumbled to the floor, my mouth dropped open in surprise.

Because there, standing in my kitchen, with a look on his face that could only be described as amusement mixed with absolute terror, was Luke.

Chapter Thirty-Six

"Jesus Christ, what the fuck!" Luke held his hands up and ducked his face behind them.

I couldn't move. I couldn't speak. Luke was here. My Luke. In my apartment. I wanted to run up and hug him and never let go. I wanted to drop down to my knees and beg him to forgive me. But instead, I scooped up Marty who had been racing around the room, barking with excitement and said quietly, "What are you doing here?"

"You scared the crap out of me," he breathed, lowering his arms and smoothing his plaid shirt over his chest.

"Well, to be fair, it's my house, I'm the one who should be here." I picked up my purse and hung it on a hook by the door while I tried to catch my breath.

"Good point," Luke said, nodding.

"How did you get in?" I said, asking a question I already knew the answer to. Terrified to ask what I really wanted to know.

He pulled a key from his pocket and held it up. "You gave me a key to check in on Marty. Remember?"

"Right." I glanced at Marty, who was happily wriggling his bum as Luke scratched him behind the ears.

"So." I crossed my arms over my chest, hoping the pressure would slow down my heartbeat. "What are you doing here, Luke?" I tried to keep the desperation out of my voice. "I've been emailing you. And texting you before that."

"I didn't get your emails or your texts," he said as he slid his hands in the back pockets of his cargo shorts, his expression serious.

"What—" I started to protest, my confusion displaying as frustration.

"Wait." He held up his hand. "I didn't get them when you first sent them."

I stood silently, waiting as requested, eyebrows raised, eyes questioning.

He gestured to one of the wooden chairs he'd pulled out from my kitchen table. "Please sit. I think my heart has slowed down enough that there is no longer any danger of me having a heart attack."

"You know," I said, continuing to stand, "you scared me too. It's not every day that I come home to an unexpected man in my apartment."

"Fair." He nodded. "In hindsight, showing up at a single woman's house unannounced probably wasn't the best plan." He grimaced. "I wanted it to be a surprise."

"Well," I said, "you definitely achieved your goal." I smiled tentatively. "Now, can you please tell me why you're here?" My body tensed as I realized this could be it. This could be the moment Luke told me to stop bothering him. That he never wanted to see me again.

Luke took a deep breath, his demeanour calm, his entire

body radiating strength and purpose. I had missed him so much. Until this point, he had been standing in front of the counter, but he now stepped aside, holding his hands like a game show model, revealing what appeared to be a cake.

"I made you a cake." He gestured again in case I'd missed it.

"Why?" I took a couple of steps towards the counter and stopped.

"Come see," he said. "It's not going to explode."

The cake was round with white icing and gold piping, made to look like a one-year AA chip, exactly like the cake I had ridiculed on the day we first met. "You are my hero," I read, and I laughed as my eyes simultaneously filled with tears.

"I thought we should properly celebrate," Luke said, his eyes soft.

"Why are you doing this?" I asked, no longer caring what my face looked like, no longer trying to hold back the hope. "Why are you here? Where did you go? Why didn't you answer my emails?"

He breathed in deeply, the pain in his expression mirroring mine. "You really hurt me that night a month ago. The night we slept together."

I lowered my eyes. "I'm so sorry," I whispered.

"I know," he said as he set his hands on my shoulders. "Let's sit. Please." We walked over to the couch and sat down.

"So, I get why you asked me to leave that night," I said after we had settled. "But why did you have to leave too? And where did you go for so long?"

He took a deep breath. "Initially I was just going to take Hannah to visit my sister in Ontario. I had some holidays saved up and Hannah was almost on summer break, so I thought I'd take her remaining schoolwork and try to recover surrounded by family." He closed his eyes as if reliving the pain. The pain that I had caused. "I couldn't be in my house. I couldn't be in the place we'd been together. I had to get away from it all."

"Away from me, you mean."

"Well, yeah." He laughed. "Of course. I told you I was falling in love with you and your response was that the amazing night we'd spent together was just about sex. You ripped my heart out. I wanted to get as far away from you as possible." He shrugged as I winced. I mean, I didn't blame him at all, but it was like a punch to the gut to hear him say it out loud.

"But then I got your first text. And it was just like a normal text. Like a 'Hey, how's it going?' text. Like nothing had happened. Like you didn't feel anything."

I lowered my head, knowing how it must have seemed but also knowing how wrong he was.

"And honestly?" he continued. "As shitty as I felt, I had been ready to give you the benefit of the doubt. I knew I had dropped the 'I love you' bomb pretty early and I knew you were skittish in that department to begin with, but after that text, I had to get even further away. I needed to escape," he said. "I needed to get off the grid."

I nodded, trying against every natural impulse not to interrupt. As much as I wanted him to answer my questions, I could tell that he needed to say this.

"Despite the fact that she's not the most outdoorsy person in the world, Hannah had been begging me to take her camping for months, so that's what we did. I found a cabin to rent in northern Ontario, completely isolated in the woods but close enough to a national park in case of emergencies. We packed all our stuff and away we went. Our own little adventure."

"That sounds…pretty?" I tried.

He chuckled. "I know that's not your jam, but it was pretty. It was gorgeous. Crystal clear water, star-filled skies; the only sounds at night were the crickets and frogs. Hannah loved it. We both did."

"So, when you say 'off the grid,' does that mean you didn't have—"

He nodded. "I didn't have Wi-Fi. I didn't have cell service at all actually."

"Wow," I said. I honestly couldn't imagine that. "What if something had happened?"

"I had a satellite phone for emergencies," he said. "And only two people had the number. Janet and Ben."

"Ben? Ben had the number?" Why hadn't Ben told me he had the number? I could feel the heat rising in my cheeks.

"Because I'd asked him not to," Luke said, reading my mind. "I had begged him not to. I needed time to get over you, and I knew if I had access to you, or if you had access to me, it would make it that much harder."

I nodded, the anger dissipating as quickly as it had risen. "That makes sense."

"But then, a few days ago, he called."

My head shot up. "What did he say?"

Luke smiled. "In true Ben form, he apologized because the reason he was calling wasn't a true emergency, but as he spoke, I realized that, to him, it kind of was. He was worried about you, Julie. He knew you were emailing me and he knew how upset you were."

A tiny dart of guilt poked at my stomach. I had finally broken down and told Ben and Kate everything—about all of my feelings and the mistake I had made. I should have known Ben would be worried.

"So, I went into a little town nearby," Luke continued, "and turned on my Wi-Fi at a café, and while Hannah played with the café dog, I read your emails."

"And?" It came out as a whisper.

"Well, my first reaction was anger, to be perfectly honest," he said as tears filled my eyes, my body slowly deflating. "I had tried so hard to force you from my thoughts." His fingers lightly clenched at his sides as if he was reliving his efforts at self-preservation. "At first I didn't want to believe you," he said quietly. "I just wanted to forget. I just wanted to heal. But then…." He trailed off, his eyes glistening with unshed tears.

I held my breath. Waiting for whatever he said next. Knowing that, whatever it was, whichever direction he'd decided to go, would change my life forever.

"Remember when you said that love wasn't worth the risk? That if you were lucky to feel that one great love, it wasn't worth all the potential heartache?" he said, eyes staring into my soul.

I nodded. "I don't think that anymore," I said, instantly

knowing it was true. Because, really? No matter what he decided, no matter what he said next, all the pain I had felt since he'd left, all the misery I had gone through, it was all worth it to feel the love I felt for him at this moment. To know that I had that capacity. To know I had the privilege of loving a man as amazing and wonderful as Luke.

"I know you don't," he said gently. "I believe you."

"Really?" I said, trying to temper my hopes. Trying to rein in the tiny bubbles of joy floating around in my chest.

He nodded, smiling. "Yes, really. And, more importantly, I believe myself. What happened that night really threw me for a loop, so much so that I started to doubt my own feelings. I started to doubt my instincts. I needed that time away to learn to trust myself again. Because, if I was being honest, I didn't believe that you thought what we'd had together was only sex. I didn't believe that the connection I'd felt was only one-sided. I knew you loved me too. I knew that you had to or everything I'd felt, everything I'd experienced was wrong. And I knew nothing in my life had ever felt so right."

I was shocked, mouth hanging open like Marty waiting for a treat. "How did you know?" I finally asked. "How did you know how I felt before I even did?"

He lifted my hand and turned it so my palm faced up, tracing the lines with his finger. "You might be surprised at this, Julie, but despite all of your efforts to shut me out, I've gotten to know you pretty well. I knew, even though you tried so hard to hide it, underneath all of your sadness and sarcasm and biting wit—"

"Hey!" I interrupted. "My wit is not biting, it's hilarious."

He laughed. "Under your hilarious wit, there was a whole lot of love that, every once in a while, would push its way through. I saw that love when you talked about Kate and Ben. I saw it when you played with Hannah. I saw it with Marty. And I saw it when you looked at me that night. I knew it was there. You just needed time to find it."

I'd given up on trying to hold back the tears and they were now freely streaming down my cheeks.

"I thought you hated me." I wiped my face with the back of my hand.

"I could never hate you. I love you, Julie." His eyes darkened and I knew it was true.

"I love you too." I reached up and touched the side of his face, making sure he was truly there, making sure he was real.

In one smooth motion, he slid his strong hands around my hips and pulled me closer and my stomach flipped.

"You're all I ever wanted, Julie," he whispered as he leaned in, our lips millimeters apart.

"Promise me you'll never leave again," I whispered back, breathless with anticipation.

"I promise."

His lips, soft on mine, parted with a sigh and I knew. Whatever heartache I'd felt, whatever pain I'd gone through, if it had all led up to this moment, if it had all led up to ending up with Luke, it had been entirely worth it.

Chapter Thirty-Seven

Six Months Later

I pulled the collar of my red winter coat up higher, burrowing my face like a turtle against the wind that was trying to whip my hair out from under my woollen hat. "Is that it?" I yelled, my voice barely making it through another powerful gust.

The van door slammed with a metallic clang and the lock clunked into place. "I don't know if we could have chosen a better day to move you in." Luke laughed and grabbed my mittened hand. "Hurry, let's get inside before we're blown away!"

I laughed along with him; there was no way a stupid blizzard could ruin how happy I was, especially when I looked up and saw who was waiting for me at the door, Marty in her arms, her face all smiles, squealing at the cold. I rested my hand on her curls as the three of us stepped into the warmth and Hannah shut the door, kissing Marty on the forehead before setting him down.

"Whoop," she exhaled. "It is not nice outside. I think we probably need some hot chocolate." She looked at me, not Luke, knowing I would do anything to make her happy.

I glanced at Luke and he gave a slight nod and a barely perceptible grin. "I think you're right," I said to Hannah. "Just let me get out of my many layers of clothing."

"Yes!" She shot her hand up in the air and scampered into the kitchen to get things ready, Marty happily bouncing after her.

I pulled off my boots, holding Luke's strong arm to steady me, and unwrapped my scarf, draping it on the wooden bench by the door. I yanked my hat off, stuffed it into a cubby and fluffed out my hair, checking it in the mirror. It had gotten longer since I'd last cut it and I was trying to decide whether to grow it out or not.

"Keep it short," Luke whispered in my ear, sending a shiver down my spine. He pressed his cold cheek to my face and then warmed the spot with his lips, making me flush. I turned and met his lips with mine. "I love you," I said and rested my forehead against his.

"I love you too," he said. "Maybe even more than hot chocolate." He winked and turned to go help Hannah in the kitchen.

As I pulled off my heavy coat, I surveyed the room, boxes of my stuff scattered amongst the cozy furnishings. Inhaling deeply, I breathed in the comforting scents of cinnamon and chocolate and finally allowed my shoulders to relax, all of the stress, all of the pain sinking into the hardwood floor. This was where I was happy. This was where I was safe. This was where I belonged.

I was finally home.

Also by Jamie

Jamie's debut novel, the romantic comedy Someone to Kiss, a hilarious and heartening take on the pitfalls of modern dating featuring Kate's love story.

As the clock strikes midnight over a disastrous New Year's Eve, Kate makes a resolution scrawled on the back of a napkin: by next New Year's Eve, she will have found someone of her own to kiss. But for the 40-something cat-mom who'd rather binge TV than brave the singles scene, the challenge is real!

Get your copy of "Someone to Kiss" here:

About the Author

Photo by
Kerry Anderson

Jamie Anderson is based in Regina, Saskatchewan, Canada. A proud Canadian and Saskatchewanian, she wanted to set her first two novels in the place she was born and raised.

She works in content marketing, has a certificate in professional writing, and has done a smattering of freelance writing, character development, and copyediting over the past several years.

She's been writing for as long as she can remember and has been reading for longer than that. She lives happily with her mountain of books, her TV, and her two plants.

Sign up for Jamie's newsletter for news on exclusive deals, special offers, and a FREE copy of Jamie's sweet, uplifting novella *Running from Christmas* as a welcome gift!

Acknowledgements

I am incredibly grateful for the many, many people who joined me in the *Love, Julie* journey. It was a tough one at times, but thanks to the help and support from so many amazing people, the end result is something that I'm very proud of.

Thank you to my publisher Tarn Hopkins from TRM publishing. She took a chance on me with my first book, *Someone to Kiss*, and continued to share her wisdom and kindness with this one, patiently talking me off the ledge as needed and graciously not saying, "I told you so," even though she very easily could have. Until I published my first book, I hadn't realized how collaborative writing a novel was and I continue to be grateful to have such a skilled storyteller in my corner.

Speaking of collaboration, thank you to Bryn Donovan for the brilliant developmental edit and for (finally) making me see that Julie could use some work. Thank you to Johanna Craven for the copy editing and Ken Darrow for the excellent proof-reading; the nerd in me gets a tiny (huge) thrill when I get to learn through all of the little nuggets of grammar feedback.

Thank you to Spiffing Covers for the cover design. I love the colours, and the image that was chosen captured Julie perfectly.

Thank you to Stacey Smith, Kendall Litschko, Shayla Dietrich, Kristine Waddell and Holly Popenia for being my first readers. Your thoughtful and insightful feedback gently nudged the book onto the path it eventually ended up going down.

Thank you again, and specifically, to Kristine Waddell for being such a great friend and for laughing when I somehow misspelled her name in the acknowledgments for *Someone to Kiss*, rather than be offended, which is probably how I would have reacted.

Thank you to Karen Kirby, Laura Weisgarber and Jodi Currie for being amazing, supportive friends, and to Karen especially for buying more copies of *Someone to Kiss* than even my parents.

Thank you to my day job friends and colleagues for being incredibly supportive, always asking how my writing is going and then sitting patiently while I talk about it for longer than they ever wanted me to.

Thank you to all the beta readers. The feedback was incredibly smart and extremely helpful, and *Love, Julie* is so much better because of all of you.

Thank you to my perfect family: my dad Kerry, my mom Catherine, my brother Chris and CJ. You all mean the world to me and I couldn't have gotten here without your love and support. A special thanks to CJ for giving me permission to pay tribute to little Marty.

Thank you also to my incredible extended family; I

am so lucky to have the best aunts, uncles and cousins that anyone could ever wish for.

Finally, and most importantly, I'd like to thank my readers. Thank you for allowing me to write sweet romances with serious themes. Writing is a form of therapy for me and I still find it impossible to believe that people actually want to read what I've written. I'm not sure if I will ever get used to that.

Despite being (hopefully) funny, *Love, Julie* is about the very serious topic of addiction. While I'm not an alcoholic like Julie, I have struggled with alcohol in the past and many of her struggles were once mine. If you or someone you love is struggling, there are places you can go for help. If you're not ready for that, I hope you talk to someone, anyone, because, take it from me, it can get better. It will get better. You just have to take that first step.